THE REDEMPTION FACTORY

SAM MILLAR'S WRITING has been praised for its "fluency and courage of language" by Jennifer Johnson, and he has been hailed by best-selling American author Anne-Marie Duquette as "a powerful writer". He is a winner of the Martin Healy Short Story Award, the Brian Moore Award for Short Stories, the *Cork Literary Review* Competition, and the Aisling Award for Art and Culture. Born in Belfast, where he still lives, he is married and has three children. He is also the author of one previous novel, *Dark Souls*, and a best-selling memoir, *On the Brinks*.

SAM MILLAR

THE REDEMPTION FACTORY

THUNDER'S MOUTH PRESS
NEW YORK

THE REDEMPTION FACTORY

Published by
Thunder's Mouth Press
An Imprint of Avalon Publishing Group Inc.
245 West 17th Street, 11th Floor
New York, NY 10011

AVALON
publishing group incorporated

Copyright © 2005 by Sam Millar

Originally published by in Ireland by Brandon in 2005
First Thunder's Mouth Press edition June 2006

Library of Congress Cataloging-in-Publication Data is available.

ISBN 10: 1-56025-860-8
ISBN 13: 978-1-56025-860-5

9 8 7 6 5 4 3 2 1

Book design by Red Barn Publishing
Printed in the United States of America
Distributed by Publishers Group West

I dedicate The Redemption Factory
to Brian, Liz and the "boys",
Jamsey, Ruari and Pearce.
A great family, and even greater friends

Prologue

T HE OLD COTTAGE resembled a great boat that had
barely cheated the storm. An outsider would laugh at
its status, especially if told it was now a prison. But
this was as much a prison of the mind as of the body: a psycho-
logical conundrum that told the sole prisoner lingering there
that if he attempted to escape it would prove his guilt – if, that
is, his former comrades hadn't already determined it.

The tide had left the shore and the smell drifting into the
cottage was strong, like bleach mingling with burnt salt. It
entered through the torn structure of the cottage, making its
presence felt uninvitingly. There were other smells inside the
confines of the cottage; of dried sweat, excrement and urine
challenging the uninvited smell, competing for second place.

Only one odour reigned supreme, gaining in strength as time elapsed: the copper odour of fear . . .

The prisoner was naked, covered only in shadows, dirt and angry purple welts. His wrists were purple stigmata caused by the "strappado" technique – a torture favoured by South American dictators in which a prisoner is left suspended from an overhanging with handcuffs until they slice deeply into the wrists.

The floorboards where he rested rose and dipped in an irregular wave, de-crucified by time and wear. A decapitated statue lay languishing in a corner, mottled with age and dung. Webs of silky dust covered a village of cigarette butts and lips of blue-moulded bread crusts.

Cold bit at him, right down to his marrow, making him shake, making him wonder if this was what they were trying to do, freeze him to death?

Abruptly, his thoughts were interrupted by the sound of feet on shells. The sound had a thickness to it, muffled, and he knew it was his captors with their wet, sand-covered boots.

The door squeaked open and a sliver of light bleached his eyes, stinging them wet. He could feel the dampness of his bones being touched by the light, a little tongue licking at his skin.

"Eat," said a gruff voice, and he felt a plate touch his exposed feet.

The meagre meals had come intermittently, disorientating, consisting of the same grey and brown greasy matter, making it impossible to distinguish between breakfast and supper. This was deliberate: no concept of time turned hours to days, days to weeks . . .

Only the ugly stubble on his face acted as a calendar, keeping him semi-sane.

Ask them, said the voice in his head. *Ask them.*

He despised the tormenting voice. He simply wanted to be left alone. Had he not been tortured enough?

Ask them.

"Can you tell me what's happening? What the decision is?" He didn't recognise the raw croak, the Judas sound that revealed his desperation.

The captors, their faces concealed behind masks, ignored the questions, allowing the silence to become heavier, more poignant.

Silence. Of course, thought the prisoner, and he almost smiled. He knew, from experience, that a perfect measure of silence had the potent power to be as ruthless and as terrifying as the actuality. It instilled fear, but so subtle you hardly realised it, until it was too late, touching you right on the shoulder.

One of the captors housed a shotgun on the crank of his elbow, cradling it affectionately like a sleeping child. The prisoner remembered the first time he saw the ugly weapon speckled with tiny freckles of rust that teased out the metal into an uneven surface. Wire wool attached itself to the gaping entrance of the barrel, and it reassured him, the gun's condition. Neglect meant disuse. It was there to scare, subdue. Nothing else.

Only when he realised that it was neither rust nor wire, but blood and hair, did the full horror of his situation sink in.

"You should be resting," said one of the captors, finally breaking the silence.

The balance of words sounded innocuous, almost caring. But the prisoner knew they were slippery and evil, like a snail captured in the sun.

The door closed, chasing out the light. He listened to the footsteps fading, hoping never to hear them again, knowing he would. Soon . . .

The morning moved on, though in the prisoner's head he found it impossible to distinguish.

He could hear the dense sound of gulls and the muffled sound of a car, thin in the background. It was raining outside, and he listened intently to the fierceness of the rain and tried to picture its needles of porcupine quills battering the sandy ground.

It was music, an oratorical salvation sent to save him, lift his spirits, and it made him wonder if, perhaps, God did exist, after all.

But the rain and music faded just as the boots treaded their way towards the door, their silent noise lurching his stomach.

The fear that had slipped a few hours ago returned, thicker, resting on his chest, affecting his breathing. There was a taste in his mouth, a distinct taste of watered metal, like a dentist drill. Only when he spat it out did he realise he was bleeding.

Good old reliable ulcer, he thought with bitterness. *I was wondering when you would show your ugly head.*

The aroma of bacon and eggs ghosted its way into the room. It was the most beautiful smell he had ever smelt, and his belly growled with anticipation. But quickly the voices came back to torment. *A good meal? You know what that means.*

A captor placed the food on the floor before backing away, into the dark. The other one – the one normally carrying the ugly shotgun – remained, watching. The shotgun was gone, replaced by a revolver.

"Why are you doing this to me? What have I done?" asked the prisoner.

Both captors remained silent, unmoving in the fading light, like foxes hiding in the dark, shrewd and calculating.

"At least allow me to look you in the eye, see your faces." Anger was building in the naked man, an emotional release. It felt good to be human again, to hear his real voice, not some cardboard echo of it. If they wanted him to grovel, cry, they would be disappointed. Bitterly so. "Are you so ashamed of what you're about to do that you can't look me in the eyes?"

For the first time that evening, one of the captors spoke, his voice slightly muffled.

"You're the one who should be ashamed. Not us. You betrayed us, our ideals – everything we fought and died for – by judiciously passing information to the enemy. I hope it was worth it, all the money?"

"That's a lie! I never betrayed anyone in my life. I swear on my family's –"

"Save your swearing. It'll do you no good – not with us. We've listened to your taped confession and the evidence against you. It was compelling. You set up three of our men to be ambushed and murdered. *They* weren't permitted to swear on family lives. Why should *you?* Now, suddenly faced with justice, you recant?"

"Look at me! Look at my body, humiliated, covered in cigarette burns, my wrists torn and shattered. Even if I said I betrayed anyone, I was tortured into it. Those weren't my words on the tape. They were the screams of a man being tortured, a wounded animal screaming for mercy. Admit it, wouldn't you have said the same lies if you were tortured? Sleep deprivation for days on end? And don't you find it a little perverse that we utilise the same torture methods we quickly condemn our enemies for? Such fucking hypocrites!"

"Eat your meal," said the captor, ignoring the questions.

"You eat it," taunted the prisoner. "Go on, prove you believe what they said about me. Eat with a good conscience. Let me see you swallow it, just like you're swallowing the lies."

The captor walked to the back of the room and looked out the window. He seemed to be studying the incoming waves, their slow movement of formless curls.

"Go on," goaded the prisoner, encouraged by his captor's silence. "Eat, drink and be merry with murder. Hopefully, the taste will always remind you of me . . ."

One of the captors glanced at his watch. "You've less than fifteen minutes. You should be making peace with God."

"God? Ha! Fuck all the gods – and fuck you, too! Remove your mask, you spineless bastards. Petrified I might come back and haunt you if I see your cowardly faces? Ha! That's it, isn't it, you pieces of shit?"

The captor walked towards the prisoner, slowly removing his mask, allowing the feeble light to expose his features.

"Take a good long look. Satisfy yourself, because this is the last face you will ever see again on this earth . . ."

It had been almost a week since the captor uttered those prophetic words, but as he sat and listened to the tape again, his belief in the man's guilt was no longer resolute. Truth be told, his belief in a few things had come under scrutiny lately, creating a residual scepticism totally alien before now. He was beginning to believe things he knew weren't healthy to believe.

He had listened to numerous taped confessions before, of other traitors and informants begging for mercy, asking for forgiveness for their dirty deeds; but there was something in this dead man's voice, echoing eerily back from the tape's grave, that began to gnaw annoyingly in his ear.

No. A million times no. I did not – arghhhhhhhhhhhh . . . bastards!

Silence. A few seconds of silence. The captor knew that those few seconds could be days in real time; time to soften the prisoner up, get him to say what they wanted to hear: ventriloquism in the extreme.

He clicked the tape off, pondering his next – if any – move. It was risky, having a copy of the original tape. Doctored copies had been make specifically for the ears of certain journalist and media outlets. They would hear the man confessing his sins, and how professional his interrogators had been. The interrogators' voices would be calm, human and almost sympathetic. The prisoner's voice would sound shaky, hesitant; a man avoiding the truth with a million lies in his head, his words stumbling like blocks of wood from his lying mouth.

Of course, very few ever got to hear the official tape, the one with the screams and denials. This would be kept for future interrogators, learning new methods, deciding what worked, what didn't.

No. The sanitised version was for public consumption; the darker, more telling tape would be archived for the selected few, for the hierarchy.

It should have been destroyed by now. He had been foolish in keeping it – if only for a few days; if only to ease his conscience . . .

From a crumbled cigarette box, he produced a cig and placed it in his mouth. The unlit tobacco tasted tired, putrid, as the flame engulfed it. Everything seemed to have the same decaying taste, of late. He studied the lighter's flame, then reached for the tape, bringing the two closer. He watched as the quivering flame from the lighter transformed into a tongue. He waited for it to speak . . .

CHAPTER ONE

Meat in All Its Bloody Glory

*"I have from an early age abjured the use of meat, and the time will
come when men such as I will look upon the murder of animals as
they now look on the murder of men."*
Leonardo da Vinci

"As long as there are slaughterhouses, there will be battlefields."
Leo Tolstoy

PAUL GOODMAN FELT like a condemned man while walking across the sodden grass leading towards the abattoir. A rosary of knots clung to his stomach, tightening at each step he took. Rain and cold nipped wickedly against his skin, stinging it. An involuntary shiver touched his spine and bowels, caused not by the weather, but by the thought that within a matter of minutes, he would be inside the building, inside the huge belly of the beast.

The abattoir was located near Flaxman's Row, the so-called industrial area beside an abandoned train station where dilapidated carriages sat glued together with rust and age. The dark, brooding weather matched his mood as he prepared himself for whatever lurked before him.

Outside the abattoir's gate, he gazed over the building. It was a mammoth, nondescript, grey cement structure, a place covered in soot – darkened stones begging to be demolished.

Dove-grey smoke drifted upward from a massive chimney, stifling the air and veiling the sky, like a ghost, formless yet controlled, as if the building were a living being, breathing steam.

There *was* something deceptively quiet and intimidating about the place, something eerily unsettling because it carried no direction of either sound or presence, like a delightful calmness, haunting, yet chillingly causing the hairs on the back of his neck to stand on end.

Paul steeled himself, unconvincingly, as he walked, trying to settle his stomach with deep breaths before making his way cautiously to the enormous main gate with its mural of strange, biblical-looking characters.

Each character seemed possessed with exaggerated muscular form of impossibly precise features mixing with harmony and attributes.

"Very nice," whispered Paul mockingly. An inscription beneath the mural read *House of Redemption*. "Creepy. What a place . . ."

Seconds later, he entered a makeshift office housed by a flea-market table and two battered chairs. The walls, once an enthusiastic blue, were now tired and defeated, with only a few drab flakes of paint still visible. Thick films of dust settled on shelves of unread books, most of which appeared to be about butchering.

The place reeked of confinement mingling with a suffocating odour of dead carpet, neglected body odour and the urine stench of flowers left in water too long – a smell normally associated with churches. It made him wonder how any human being could voluntarily cope with such stench. More importantly, how the hell would he manage, if he got the job? He didn't *want* the job; he *needed* it.

An unruly pool of shadows lounged in the room as light splintered in from a cracked window resting on the face of an unhealthy looking young woman – who was about the same age as Paul – occupying one of the chairs, varnishing her fingernails. So skinny, she resembled a stick insect. Her head was enlarged, disproportionately, and drooped burdensomely on her skinny frame, like an over-sized daffodil. Tiny bald spots speckled through her thin, greasy hair, and Paul noticed a scant line of discoloration where hair had recently been removed.

Her skin was stony-white and moist with perspiration, like the sheen of patent leather. There was something terribly weird about the texture of the skin, though not by the multitude of tiny pinhole-dots mapping her face – presumably destroyed by acne – but by the reflective gleam of light sporadically released from it, reflecting like miniature rhinestones nesting there. For a brief, terrible second, it made Paul think of his mother's skin, how it always glistened in the morning sunlight as the alcohol rose to the surface, seeping through her pores . . .

"What d'ya want?" asked the young woman who, not bothering to glance in Paul's direction, continued on her fingernails, seemingly fascinated by them. A faint odour, like a residue of hospital, of medicines and disinfectant and illness, oozed from an opening in her shirt. Each time she moved, the odour became sharper. It was an odd smell and made him uncomfortable, gripping him with the feelings of his first day at school, the loneliness which had engulfed him in that imposing place, the shame and humiliation upon realising he had wet his pants in his anxiety. A simple shame, but a shame that would remain for ever.

Paul found the young woman loathsome, but cleared his throat, as if dislodging phlegm would ease the tension with one good cough. "I've come for a job. I was told there was one up for grabs."

"Yeah? Who told you that?" She had yet to look at Paul.

"Stevie Foster. Told me on Thursday that there was a –"

"That weasel never told the truth in his life," she interrupted, still not looking in his direction. Her shrill voice was coiled with resentment and smothered anger. "Told me he had a two-pound dick."

Paul didn't know if he should laugh or continue with the conversation. His nerves got the better of him. "No one has a dick that heavy. It would be massive." He began to laugh nervously.

"Weight? Who said anything about *weight*? Oh, he *has* a two-pound dick. His problem is that it's the *size* of a two-pound coin," she replied, not missing a beat. "Stevie's problem is that he can't keep a secret or lie convincingly."

Paul grinned.

"What's your name?" she asked, blowing on the dampness of her fingernails.

"Paul Goodman."

For the first time, the young woman looked up. Her eyes – focused and intent – were the greenest he had ever seen, as green as the skin of an iguana. They looked hungry, ready to eat. But something beyond hunger hid in there. Something cunning and malevolent. "Are you?" she asked, smiling a smile that was neither pleasant nor natural, but smug and slightly sinful.

Immediately, Paul thought of a snake, its bad skin flaking on the table. He wondered how such a massive head simply did not break away from the neck. She looked the type of woman who asked for trouble out of pure boredom.

"Am I what?" asked Paul.

"A *good* man." She laughed, but a laugh meant to hurt. "I prefer my men *bad. Very* bad . . ." Pushing herself away from the table's lip, the young woman walked towards a door directly behind Paul, knocking once before entering. A moment later, she reappeared. "You can go in . . . *good* man. Shank will see you. But don't say a word until he speaks to you. Understand? He doesn't like to be disturbed while he's *thinking.*" She smirked, and once again Paul thought of a snake.

Directly outside the door, a burly figure stood, unmoving. He was dressed entirely in black. From ear to ear, a horseshoe of bristles shadowed what little skin his face revealed. His demeanour was that of confident bouncer waiting for some fool to step out of line, and there was little doubt in Paul's mind that this was the legend known as Taps.

He had earned the nickname Taps as a young enforcer for the local gangsters in the neighbourhood. Any time someone couldn't understand "pay up", Taps was sent to teach them elocution lessons, usually with a baseball bat, but sometimes with only his bare hands, the size of dogs' heads. The victim would be beaten to an inch of his life, a bloody pulp of bones and blood. Released from hospital, the victim, if fortunate, would emerge balanced on crutches, tap tap tapping his way home.

Taps never once killed anyone – an envious achievement considering the numerous bodies he transformed. Some said he was lucky never to have killed, but they were wrong. Luck had nothing to do with it. He was a professional, a brilliant surgeon-in-reverse who knew precisely when to stop.

Paul smiled feebly and nodded. Taps ignored him.

Shank's office was badly lit, and it took a moment for Paul's eyes to focus, moving on the blurred features.

On a table sat a bust of a severed pig's head, its languid tongue resting between yellow and bloody teeth. A tiny plaque beside the bust read: *It is easier to forgive an enemy than to forgive a friend: William Blake (1757–1827).*

Skeletal statues lined the room. One particular figure was so repulsive Paul could not look at it directly, momentarily averting his eyes from it.

A female skeleton held a tiny skeletal frame of a baby in its hand. It was a shrine to the Virgin and her son, and in a perverse way, the scene evoked love stripped, literarily, to the bone. The bones had been bleached so thoroughly their lines held dark, almost carbon shadows.

Paul found the scene repulsive, almost sacrilegious, despite his irreligious views. *Repulsive,* yes, but thoroughly *compulsive* as he glanced at it again, allowing his eyes to rest upon it.

The figure of Shank sat behind a desk. He appeared massive. Even while being seated, his bulk dwarfed the room. His head housed not a stitch of hair, and immediately Paul thought of the lollipop-sucking cop from an old TV show. Shank's skin had the pinkish tone of a healing wound. A trellis of wrinkles covered it in thick layers guarding eyes as dark as the undersides of decayed leaves. *He has the look of a total bastard,* thought Paul.

A cigar smouldered in an ashtray, long forgotten by its owner.

Shank appeared engrossed in a jigsaw puzzle on the table. It looked like an unfinished picture of an angel.

Paul found it strange for such a large man to be doing jigsaw puzzles – and puzzles of angels, into the bargain. The puzzle held the same withered appearance as the large painting on the outside of the abattoir and was similar in design to the paintings on the wall.

"Blake," replied Shank, as if reading Paul's mind. "All the pictures in here and throughout the building are from the brilliant mind of William Blake. The greatness of any painting is measured by its ability to keep surprising us, revealing something new every time we go back to look at it. If you look closely enough, you can see a woman's face on the chest of the angel, over in the corner. If you look hard enough, you can see all sorts of things . . ."

Shank's voice was deep, confident with power.

Not knowing what to say, Paul said nothing while he stared at the angel's chest, searching for a woman's face.

He failed to find it.

"You've come for a job in my abattoir?" said Shank, glancing up from his task.

His eyes are impossibly black, like milk-less coffee, thought Paul. *They have no pupils.*

"Yes. I was hoping –"

"Hoping? Ha! I would leave that at the door, Mister Goodman. Only reality exists here, not tidy little words like hope. Think you can handle working in a place like this? Think that just *any* person can work in this place? Think *you* can work in the House of Redemption?" asked Shank, holding a piece of the jigsaw puzzle between finger and thumb, seemingly debating its niche. "Think you can work in a place without hope, and that you've got the stomach for it, Mister Goodman?"

Stomach wasn't part of the equation – a pay cheque was. "I don't have any problems with my stomach," replied Paul, his words full of false confidence. He hardly recognised his own voice. It sounded like tin, shaky, cowardly.

Shank gently placed the jigsaw piece into place and nodded to himself. "This place is like a jigsaw puzzle, Mister Goodman. One piece out of place and nothing is achieved. We are all soldiers in the same trench, all fighting the same battle."

There was arrogance in Shank's voice that seemed strangely justified as he reached for a cloth to wipe his hands. "Well, tell you what, Mister Goodman. I'll do a deal with you. I'll show you about the place, and if you don't vomit or faint . . ." Shank smiled a tight smile, forced and devious, and immediately Paul thought of the girl with bad skin and large head, the girl who resembled a snake. "Okay?"

Paul nodded.

"Let's go," commanded Shank, laughing. "Let us prepare for the shadows of the dead."

Paul moved for the door, but not before Shank told him to wait, he had something for him.

"Here. Put this on. Don't want your head getting hurt, do

we?" Shank handed Paul a yellow hardhat. "All would-be recruits wear *yellow* until they have proven their worth. Green is for the apprentices; red for the qualified butchers. Black, like this one I'm wearing, is for the boss. There only is one black hat in here. Understand, Mister Goodman?"

Paul nodded. He wished he were some place other than here. What he would give to be in the Tin Hut, playing snooker, listening to his best friend, Lucky, talking a load of shit.

"Oh," continued Shank, stopping at the door. "You just could be blessed to spot one or two gold hats. Those are . . . warriors." He smiled a scary smile. "They are people who were born to be butchers of creatures . . . blood and death is second nature to them. They are dedicated to their craft. So, a little piece of advice: if you do happen to see a gold hat – pretend you didn't. Avoid their attention without causing unpleasantness. That's one of the important survival skills in here. They don't like people staring at them. No, not one bit . . ." Shank laughed.

A shiver touched Paul despite the freezing temperature already mounting in the room and throughout the building. He wished Shank would stop lecturing. It sounded degrading, full of malice.

Resigned, Paul placed the hardhat on his head, knowing it was two sizes too big, and walked out the door and up the stairs, directly behind Shank. He knew he looked stupid in the yellow, oversized hardhat, but realised this was all part of the game played by Shank.

Two enormous steel doors were pushed aside by Shank, who, like a ringmaster, indicated for Paul to enter. "Feast your eyes on the beauty of death and you will know that this place has no equal."

Hesitating, Paul stopped, as if to take a breath of air.

Shank grinned before pushing Paul ahead. "Doubt is the gate through which slips the most deadly of enemies, Mister Goodman. Hesitate and you die. Surely, we don't want that on your first day, do we?"

Reluctantly, Paul entered, and immediately felt as if an invisible hand had slammed against his stomach. The place was massive and held no boundaries. It was breathtakingly horrible, like the Sistine Chapel blooded by barbarians, seething with rage in a hideous frenzy of activity. Its dank coldness reeked with tension, void of all things human. The massive floor was littered with sawdust chips speckled red with imperfections, while above him thousands of withered electric wires hung dangerously like spindly skeleton bones on a giant spider. There was a sense of danger about the place, a sense that someone was going to be killed before the day was complete.

Ruddy violins of sheep carcasses captured on unforgiving "S" hooks dangled grotesquely from above, mingling with dead, cello-shaped cows, like a bizarre scene from Hieronymus Bosch marrying the surrealism of Salvador Dali.

More of the same type of biblical paintings, such as those in Shank's office, lined the walls. There seemed to be hundreds if not thousands of them, and like those intense displays, the eyes in the surrounding pictures seemed to stare at him – at everyone – like sentinels on duty, illuminated by garish fluorescent lights.

Workers were saturated in blood and moving in perfect harmony, as if part of some farcical play performed for an invisible audience. They all seemed to be talking at once.

"Ladies and gentlemen! Your attention, please!" screamed Shank, his voice rising above the skull-rattling noise of machinery.

But if the workers heard his voice, they showed nothing, continuing with their hacking and sawing of meat, some of which was dead, some of which was clearly not.

"A contestant has entered our domain, our magical kingdom of life and death. He believes he is our equal. What say you?"

The workers were as bloody as the mangled wreckages of meat they hacked at, and distinguishable only by the tiny whiteness of their eyes, teeth and fingernails. They continued working their endless preparation of death as if they were immune to the question uttering from Shank's mouth.

Paul's nostrils began to flood with a stomach-churning smell. The same stinking stench from outside the building came at him with force, but more powerful in its taste of rotten flesh, and of fear and hate oozing from the ruins of carcasses and their tormentors.

One group of workers, their faces obscured by the steam rising from giant mugs of tea cradled in their massive hands, sat comfortably in a corner, seemingly immune to the chaos all about them, talking, reading newspapers roughly handled by reddened hands. Other workers devoured meals of fried eggs and freshly slaughtered meat, wiping their stained mouths with bloody, ragged handkerchiefs and soiled aprons.

Paul felt his stomach move at the thought of eating a creature he had seen alive minutes ago. How could their stomachs hold down the food? He felt his head go light and wondered if he was going to vomit, if his resolve would evaporate?

Swiftly, he remembered Shank's warning about fainting and vomiting and he willed himself to win, not to succumb. He needed this job, badly. He would not leave this terrible place without it.

"Are you feeling okay?" asked Shank, grinning. "You look pale. Perhaps we can arrange a visit for some other time? It's nothing to be ashamed about, Mister Goodman. Many are called, but few are chosen . . ."

Paul barely collected himself sufficiently to frame a thought. "Thank you for your concern, Mister Shank," he replied. "But I'm fine. More than fine . . ."

"Good!" replied Shank, slapping Paul's back. "That's what we want to hear. Isn't it, ladies and gentlemen?"

No one heard. If they did, they did not answer.

Shank walked ahead, talking loudly, his voice filled with pride. "My abattoir is the biggest single killing unit in the country. The major activities involved in the operation of the abattoir are slaughter and chilling of carcass product, boning and packaging, as well the drying of skins for leather. Nothing goes to waste here, Mister Goodman. *Nothing.*"

Moving swiftly, Shank walked towards a cluster of open doors, followed closely by Paul.

"Over there, to your left, are the by-product rooms housing dripping, fertiliser, oil, sinews, hoofs, hair, glue, bones and horns." A sound kept interrupting the flow of Shank's words, a sound so soft it was barely perceptible, of muffled voices emanating from somewhere inside. Only the terror in the sound sharpened its appeal to be heard. The voices weren't loud, but their clarity grew.

Paul traced the sound from some place near the upper

entrance, an independent floor governed by a cluster of red-hats who stood menacingly about like a hierarchy of Spanish Inquisition cardinals about to pronounce death on a heretic. There was an absence of movement, a core of quiet and stillness complete, as if they were waiting on a photographer. He had the edgy feeling that all the activity must mean something, even if he couldn't make any sense of it.

As if in trance, Paul followed the sound, followed its Pied Piper magnetic power even though he didn't want to. For a brief moment he thought he saw the flash of a gold hat and felt his resolve being undermined a little by Shank's words not to look at the gold hats, as if they were Medusa, capable of turning flesh to stone.

Turning his head slightly, Paul watched as bewildered creatures entered one end of the large room, only to emerge naked, humiliated and dismembered at the other atop a large conveyer-belt slithering its way ominously in his direction. The workers moved quickly on the creatures, in a frenzy of activity, infected by the fervour, their hands gesticulating like traffic cops on too much caffeine.

The gold hat was screaming instruction at the workers. "Keep it tight, Raymond, you stupid fuck! The cows are trying to leap over the barrier. Stun the bastards, will you!"

Galvanised by the smell of blood, some of the cows, in a futile attempt to escape, were attempting to leap the barrier. Raymond, a tall skinny young man, looked confused by the rush of cows heading dangerously in his direction.

"Careless, Geordie!" shouted Shank angrily at the gold hat. "Bloody careless. They've squeezed out of the stunning tongs and head bars. *You're* in charge, but you're losing control of the situation. The animals have taken over the farm. Fix it!"

Without hesitation, Geordie grabbed the stun gun from Raymond's hand, pushing him backwards towards the crushing beasts, regardless of his safety. There was a unity of purpose in Geordie's movements.

Seconds later, the *spa spa spa* sound of the stun gun began, isolating the brain of each creature as the tiny metal pellets hit home at the back of the skull, devastating all feelings in the body.

As each beast buckled to the ground, it was quickly set upon by the angry butchers, raging that the creatures had humiliated them in front of Shank. Most of the cows had their throats quickly slit, but a few not so fortunate suffered a slow and agonising death of stabs wounds to the body. A bloody highway of intricate veins and vestigial nerves were strewn everywhere, some ticking with shock.

"Look at them move, Mister Goodman. It's almost like poetry in motion," said Shank, admiringly. "You know, sometimes I think they see the faces of their wives in those cows . . ."

Paul said nothing. He was numb. He had never witnessed anything on this scale before, never imagined this was how his Saturday fry originated. He felt shame, disgust and hatred for the grinning faces. He had no other option than to look away.

"It's a great form of anger-management, is slaughtering," continued Shank. "I could make a fortune selling this therapy – and it would work. Not like the nonsense of sitting on a couch and telling some shrink your problems. How can sitting on a couch and making a fool of yourself be beneficial? It's all baloney. Voodoo magic and hogwash. No, this is the real thing. None of my butchers go home with anger in their hearts. It's all released here, in the Bloody Garden of Eden. Isn't that right, Geordie?"

Geordie turned to face Shank.

"Who's this idiot? Another tourist come to visit Grisly World?" asked Geordie, ignoring Shank's question. "And why is he staring at me? Think I'm a freak, Idiot? Never see someone wearing scaffolding?"

To Paul's horror and disbelief, Geordie was a young woman. Steel leg-braces looped the outside of her legs, and as she walked menacingly towards him like darkness on the move, her limps becoming more pronounced in their vertical stiffness. Her eyes were mirrored bullets, lethal in their intensity and savagely focused, bleaching the depth of his bones. Shadows jiggled on the wall behind her, seemingly human, following her every move. She seemed to have deliberately set her face into an expression that no worker could misinterpret: *Don't fuck with me*, it screamed. Now it said to Paul: *Fuck off; your kind isn't welcome here.*

"Easy, Geordie," said Shank, grinning at the look on Paul's face. "Calm your arse down. I don't want you killing a would-be recruit on his first day. This is Mister Paul Goodman. He's passed all the tests. Almost. Hasn't fainted once. Hasn't even shit his pants. He's defeated the lot of you." Shank laughed. It was full of scorn and disdain for Geordie, for the workers.

From a gold container, Shank removed a cigar, sniffed its leaves then lit it. The tobacco crackled, and for a second, his face became invisible, lost in the mist of smoke.

"Has he, indeed? Not shit his pants? Well? What are we waiting for?" said Geordie, her eyes never leaving Paul's. "He's either with us or against us. Time for Paul the Baptist to find out if he's a heathen or a butcher. Take him away!"

They came at him from every direction, like ants, their hands grabbing and pulling him to the ground. Within seconds his clothes were ripped from him and he was carried trophy-high, naked. He felt he was losing his mind, as if this was one of those nightmares you awake from only to find yourself paralysed with fear at what your mind has done to you, recognising it as valid and real, but that perhaps it never really existed to begin with.

"What? What are you doing?"

His mind wasn't working right, as if it were wrapped in putty. Everything was soft and filtered, even the noise around him. He felt as if he wanted to throw up but didn't have the energy. He became light-headed. The sensation was one of floating away. Somehow, it was important that he stay on the ground. He blinked his eyes to try and clear his thinking. There were white spots behind his lids. They turned black when he opened his eye. He watched them, dancing across the ceiling. What was it about spots? There was something important but he couldn't remember. Maybe it would come back to him, he thought, and closed his eye once more. He screamed to be released, but the mob only screamed louder, laughing, encouraged by his fear and helplessness. Now he felt as humiliated and as naked as the beasts whose deaths he had witnessed a few minutes ago.

"Baptise. Bap-bap-tise. Baptise. Bap-bap-tise," they chanted, almost in song. "Baptise. Bap-bap-tise . . ."

The more Paul struggled, the tighter their grip on him became. He fought off the twin impulses to scream and kick.

Within seconds, he was drained and felt his body go limp, like paper damp with water.

"Now you're learning," whispered Geordie into his ear. "You can struggle, Idiot, but you can never win. Not here, not in this place. Never *ever* in this place . . ."

Unexpectedly, the crowd stopped and eased him to the floor, gently, as if he were something fragile, a tiny baby newly born.

"John and Alfred? Take his ankles. Raymond? His left hand; I've got his right. The rest of you stand back," commanded Geordie.

"What are you going to –" But before Paul could complete his question, he found himself being hoisted into the air.

"Ready lads?" said Geordie. "One . . ."

"Hey!" shouted Paul, fear in his voice, as he felt his body swaying to and fro. "What are you –?"

"Two . . ."

"Look, okay. You win. Please . . ."

"Hope you can swim, Idiot. *Threeeeeeeeeeeeeeeeee!*"

He remembered sailing through the air, naked, and the truly exhilarating experience of what birds must feel at the start of take-off. A swirl of colours passed over his perspective. He remembered his penis wobbling from side to side, making horrible slapping sounds, as it winked at him like a one-eyed pirate.

Only when he realised that they had tossed him from the third floor and that he was falling quite rapidly towards his death, did he scream.

Some ray of hope, perhaps augmented by his closeness to death, seemed to fill him with adrenaline, dulling the fear inside. His life didn't fly before him in a blink of an eye – as was rumoured in near-death experiences – but when his face and body crashed into the red carpet beneath him, killing him instantly, he did piss himself.

Red. What would the world be without it? It is the most attractive of colours, primary in its superiority. Roses, apples, wines and Valentines. Red sunsets and hot love. Red is the component and attribute of power, vitality, passion, anger and excitement. All are governed by red. But without doubt, the most important of all reds is blood. Without it, we are nothing. It is a life-giver.

When you come upon an action at the precise moment of occurrence, movement is frozen, sound waves do not propagate, and what you see is not real. And so it happened, spreading through Paul's whole being as he found himself swimming in blood – lakes and seas of the stuff – knowing if he didn't do something very quickly, it would not be a life-giver but a life-taker.

His head came to the surface, only to find the rest of his body being pulled back down by the blood's magnetic power. He was a good swimmer, loved to swim, but this thick liquid was unlike water. It had more in common with a swamp, and the more he struggled the stronger it became.

The workers had surrounded the massive blood tank, cheering him each time his head rose to the challenge. He didn't know how deep the tank was, nor how wide, but it seemed endless. Yet, he believed he could accurately form a picture of how the tank had been apportioned for all the running blood oozing and streaming from the unwilling throats of cows and sheep. Only now did his brain kick in, telling him how he had hit the red carpet of a swimming pool full of animal blood, doing a massive belly-flap before quickly sinking like a stone, his body rapidly losing buoyancy.

The blood disorientated him, his direction, as did his sense of survival, which he would have had if he were drowning at sea, in beautiful salty water.

Each gasp of air released a mouthful of blood. He remembered the beautiful voice of Shank telling them to bring him up, he's had enough. Then the hateful words of Geordie saying no, others have lasted longer, test him, test the bastard Idiot.

"Out, I said. Take him out – *now*," commanded Shank, no longer tolerating Geordie's defiance.

Hands quickly reached into the pool and retrieved the bloody body of Paul. He resembled something which has just crawled from the womb, all bloody and slimy, slithering and squirming on the floor, a dead thing somehow reactivated. When he coughed, great bubbles of orange and pink emerged from his throat gushing out his mouth and down his nostrils and slowly but surely he realised he was still alive – barely.

"You showed favouritism, Shank," accused Geordie. "He still had ten seconds left."

"Perhaps," replied Shank, removing a pocket watch from his waistcoat before smiling. "Perhaps your watch is simply wrong? Eh, Geordie?"

Geordie glared at the motionless body at her feet on the unforgiving hardwood floor. She knew there were certain lines even she could not cross. But she also knew there were lines needing to be crossed. "He still hasn't toasted our health, yet," she said, smiling deviously. "Even you can't deny us tradition, Shank."

Shank though for a moment. "He'll do it. I've no doubt whatsoever. Isn't that right, Mister Goodman?"

Paul could hear the words falling in his direction, but he could not understand their meaning. Hands pulled him up and steadied him against the massive metal pool.

"Almost home, Mister Goodman," said Shank staring directly into Paul's eyes, like a trainer who had just witnessed his boxer take an unmerciful battering.

You've almost got the job, Paul, said the voice of his mother in his head. *Show them what a man you are, show them good and proper,* she encouraged. *And don't forget all that meat for free each Friday. We'll show the whole street it. Steak and sausages and chops and . . .*

"Here you go, Idiot," said Geordie's voice, breaking his thoughts. She held a pint glass full of warm blood to Paul's mouth. "Drink it down, deep to your stomach. Drink and the job is yours. Isn't that right, Shank."

Shank said nothing. There was nothing he could say. All were watching. All remembered their own bloody initiation in the pool of horror and pint of terror. There would be no exception.

You can do it, Son, enthused his mother's crackly voice. *One great gulp and it's all over. Think of it as a pint of coloured Guinness. You can do it . . .*

"Do it. Do it. Do it. Do it," chanted the crowd who had now gathered, surrounding Paul in a circle. "Do it. Do it. Do it . . ." On and on they went, hypnotised by their own sound.

The smell in Paul's nostrils made him think of OXO cubes. He loved OXO cubes, especially on winter nights. He knew he would never touch another one again as he brought the pint to his lips, dreading the stench, not wanting to look behind Geordie's shoulders, knowing a tiny calf lay staggered and drained, strung up by its skull, its long legs dangling as a small pool of blood grew from it, the same blood resting on his lips, its taste of salty iron familiar from his past as a brawler.

You can do it, said a voice in his head. It sounded like Shank's voice but it was probably his mother's. *One great gulp for mankind . . .*

An urgency for completion filtered through Paul, as if tiny threads of his brain were becoming unstitched. In his mind, he was in an arid region, scorching heat piling down on him, sandstorms flaying his skin. He felt his tongue swell through parched and peeling lips. In was only a matter of time before he was dead, the sand covering his body.

When the oasis came into view, it was the most beautiful sight he had ever witnessed. He drank from its water, greedily, and believed it to be the greatest taste he had ever tasted, gulping it down, disregarding the strange lumps floating on top.

Thirst. Thirst. Thirst . . .

"Good man, Goodman. Well done!" exclaimed Shank, shaking his head in admiration. "Well bloody done, indeed, Mister Goodman!"

The crowd joined in, whistling and cheering, even those who had wanted him to fail, to die before their eyes, begrudgingly joined in the congratulations.

Paul said nothing. He didn't trust himself. The pint of blood sat in his stomach like an angry fist.

Well done, Son, said the voice of his mother. *You've done us proud. I'll have a big mug of tea waiting for you when you get home. Wait till Maggie Mullan hears this. Her and her skinny pork chops on a Sunday. I don't suppose you'll be wanting a bit of bacon with your spuds . . .?*

"Raymond? Take Mister Goodman to the shower and see that he gets some overalls to go home in. He starts Monday morning, six o'clock sharp. Is that sound, Mister Goodman?"

For the first time since entering this marvellous and terrifying place, Paul smiled.

"That . . . that is sound, Mister Shank. Very sound, indeed. Thank . . . thank you."

Once outside the abattoir, Paul felt free. He inhaled the cold air with the same vigour he had used when he thought he was drowning in a sea of stinking blood mixed with sounds and vibrant sinister smells.

It was dark now, with evening dominating the hazy distance, seemingly in all directions at once, squeezing out the last measure. Only the rough, rising shapes of trees and rusted vehicles, with their small properties of light and sound, were sharp enough to make a clear image in his head, to help guide him home, not towards the moonlit fields that spread as far as the eye could see, but towards the dark and ominous woods that towered behind the abattoir. The smell of dinners being prepared in far-off homes floated on the soft breeze, signalling the close of day.

The image of the mysterious Geordie, her legs shackled and imprisoned for ever, surfaced again in his head. He knew she was watching him from a window, but he didn't look back, even though he wanted to. He wanted to see her face. Was it filled with defeat? Hatred? Indifference? He wanted to look back, but didn't. He was just glad to be going home.

CHAPTER TWO

Dreams of Darkness and Delicious Death

"In dreams begins responsibility."
W.B. Yeats, *Responsibilities*

"There was a door and I couldn't open it. I could not touch the handle. Why could I not walk out of my prison? What is hell? Hell is oneself, hell is alone, the other figures in it merely projections. There is nothing to escape from and nothing to escape to. One is always alone . . ."
T.S. Eliot, *The Cocktail Party*

DREAMS, TO PHILIP Kennedy, serve a very specific purpose. They say dreams have no colour, but Philip Kennedy knows that to be untrue. His dreams are in red.

Sometimes the red is as placid as oil on a candle's drip and is almost calming. Sometimes it beads his brow with sweat. But always, that horrible whispering, accusing voice: *Why? Why me? Why why why . . .?*

Through sheer force of will, he smashed the present night-mare's iron grip, waking breathless in the raw-boned darkness, almost as if he were a dream, a ghost, a figment conjured out of need.

He'd had a headache for four days. It wasn't his first – he had a history of migraines, but usually, by morning, the pain was gone. This was different. The headaches had left a residue of pain unlike anything he had tasted. He believed that the young man who had visited the shop two days ago, inquiring about snooker cues, had sparked all this. Not forgetting, of course, Catherine's treacherous, but clumsy sleight-of-hand . . .

Everything began spinning around him as the remnants of last night's alcohol coursed through his veins. In his head, he heard the unmistakable sound of someone trying to ease a cork from a neck of a bottle. It was an enticing hum, and the un-natural progression of his thoughts lead repeatedly back to this imagined sound until he could no longer tolerate its torturous call.

Rising, he poked the patches of darkness until he found the open cabinet and skilfully fiddled a slab of wood from its place, pulling it out before capturing the bottle of whiskey with its torn label and lying words. Frantically – but expertly – he mixed the stale water from the rusted jug with just the right amount of alcohol – not so much that you could smell it but more than enough to give it that little kick. *A little kick in the arse . . .*

Impatiently, he swished the diluted alcohol through his teeth, swallowing the amber liquid, repeating the exercise until the taste returned to his tongue, burning it with intensity, wishing he could explore the bottle again and again, for ever and a day, never ending its flow, admiring the simplicity of its power.

The throbbing slowly began to subside, and he felt only numbness and depletion while walking to the window. *Air. Need some air . . .*

He wrestled the reluctant window open and poked his head outside its frame, as if preparing for the guillotine. Above him the sky was disturbing and grey. He could see bellies of clouds moving overhead and thought about rain. He thought about a beach . . .

In due course, he made his way downstairs to the shop, focusing his thoughts upon routine tasks, passing Cathleen's bedroom, stopping at the toilet to relieve himself in the sick light of the dingy space.

The shop itself was carefully arranged in a dimly lit, fragile ecology of handmade cupboards and drawers. The displays before him presented shelves of silverware lounging on black velvet with plenty of separation between each item. Cathleen didn't believe in crowding the more expensive goods in the shop.

Tools, manually and electrically driven, lined the far walls like trophies and weapons; do-it-yourself books poked from wooden crates. Once, they had belonged to the men from town; now they belonged to Cathleen, held by the power of ransom. She would never use any of the tools, of course, but that wasn't the point. What she had, they didn't. She always laughed at their feeble excuses, how they always said for a couple of days – a week at most. But the week would turn into a month, and before long, the docket would have accumulated enough late-payment penalties to make payment unattainable.

Getting the goods from the bad . . . *Never borrow,* was her motto. *Be the one everyone owes. Foster suspicion. That's the power. The true power. Taking the goods from the bad.* She loved that last saying. Thought it up one Sunday at church. *Take the goods from the bad, the scum, because that is all they are – will always be. Scum.*

Without exception, his preferred items were the collections of old books – some of them first printing editions: Nietzsche, Tolstoy and Kant shoulder to shoulder with Shakespeare, Socrates, Shaw and Joyce.

One of Kennedy's favourite books, *The Ragged Trousered Philanthropist,* was beginning to look a bit ragged – a bit like its hero – its spine withered and tarnished. It was a first edition, and more care should have been granted it, but he couldn't resist rereading it every chance he had, regardless of how many times he had read it.

Catherine had threatened to burn the book, along with all the others, but quickly recanted seeing the storm in his face. *Weather is always unpredictable, but especially the storm . . .*

The Ragged Trousered Philanthropist sat next to *Don Quixote,* his favourite.

He loved the smell from the books, the musky smell of opium which never failed to bring back the lanced days of childhood memories; of a childhood he hated and feared, but would give everything he owned to be transported back to that time.

Kennedy walked out on to the street and pulled the rusted shutters up from the shop's front, casting a feeble light into the entrance of the shop, revealing more items "rescued" from the hands of their owners: Sunday suits lined up like naked carcasses in the local abattoir for all to see – a million threads, a thousand buttons, a universe of heart-breaking stories captured and exposed, humiliating the one-time owners; an army of candlesticks and lamps granted no light, only a silvery coating of cobwebs falsely glimmering with life, each tagged with the sale price; women's shoes surpassed men's boots, as did the wedding rings of dainty fingers; blocks upon blocks of bed linen accumulated from floor to ceiling, standing like giant pillars of cloth, all mixed in the melting pot of personal heirlooms, too numerous to calculate.

Unenthusiastically, he made his way back to the shop, towards the kitchen.

Dirty plates loitered in the sink, grease congealing. He decided to make some coffee before preparing breakfast for Cathleen, his sick wife.

The thought of entering her room, seeing her sitting atop the bed, her nylons knotted about her massive ankles, made him shudder. Occasionally, she would wink, just as he prepared to leave, a wink that said: *Don't forget my bedpan, darling. I had a terrible night last night. Must stop eating those prunes, even though I am quite partial to them.* All this, while spreading her enormous, unnaturally white legs wide across the bed in an unspoken declaration of territorial rights.

Cathleen had already survived two husbands, both of whom rested side by side at the local cemetery like bookends of death. Unfortunately for Kennedy, there would be little chance of husband four – or wife two.

It had been over two years since he had been in that bed, but Kennedy thanked God for small mercies. Over the years, Cathleen had piled on the weight at an incredible rate, as if preparing for the *Guinness Book of World Records*. Her one-time lovely face had been consumed then camouflaged with layer upon layer of candle-grease fat, until he barely recognised her as the woman he had first met.

In the kitchen, Kennedy found a bunch of bananas in a fruit bowl on the dining table. They were dull yellow, with large brown spots the size of thumbs. Tiny fruit flies hovered above them quietly, drifting back and forth above the shine of the table. Aimlessly, he sliced through a banana, dicing it before mixing it with her bran, the horribly disgusting bran she used to *clear her plumbing*.

With all of the darkness lifted, the light in the hallway seemed more intense, spotlighting his every movement as he entered her room without knocking. She didn't like him not knocking. Good.

A faded illumination escaped from a neck of a tiny bedside lamp, competing against the bluish glow of the ever-present television screen flashing on Cathleen's sagging, alabaster belly. *Flicker, flicker, flicker.* Her left leg was wrapped in plaster, a remnant from an accident two weeks ago.

The television murmured softly in the background, showing highlights from a food programme in some faraway, rain-drenched place.

Catherine's turret-shaped eyes never left her husband's movements. She was first to speak. "Didn't sleep . . ."

a wink last night, he finished in his head.

". . . a wink last night," she sighed.

"Have you been taking your sleeping pills?" he asked, not giving a damn.

"This pain is terrible. It seems to be getting sharper. My bedsores are . . .

. . . *becoming unbearable.*

". . . becoming unbearable." A moan escaped her large

mouth. "This morning, I was depressed for no conceivable reason whatsoever. Imagine that. Why on earth would I be depressed?" The derision in her voice was sharp.

"The dosage. Doctor Moore should increase the dosage, for you," replied Kennedy, instinctively.

Cathleen had been instructed to take insulin three times a day and to keep an eye on her blood sugar. Three of her toes had been amputated over the last six months, and Moore had warned her, constantly, that her health would rapidly deteriorate if she didn't watch what she consumed. But Cathleen had more interest in a slab of cake, a box of Quality Street, all washed down with a nice hot mug of chocolate, than she did for any annoying needles and vegetable diets.

"I keep asking God what I've done . . ."

. . . for Him to place this terrible cross on my shoulders.

". . . for Him to place this terrible cross on my shoulders."

In his head, Philip pictured Cathleen nailed to a cross. The nails were covered in rust from the smelly sweat oozing from her. He was at her feet, in the garb of a Roman soldier, spear at the ready to finish the job. She was asking for water. He smiled before shoving the bedpan in her face, his mind playing out every delicious detail in slow motion.

Catherine sniffed suspiciously. "You've been drinking."

"And you've been pissing," retorted Kennedy, his eyes flashing at the overflowing bedpan. "How you can smell alcohol over the stench of your own piss is beyond me."

"You're a king bastard," hissed Catherine. "You put me in this situation. Helpless, depending on you."

Kennedy smirked. "You put yourself in that sickbed, not me – you and your nose."

"Make sure you open up early today. It's Friday," replied

Catherine, quickly ignoring the innuendo. "The bastards always have money on Friday. Don't be soft on them, like you were with Biddy Black, last week."

Biddy was the weekly housekeeper. Kennedy had allowed the unfortunate woman to regain possession of her dead husband's wedding ring without the added interest, never realising he had been set up by Cathleen, who had suspected him of going soft. Even though her sickness was slowly eating her ability, being stationery did not retard her power one iota.

What a fool he had been, never suspecting that that bastard Biddy Black had been on Cathleen's payroll. But he remained silent, keeping his expression neutral; knowing the flaw of most arguments is the inability to anticipate the rebuttal.

Placing the breakfast on a side table, he turned to leave the room, ignoring the dishes from last night.

"Maybe I should hire a food taster?" she said, her face a spider's web of suspicion as she glanced at the greasy contents resting on the tray. "Perhaps it's only my imagination, but there seems to be a bitter taste to the food you've been cooking me, lately."

"Perhaps the bitterness isn't in the food . . ."

"Perhaps you didn't cause me to fall, either, almost breaking my neck?" Her wrinkles fell into angry ellipses framing the centre of her face.

Kennedy shook his head. "Not this nonsense again? I warned you about that loose carpet at the top of the stairs, months ago. Told you to be careful. Thank God your weight cushioned the fall . . ."

"Bastard," she hissed.

"You shouldn't talk about God like that. It's disrespectful."

"You think you're so smart, don't you? Think no one will believe that it was you who pushed me, tried to kill me?"

"Kill? Don't be so dramatic. You were embarrassed by your fall. It was your weight and carelessness that caused it. A loose nail, an upturned corner of carpet. Everyone knows that," Kennedy smiled. "You really must stop watching those old Agatha Christie movies. They're feeding your imagination. Why on earth would I harm you?"

"You know damn well . . ."

"Do I? Tell me."

"Stop playing games! You think I have something, something belonging to you."

Kennedy's face tightened, slightly. "Do you?"

Catherine looked away from his eyes. "No . . ."

"Good. That's that sorted. Nothing to worry about then. Now, eat your breakfast. I done your pancakes just the way you like them."

Catherine shuddered slightly. "I'm not hungry."

"Nonsense. We need you to get your strength back as quickly as possible. The shop is a disaster without you. Also, you'll be able to help me search for an item I seem to have . . . misplaced. You know how annoying that can be, believing you've placed it someplace only to find it gone when you check. Maybe my old memory is no longer as reliable as it used to be. Anyway, that's why I need you to help me search for it, when you get better." He removed a knife from the tray, and expertly sliced a pancake into four parts. "Open wide."

Reluctantly, Catherine's mouth opened partially. Kennedy squeezed a pancake patch in.

"Close and chew. It's important to always chew your food. We don't want you choking. Do we?"

The chime of the shop's bell echoed up the stairs.

"Must go," said Kennedy, leaving the remainder of the pancake resting on a plate. "I'll bring your lunch up, later. I'm making your favourite. Chicken soup. Yum yum. That'll soon have you on your feet." Kennedy smiled and winked, then closed the door behind him, gently.

Catherine quickly reached for the bucket beneath the bed and spilt her guts into it.

CHAPTER THREE

Lucky

"Tell me thy company, and I'll tell thee what thou art."
Miguel de Cervantes, *Don Quixote*

"Keep your fears to yourself, but share your courage with others."
Robert Louis Stevenson

PAUL HAD REACHED the entrance to the Tin Hut – the local snooker and drinking hall – just as the familiar voice asked, "What the hell are you doing with a brush shaft? This is a snooker hall, lad. Not the abattoir's annual sweeping contest."

Paul didn't want to think about the abattoir. He would be back in that place in less than thirty hours. Like a prisoner on parole, he dreaded the thought, but knew he had no other choice. He had been out of work for almost a year – his longest stint of unemployment – and the abattoir seemed the best opportunity to rectify that. He hated the thought of getting the job but, paradoxically, knew he was lucky to have secured it. His financial situation left him in no doubt about that, not to mention his mother who never failed to tell him that he should be married by now, giving her grandchildren. Of course, that was a load of nonsense. The last thing his mother wanted was to be in close proximity to people less than two feet tall with rubbery faces. She didn't hate kids: simply could no longer tolerate them, their shitty smell and non-stop mouths, as if the one child in her life had drained her for ever.

"Funny you should mention the abattoir, Lucky, because by the time I'm finished with you and the rest of the would-be challengers in there, it *will* be a slaughterhouse. Make no mistake about that. And that lucky charm of yours won't help, either."

Lucky raised his wrist and kissed the gold bracelet dangling from it. *There's only one Lucky* it proudly proclaimed.

"The day you beat me at snooker is the day I give this to you."

They both grinned and entered the Tin Hut.

Once inside, Lucky volunteered to buy a drink.

"Performing a miracle, Lucky? Where the hell would you get the money for two pints?" smiled Paul.

"Well, the way it works is that you're suppose to stop me, preventing my hand – which is strategically placed in my pocket – from coming out, saying – *demanding* – that under no circumstances will I, Paul Goodman, allow a drink to be bought by my best friend, Lucky Short, tonight, because of the wonderful news that on Monday I, Paul Goodman, start my new job at the slaughterhouse."

"I see. But what if your best friend has no money until payday, next week? What then?"

"Credit, me old bucko. Terry Browne knows you now have a job and will be more than willing to put a couple of pints on the slate."

Paul laughed. "You better hope I don't get fired on my first day, my best friend, because it'll be those dancing legs of yours that'll be getting smashed by Terry, not mine. Now make yourself useful. Go over and put our names down for the middle table. I'll get the pints."

While Paul waited for the pints to be pulled, he glanced back at Lucky, who was arguing with someone about being next for the best table in the place, the middle one. It had few rips in it and was almost perfectly balanced, with little or no sliding to the side.

"Suckered in for a free drink from that lazy pissy whore, Paul?" said the owner, Terry Browne, a one-time boxer and trainer. People Terry didn't like were pissy whores. Nearly everyone in the hall had been a pissy whore at one time or another. Only yesterday, Paul had been a pissy whore. Now, with a potential job, he was Paul, a customer with credit.

"He's okay, Terry. Just never had too many breaks in his life," replied Paul, smiling.

"Breaks? The only breaks that pissy whore is interested in are the snooker breaks he makes – and even those are crap." Terry shook his head. "Does he still go to the Boom Boom Rooms for those dancing lessons? Still thinks he's the next Fred Astaire?"

Paul nodded.

"I'd like to give him a good kick up a stair, the pissy whore. I blame him on you no longer having any interest in boxing. You had a lot of potential. A lot of potential."

"Lucky didn't stop me. I just lost interest in getting my head knocked off every time I entered the ring – all of ten seconds," laughed Paul, wishing the pints of Guinness would hurry up and settle. Terry believed that pulling a pint of Guinness was an art, a slow and delicate art, and God help the person who asked him to hurry it up, destroy his masterpiece.

"Don't be daft," said Terry, crossly. "You had potential. Always. Don't let any of these pissy whores tell you anything different, especially that pissy whore Lucky Short. What the hell you ever saw in that walking failure, I'll never know . . ."

Paul just smiled. There was little point in even contemplating a disagreement with Terry, whose middle name was Opinionated. Instead, he watched the beautiful creamy white of Guinness harden, transforming itself into a vicar's collar, while his mind strolled back to yesteryear and the first meeting he ever had of Lucky Short . . .

Imagine having the nickname Willie Short, of having to carry it with you as a young boy through school years, through the pimply, squeaky voice of adolescence. Can you imagine a worse fate?

Try this.

What if the nickname wasn't a nickname but your *real* name?

Willie – Willie Short – couldn't fight to save his life, let alone defend a name he despised. Fortunately, he possessed exceptional fortitude, comfortable with the probability of humiliation at all times. Even some of the girls in the street used to beat him up – usually on a Thursday night after being hyped to the gills by Emma Peel in *The Avengers*. "Is your willie short, Willie Short?" they would tease mercilessly, as only girls can tease.

Paul Goodman was Willie's best friend. Actually, Paul was Willie's *only* friend and ended up fighting most of his fights for him, as friends tend to do for friends. Not a week went by when Paul couldn't be seen with a black eye or busted lip, or some other war wound meant for Willie, whose war cry was: "I'm getting Paul Goodman for ya! He's a famous boxer, ya know! Won a silver medal at the Olympic Games . . . beat the shit out of Mangler Delaney . . ."

It made no difference that Paul had never fought at the Olympics and that the only meeting between the notorious Mangler and Paul ended up with Paul having a new identity done to his face that lasted two weeks.

Paul and Willie had met quite by accident, and depending which friend you listened to, each had a different rendering of the occasion.

One Friday night, Paul had just had his face and spirit battered by Mangler, who seemed driven by the hatred of Paul's handsome face, wishing to make it as ugly as his own.

Delaney was an evil-looking young lad who would grow up to become the local undertaker. Years later, Paul often reflected that perhaps the boxing was only Delaney's apprenticeship, whetting his appetite for what really was his calling: burying the dead.

His face covered in a family of forget-me-not bruises tattooed firmly to his skin, Paul called in to the local café. He wasn't really hungry, but his spirits needed a bit of a lift. Afterwards, he would head home, just in time for his favourite sports show, *147*. He had never missed the show, where snooker players tried to reach the magical break of 147, immortalise their names and have a holiday – all expenses paid – thrown in for good measure.

Snooker was his real passion, not boxing. Boxing was an ordeal inflicted upon him by his mother, who kindly enrolled him at the local boxing club in the misguided belief that it would somehow make a man out of him. He was twelve. What young boy wants to be a man at twelve? All Paul wanted to be was a kid.

Paul figured at least fifteen people were in front of him in the queue and quickly tried to calculate how long it would take before he reached the counter. He prayed he didn't get Annie Parson. She was at least 100 years old and had old battered hearing-pieces in both ears, forcing you to scream at the top of your voice. Tiny brown lumps of earwax covered the pieces, making the chance of hearing nil minus zero.

Annie was an extremely ugly old woman whose nasal hairs dangled like spiders legs, and her foul breath always smelt of tobacco and mints. An army of moles littered what little skin she had, and it was said that if you joined all the moles together – like "join the dots" – they would mutate into an image of Elvis Presley. People said she was good at reading lips as well as tea leaves. Paul believed neither, only that she turned his stomach.

As he eased closer to the counter, he prayed to God to give him a break, just like the break he wanted for Alex "Stormy" Jennings, his favourite snooker player, who hoped for the magical number tonight.

Don't let Annie serve me, God. Please, show some mercy . . .

But there'd be no mercy tonight. Not at the boxing. Not at the café.

"You'll have to speak up, ya little bugger! I can't hear a word you're saying!" boomed Annie, her midget frame perched atop a milk crate barely reaching the lip of the shop's wooden counter top.

Ah, fuck. She's no teeth in. I'm gonna throw up. There's juice on the tip of her nose. It must be snot. Oh, fuck . . .

"Speak up, ya little bugger!"

"I said a fish supper!" screamed Paul, right back at her hairy face. "No salt or vinegar."

"Vulgar! Who're ya calling vulgar, ya little bugger! I've a good mind to call our Anthony! He'll show ya, ya little bugger!" Annie's brother Anthony, the owner of the cafe, was about ninety years old, aided by two walking sticks. He wore clothes two sizes too big and squeaky shoes. You heard him before you saw him.

"No! I just said no salt or vinegar!" Someone started giggling behind Paul. Within seconds, the giggle was contagious. They were all at it.

"Give her a kiss, Paul. Stick your tongue in her mouth," someone shouted, making the laughter louder.

Paul glared back at the crowd, hoping to catch the owner of the smart mouth.

Five minutes later, Annie handed him the steaming package, but not before drowning it in salt and vinegar. The vinegar was seeping heavily through the thin paper. It felt disgusting, like a baby's soiled nappy, and was probably unfit for human consumption.

"In future, you watch your language, ya little bugger!

Coming in here with your face dripping blood all over the place. We run a respectable establishment here. The next time, you'll not be served! I can read lips, ya know!"

Paul quickly grabbed the package from Annie's withered fingers. "There'll be no next time, you old witch! I'm going to Harry Bunts, in future."

"Anthony! *Anthoooonnnyyy!*" screamed Annie. "The little bugger said I had a hairy cunt! Anthony! *Anthoooonnnyyy!*"

The place went into uproar while Paul made good his escape.

Resigned that *147* was gone for another week, Paul rested his tired back against the café wall and opened up the package. The steam rose to his face, the aroma making his stomach growl with anticipation. Like a starving wolf, quickly he devoured the contents and waited.

"That was you who shouted for me to stick my tongue in Annie's mouth. Wasn't it? Don't lie, it'll only make matters worse for you," said Paul, grabbing a boy as he emerged from the café.

Startled, the boy almost dropped his package of chips. "Yes," replied the boy, offering no defence. "I just thought it was funny. I'm sorry . . ."

"Well, it wasn't."

"Your face looks a right mess," said the boy, leaning his face into Paul's. "How many of them were there?"

"Perhaps you would like me to leave *your* face like this? And what are you blabbering about? It was one person, Mangler Delaney, in the ring. I just had a bad night."

"You can say that again. Your face looks like a balloon – a battered and bloody balloon."

"Do you even know who Mangler Delaney is? He won a

silver medal at the Olympic Games, that's all. And I managed to stay in the ring with him for a good two minutes."

"A *good* two minutes, eh? Lucky for you they weren't a bad two minutes," smiled the boy, stretching out his hand to be shaken. "Anyway, my name is William. William Short."

"Never fucking mind, Will*ie*. Now move, out of the way. I've got to get home." Paul wanted to get home before any of the street gangs witnessed his defeated face. They would perceive him an easy target. His life wouldn't be worth living if word got out that he wasn't such a great boxer, after all. Going to the local boxing hall was the only thing that had placed doubt into the minds of the gang members. *Don't fuck with him; he's a boxer, ya know . . .*

Paul knew he would relinquish that life-saving doubt if any of them spotted him, vulnerable and battered.

"My da has great stuff in the house. Magic cream, he calls it. Your face will be like new, once you put it on. Wanna try it?" asked Willie.

No, Paul didn't want to try such nonsense. He didn't even want to be seen talking to this non-ranking non-person.

"I saw Badger Lumley and his gang over near Alexander Street," continued Willie. "That's where you live, isn't it? That's where his gang was lurking. But cheer up. My da says that gangs are where cowards go to hide."

For a split second, doubt and possibly fear registered in Paul's eyes. Badger alone would be no problem. But with his gang . . .? Paul quickly calculated how his face would be like a red rag to a bull once Badger spotted it. He would fancy his chances. Paul would be regarded as a wounded animal.

"Where do you live?" asked Paul, reluctantly.

"King's Court," replied Willie, enthusiastically. "A two-minute walk. That cream'll do the job – guaranteed."

"Guaranteed?"

"Cast-iron."

They kept to the safety of badly lit streets. The darkness covered Paul's wounds, and he was grateful. If only this nuisance would stop asking questions and doing that stupid tap dancing.

"Ever watch Gene Kelly in *Singing in the Rain?*" asked Willie, undeterred by the anger in Paul's stormy eyes.

"Rest your bucket-mouth," whispered Paul, menacingly. "You can be heard a mile away."

To Paul's chagrin, Willie began doing quick spins and high kicks, before bursting into a melody. "I'm singin' in the rain. Just singin' in the rain. What a glorious feeling, I'm happy again. I'm laughing at clouds. So dark up above . . ."

All I need is for it to start bucketing and this maniac to start bouncing off lamp-posts. He really does think he's Gene Kelly. Scary. Very scary, indeed.

"The sun's in my heart. And I'm ready for –"

Lightening-fast, Paul grabbed Willie by the shirt. "I know what you'll be ready for if you don't shut up. You're bringing attention to us, you maniac."

Defeated, Willie continued the journey in silence.

It wasn't a two-minute walk. More like seven minutes. But when they reached Willie's house, Paul felt relieved, as if reaching the sanctuary of a castle.

"Wait here, mate. I'll be back in a second."

Mate? No, that isn't part of the deal, thought Paul, watching the figure disappear up the stairs. *Cream and goodbye.*

Willie's judgement of time seemed totally out of sync with

reality. A second turned into a minute; a minute turned plu-
ral; and just as Paul turned to leave, Willie came rushing down
the stairs, taking the steps two at a time.

"Sorry, mate. I couldn't find, it for a while. He had it hid."
Willie was breathless. "Here, get that slapped on your face.
Bloody magic, that stuff. My da swears by it."

"Put it on here? Now?" asked an incredulous Paul. "Go
home with cream all over my face like some woman out for
the night? Wouldn't I look the right one? Are you trying to
wind me up, Will*ie*?"

"No! I wouldn't do that, mate. But my da uses that every
night. He'd go totally buck-mad if it was gone."

"Buck-mad? I'm the one who must be buck-mad, listening
to a raving lunatic like you." Despite his reluctance, Paul knew
he had little choice, and slowly he dabbed the cream all over
his face. It felt unnatural, girlish, but he was encouraged by the
words of Willie.

"You can hardly see the cream, mate. And in the dark, no
one will notice it. I'm telling ya, my da –"

"I know, swears by it. And stop calling me mate. We're not
mates. Understand?"

"Okay, Paul," smiled Willie, undaunted.

"How come you know my name? I never told you it."

"Are you kidding? Everyone knows you. Paul Goodman.
The man you don't fuck with."

Paul felt his face go red and wondered if it was the cream
burning his skin?

"Well . . . here, take your cream . . . thanks."

"No sweat, Paul. Do you want me to walk you home?
Badger and the gang will be over at –"

"No! No . . . I'll manage."

It was only the next morning, when the miracle happened, did Paul appreciate the strange encounter he had had with the even stranger William Short. The swelling in his face had mysteriously disappeared. Only a few lines of damaged skin tissue turned purple and blue revealed any trace of the hammering the night before.

"Amazing. Afuckingmazing . . ." whispered Paul, studying his face in the mirror, delighted. He was so delighted, in fact, he decide to call over to William's house to thank him.

When Willie saw Paul at his door he couldn't believe it, such was his joy. No one had ever called for him. No one. So startling was this development that the neighbours glanced out their windows, witnesses to an event they believed was not possible.

"Look," said Paul, sheepishly, "I just want to say thanks . . . you were right, the cream was magic. Even *I* swear by it, now."

They both laughed. Willie's mother, working in the kitchen, smiled. It was a long time since she had heard her son laugh. Willie's father, upstairs preparing for the afternoon shift at the steel works, nodded to himself. He always knew his son would be okay

"Can you get me the name of that cream? I'm gonna tell my trainer about it. He'd love that sort of thing."

"You can get it over in Thompson's."

"The chemist shop?"

"Yes, over on Clifton Street."

"What's it called?"

"Easy Shift. It's haemorrhoid cream."

"Hema what cream?" asked Paul, puzzled by this strange sounding name.

"Haemorrhoid cream. You know, piles."

"Piles? Piles of what?" This was becoming more confusing. Paul wished he hadn't asked now.

"*Piles.* You know, those things old people get up their arse."

"Up their arse . . ." Paul felt bewildered "What the fuck do you mean? What's up their arse?"

"Piles – haemorrhoids. Bunches of swelling blood, shaped like grapes. Old people stick the cream up their arse to make the swelling go down. My da uses it every single night. Swears by –"

"*Arse cream?* You made me stick arse cream all over my face? Are you fucking mad? If this ever gets out I'll be called Arse Face for the rest of my life, you mad bastard." Paul made a lunge for Willie, but it was too late. The front door had already been slammed. "You ever, *ever* breathe a word of this, Will*ie,* you're dead," hissed Paul, threateningly through the letterbox. "Do you hear me?"

"You're my best mate, Paul. I would never tell a soul. Honest . . ." replied Willie, hunching down to speak to Paul through the other end of the letterbox. "The moment I saw you, I knew I wanted you for a friend – a best friend. I'm so lucky . . ."

"I was over near North Queen Street, yesterday," said Paul, handing Lucky his pint. "There's an old pawnshop at the bottom of the New Lodge with a great collection of cues. In about four weeks, I'll have one."

"Listen to Rockafella," grinned Lucky. "Just make sure you get me a few pints in between, before you start setting the world on fire with all your money."

Hugging their pints of Guinness, the friends strategically sat themselves down in the far corner, their backs against one of the two potbelly stoves heating the Hut on cool nights like this. Paul felt a satisfying glow emanating from the pregnant belly of the stove, plus they had the advantage of seeing the competition in action, warming up in the rows of snooker tables.

"The owner – some old man with sideburns like Elvis – didn't seem too enthusiastic when I started asking him the price of some of the cues," continued Paul. "It was almost as if he didn't want to sell any item in the place."

"That's Philip Kennedy. He's not the owner. His wife is," said Lucky, sipping on the beer.

"Still, you'd think he'd be only glad of a sale. Didn't look like they were doing too much business, when I was there."

"Would you listen to yourself, bursting with so much money you don't know what to do with it. Anyway, if you knew that poor bastard's wife, you'd understand why he looks so fucking miserable. Cathleen 'Zipper' Kennedy. Know her?"

"Unlike you, Lucky, I've better things to do with my life than to know everyone in this town."

Lucky took another sip of Guinness. The only thing better than a nice cold pint of Guinness was a nice cold pint of *free* Guinness.

"Cathleen came from a well-to-do family. Rumour had it she looked like Marilyn Monroe . . . only ugly. Her da – Jacky Denver – was in the scrap metal business. Loaded to the gills, the bastard. Years ago, he bought an old rusted ship down in the docks, repainted it and sold it to a dictator in some tiny country. Made a fortune – as well as all the headlines. Anyway, when he died he left most of his money to the Church – probably trying to buy his way into heaven. Cathleen received a few crumbs, and from the crumbs came the pawnshop. Not much really, when you consider what her da owned at the time. You can imagine the bitterness eating away at her arse, all these years. A princess relegated to a pauper."

"Well, she stills owns more than most people in town. Fair play to her," Paul managed to say, just before the smirk appeared on Lucky's face.

"Fair play, you say?" Lucky sipped the Guinness slowly, peering over the glass with razor eyes. Paul knew that look could only mean one thing: he, Paul, had walked right into a big pile of shit.

"Fair play, you say?" reiterated Lucky, placing the glass on the table, smiling his fox-with-a-chicken-in-its-mouth smile. "She wouldn't know fair play if it bit her in the arse. Do you know why she is called Zipper?"

Paul didn't answer. There was no point.

"She was also one of the main moneylenders in town. A great bitch of a woman. She carried her own bankroll, hid inside a concealed, zipped-up compartment of her sanitary towel, to deter would-be robbers. Shit, you'd have to be brave to venture near her undergarments. Talk about bloody blood money!"

Paul laughed so loud that snot and beer went flying from his nose, forcing him to snort back the snot just to breathe. "Get the fuck out of here! You just made that up, there now." Paul wiped his face with the sleeve of his shirt.

"If I could make that sort of shit up, I'd make a fortune as a writer," grinned Lucky. "They say she still carries her money in one, even though her days are long gone. Can you imagine the look on the undertaker's face when he comes across that? A sanitary towel on an old woman, and it stuffed with money? Fuck! What I'd give to be there when that pops out."

They both laughed, quietly this time, heeding the warnings from serious faces painted on the snooker players.

"Do you want to hear something even funnier?" asked Lucky.

"Funnier than Zipper?"

"Rumour has it that her husband, Philip, was a member of some sort of gang, years ago. One of their top men, I heard."

"A gang? That old guy? What kind of gang?"

"It's hard to pronounce their name. One of those secret gangs that everyone knows about! Something like N R Key. You know, one of them that goes about causing mayhem, shooting people and all."

Paul grinned. "Don't be daft. That old man couldn't hit the toilet when he pisses. This time, Lucky, you've out-exaggerated yourself, mate. Could you picture him holding a gun, his hands shaking like jelly, before he shoots himself in the foot?"

"I'm only telling you what I heard. He was a bit of a hard man, in his time. Happens all the time, doesn't it?"

Paul grinned. "What happens all the time? You not buying a drink?"

"Go on, grin like a fucking baboon. Suits you right down to your red arse. Time. That's what I'm talking about. It mellows a person. Doesn't it? All that fighting has to do your head in after a while. Right? The old bones and reflexes no longer working. You want a bit of peace in your old age.

Right? Anyway, it's the quiet ones you need to keep an eye on. You can't tell a book by the trousers it wears."

They both laughed.

Apart from the bright lights hovering over the tables, the snooker room was a dark chamber of faded green wallpaper and woodworm-infested trimmings. A dim light was oozing through orange curtains, painting everything in a misty colour of burnt copper. Racks of skinny cues lined the hall like rifles equipped for war. A montage of battered photographs – depicting snooker heroes – covered what the green paint missed.

"Now, tell me again about all those workers," encouraged Lucky. "Seem a right bunch of nutcases. Thank God it's not me working in that place. Did you get to see Shank, the owner? Heard he's a real hard fucking case."

"*See* him? He gave me a personal tour of the shit-hole. Do you know who he looks like?"

"No. Surprise me."

"Do you remember that cop on the old TV show, years ago? The one who always sucked a lollipop and said something like 'who loves ya, baby'? Big baldy head, all massive and lumpy? I can't remember his name, but he's a spitting image of him, only more muscular. Looks like two men built into one."

"Yes. I think I know that cop show. What the fuck was his name? Ironside, wasn't it? That was it," stated Lucky, grinning, appreciating his knowledge of all things useless. "I'm 100 per cent certain. Ironside was his name."

"No. He was the one in the wheelchair. He had plenty of hair."

"Fuck! You're right. Now I'll torture myself all day until I get his fucking baldy name. Wish you hadn't told me."

"You asked."

"Did you get to see Taps? What's he look like? I heard he makes King Kong look small. And what about that tattoo in his mouth? Is it true, or what, about his smile?"

It was also rumoured that Taps had the words YOU ARE LYING tattooed on his gums, visible only when he smiled; the smile soon becoming a poisoned chalice for the recipient.

"He didn't smile at me – thank fuck. And as far as the rest of the workers, well, I can honestly say that you, Lucky boy, would not last a minute in there. Geordie would have you for dinner."

Lucky killed the last of his Guinness, belched before commenting. "You might be surprised, Mister Tough Guy. I may not be a boxer, but I could still end up kicking Geordie's balls in."

"I would be more than surprised, seeing as Geordie's a girl," laughed Paul. "And a handicapped girl, into the bargain."

"A girl, working in the slaughterhouse? And handicapped? You don't think I could beat a wee crippled girl? Have you no respect for me as a mate?" Lucky sounded wounded.

"Don't worry about that. She's not your average girl. In fact, she is unashamedly frightening."

"To look at?"

Paul thought for a moment. "No. Actually . . . she is quite pretty. But there is something about her, all that anger, as if it is all bottled up, ready to explode at any minute. She probably – deliberately – picked the abattoir to release all that anger on the creatures in there – human as well as animal . . ."

Paul seemed to drift, as if something was coming to him,

hazily, something in a thought that refused to linger more than a second, then was gone when Lucky interrupted by saying, "Speaking of the abattoir. How are you fixed for getting some steak for my ma? She'll give you half of what Norton's charge."

"I haven't even done a day's work in the place and everyone is hitting me for cheap meat."

"Yes, but I'm not everyone. I'm your –"

"Best mate. Yes, I know the routine. Know the script. I'll see what I can do," said Paul. "Anyway, I doubt if I'll be getting much cheap meat. Doesn't look like a charity shop to me."

"You're entitled to it, mate. Stevie Foster told me that when he worked in there he was allowed as much meat as he could carry. Buckets of it."

"I wouldn't put too much credibility in any word Stevie says. Told the girl in the abattoir he had a two-pound dick."

"A two-pound dick? A *two-pound* fucking dick? Fuck the night! And I thought I was the lucky one!"

Paul smiled before relating the conversation with the strange girl in the office.

Now it was Lucky's turn to almost choke. "Oh, shit. That's great. A two-pound dick reduced to a two-ounce prick."

"Just keep it to yourself. I don't want to offend him."

"Talking of Stevie, there he is now, walking in the door," said Lucky, nudging Paul. "Shouldn't you be buying him a pint, just to show your appreciation of getting the job?"

"Give me time. I've almost reached the limit of my sub from Terry. I'll not have a penny in my pay packet, next week, if this keeps up.

Paul ordered a pint to be sent over to Stevie. A few seconds later, Stevie waved a thank you.

"Bet he wouldn't be waving if he knew you were telling everyone he had a dick the size of a coin," smiled Lucky, mischievously. "Little did he know it was a *toss up* to see if you would get him the pint."

"Very funny. Drop it. Okay?"

"The next time we have a dispute as to who should go first in snooker, we should toss Stevie into the air."

"Enough. Okay? He's looking over here, in this direction. I want a peaceful night. No hassle."

"That makes a *change,*" smiled Lucky, refusing to allow the topic of Stevie Foster's penis to die.

Shaking his head, Paul grabbed the empty glasses and headed for the bar, hoping to avoid Stevie sitting at the far table.

"Thanks for that pint, Paul," said Stevie, magically appearing at Paul's side, an almost empty glass in his hand. Paul could see Lucky in the background, holding his hand down at his crutch, making a circle with finger and thumb, and pointing in Stevie's direction.

Forcing a bubble of laughter back down his throat, Paul thanked Stevie for getting him the job. He decided not to mention the weird girl behind the desk, or indeed, any of the others.

"Another pint, Stevie?" asked Paul, knowing the answer before the smile appeared on Stevie's face. "Three pints, please, Terry."

Terry glared at Stevie. Another pissy whore.

"Brilliant, mate," said Stevie, ignoring Terry's look. "I'll see to you next week. I'm due a wee bit of money. Anyway, how did it go at the abattoir? Any problems? Hope you told them you knew me. I've got a lot of pull in that place. I knew that once you mentioned my name, the job was yours."

"Yes, everything went well. I got to meet Shank. He gave me a tour of the place." Paul thought it best not to mention the bloody bath ceremony.

Stevie's left eyebrow curled into a hairy question mark. "You actually got to meet him? That must have been an experience?"

"An experience? Big deal. He owns an abattoir. Who gives a shit?" replied Paul, faking bravado as he removed a cigarette from a battered packet. He lit it, and it sizzled in the air, cracking and spitting with dryness.

Terry interrupted the conversation, placing the filled glasses on the counter, before walking away, shaking his head.

"Shank did time in jail," whispered Stevie. "He never leaves the abattoir, they say, because he is wanted in other countries for murder and racketeering."

Paul shook his head, believing this to be another of Stevie's boasts. "Don't talk shit. Yes, Shank is a scary and intimidating character – but a murderer? C'mon!"

Stevie sucked on his pint, then licked his lips, tasting the remnants of Guinness skidded on them, before continuing.

"You know the loan shark, Jack Daley?"

"Yes," replied Paul. "Of course. Who doesn't?" Daly was a thug in a league of his own. He was the high priest of violence. Loved it. Loved its taste and sounds, its power and what it could do to those weaker. He was the type of scumbag that you could kill with a clear conscience, putting a smile even on the face of the gods. Few people in town had escaped his fists.

"Well, look upon him as a loan *sardine* when comparing him to Shank. Daly worships the man, fears him."

Paul laughed. "Daly fears Shank? Come off it, will ye? How the hell would you know?"

Stevie glanced over his shoulder, making sure no one was in earshot.

"I remember years ago, as a kid, Daly coming to my house looking for my da. Apparently, my da owed money to Daly – as most people in town did, in those days. I remember peeping from behind our parlour door, watching Daly putting the heavy hand on my da, telling him he had one hour to come up with the money, or else . . ."

For exactly ten seconds, only the sound of snooker balls kissing could be heard while Stevie paused dramatically.

"Or else?" said Paul, eventually, irritated by Stevie's drama.

"Or else Daly would have to work him over, put him in hospital for a few days . . ."

A few more seconds elapsed.

"Is there a end to this story? Or do I guess it?" asked Paul, becoming more irritable.

"Well, I couldn't quite hear every single word, but I heard one word, and that one word changed not only the features of Daly's face, but the entire direction of the conversation."

"And that one word . . .?"

"Shank."

Paul laughed. "I see where we're going with this. Shank then takes control of your da's payments and your da ends up paying double to Shank, in the long run. Smart da," laughed Paul, sarcastically.

"No. Not exactly. It seems my da saved the life of Shank's

cousin during the war – he even got a medal, or something like that – and Shank couldn't do enough to help. We never had another visit from Daly again. In fact, any time when Daly saw my da walking down the street, he would cross over to the other side, fearful of offending a friend of Shank. Now, do you understand the power of Shank?"

"I wished you hadn't told me all this. Now I'll be crapping myself every time I see Shank." Paul took a taste of his cigarette, allowing it to burn inside his lungs.

Stevie laughed. "You'll never see him again. That was probably a one-off encounter you had. All the time I worked in there, I only saw Shank once." Stevie took a longer sip of the pint before continuing. "What did you think of Violet?"

"Violet?"

"The receptionist."

"Oh, right. Yes, quite a pleasant person."

Stevie chuckled. "Now, I know she's not too great to look at, but you should see her in bed! Fuck! Couldn't get enough of me. The only real problem with her is she can get quite nasty at times. That's why they call her Violent Violet. She's as charming as a crocodile. Her vocabulary begins with the first four letters of the alphabet – as well as the sixth, of course."

"I'll be honest. She put the shit up me more than Shank did."

"She would, wouldn't she? Being Shank's daughter, and all."

"Shank's . . .?" Paul was relieved that he hadn't made any derogatory remarks about Shank in her presence.

"You know, she was almost killed in a car crash a few years ago, as a kid. Went right through the windscreen of her uncle's car. Fortunate to be have survived. The plastic surgeon did a great job on her face but was unable to remove all the millions of tiny fragments of glass encrusted in it. You noticed that, didn't you?"

Paul had a horrifying flashback to the office, Violet sitting there. Now he remembered, the strange texture of her skin, how it seemed to . . . gleam.

"I'm not kidding," enthused Stevie. "When you turn the lights off, her face turns into one of those mirror balls you see floating from the ceiling in the old disco movies."

An image of Stevie doing his impersonation of John Travolta flashed in Paul's mind. John Revolting, more likely. He wondered if Stevie had any info on Geordie.

"There's a girl in there, in charge of the butchers. They call her Jeanie or something," said Paul, trying to sound casual, deliberately mispronouncing Geordie's name. "Know her?"

Stevie paused for a second. "Jeanie? I'm trying to think. Can't remember any Jeanie. It's been a couple of years since I worked in there. Probably all new workers. Can't say I know any Jeanie, mate. Sorry."

"She . . . she . . . seemed to have bad legs, I think. Walked funny."

"Walked funny . . .? Oh! You mean Geordie, not Jeanie. Fuck, how could you forget her, once you've spotted her? Walks like Long John fucking Silver with woodworm."

Paul smiled, hating himself for its falseness, his silent acceptance of Stevie's words.

"Hmm. Yes. Now that you've mentioned it, I think her name *was* Geordie."

"No thinking about it, mate. The devil broke the mould when he created her along with her sister."

"Her sister?"

"Yes. Violent Violet. Not notice the resemblance?"

Paul thought for a moment. "I never got that close."

"Good. Keep it that way, mate. Two real fucking nutcases – just like their da. Biggest mistake I ever made was going out with Violet." Stevie shivered, involuntary. "Keep this to yourself, mate, but that fucker threatened to slice off my dick when I told her I no longer wanted to see her."

"Fuck . . ."

"That was the main reason for leaving. She made my life a living hell in there. Just keep away from her – from the whole lot of them, mate. They're a strange family . . ."

Before Paul could interrogate Stevie further, Lucky began to signal frantically that a table was free.

"I've got to get back over to Lucky. Thanks again for the help in getting me the job, Stevie."

"Any time, mate. Just keep your distance from the Sisters Grimm and keep your dick in your pocket."

CHAPTER FOUR

A Taste of His Own Medicine

*"Doctors will have more lives to answer for in the next world than
even we generals."*
Napoleon Bonaparte

*"Do not meddle in the affairs of wizards, for they are subtle and
quick to anger."*
J.R.R. Tolkien, *Lord of the Rings*

CATHLEEN SENSED BRIGHTNESS and felt her face getting warm. She awoke, as if from a coma. Her head was throbbing from painkiller dregs, dregs her body was finding increasingly difficult to tolerate. Finally, focusing her eyes, she was somewhat startled to see a young man standing at the side of her bed.

"Who the hell are you?" she asked, looking suspiciously at the man. "And what are you doing in my bedroom?"

The man was checking something scribbled on a pad while

his fingers negotiated a pen. The pen rolled with a life of its own, back and forth between his fingers, magically, like water over pebbles in a stream.

Trying desperately to shake the lethargic feeling in her reluctant body, Cathleen wondered if Philip had put sleeping pills in her soup. "I'll ask you for the last time. What the hell are you doing in my bedroom?"

If he heard her, he didn't acknowledge it.

"Are you deaf? Who the hell gave you permission to enter my room? That bastard downstairs, no doubt."

The man looked at her, shocked, not accustomed to being spoken to in such a manner. An hour ago, Cathleen had used the bedpan, and the look of disgust on the man's face could not be hidden. The foul smelling stench of dead cigarettes and cold, greasy food mummified the room, competing with the rancid reek that oozed menacingly from the bedpan.

"No, I'm not deaf, Mrs Kennedy. If you would be kind enough to have some patience, I'll be able to speak to you directly."

"Speak to me directly? Speak right now, or get the hell out of my room. How's that for patience?"

The man's face flushed. He couldn't believe such impertinence. Surely even these people had basic manners?

"My name is Doctor Ferguson. I have been asked by Doctor Moore to attend to you while he is at a conference. Now, if you don't mind . . ."

"But I do mind, *mister*. You're not a doctor to me. You look like you just left school. You've still got pimples, for God's sake. Show me some identification," she insisted. "For all I know you could be the window cleaner, or a burglar. You're probably working for that bastard, Philip. Come to poison me, eh? Think I'm that stupid?"

Moore had warned Ferguson about Cathleen Kennedy; yet, he found her lack of respect shocking and intolerable. *Why hadn't Moore allocated the weekend shift at the RVH to me, instead of this old dragon's lair? Revenge, no doubt. Teach me a lesson in humility. Moore has more in common with the dragon and his precious working-class background than he does with me.*

"Are you deaf or simply as stupid as you look?" quizzed Cathleen, wondering why he was staring at her, his mouth saying nothing. She glared at him with an expression of tested tolerance on her haggard face, like a schoolmistress about to administer the cane.

Ferguson's face had turned from an exasperated pink to a furious reddish-purple. Reluctantly, he removed a card from his wallet and held it out for Cathleen's inspection.

"No one has come to poison you, Mrs Kennedy. We are all here to help."

"Help? Don't make me laugh." Barely satisfied, she granted him permission to continue with his reading of the pad and his nervous trait with the pen.

"I see you've had three of your toes amputated, Mrs Kennedy," said Ferguson, his eyes never leaving the pad. The pen in his right hand scribbled something, and then went back to snaking between his fingers.

Cathleen forced a movement in the bed and quickly flashed her right foot.

"Wouldn't it be better if you actually *looked* at the offending foot, *mister?*" She wiggled the remaining two toes – the big toe and the tiny one – at Ferguson's face. The remaining toes resembled the "V" sign.

Disgusted, Ferguson scribbled more.

"Moore claimed that by amputating I would remain one step ahead of death, but if he removes any more of my toes, I'll not be able to step in any shape or form," said Cathleen, wryly, her eyes glued to the face of the young doctor. He reminded her of someone, but she couldn't quite put a name to it . . .

"If you do not stay active, Mrs Kennedy, or watch your intake of carbohydrates – especially liquor – the sugar in your blood will eat your insides. Your veins and arteries will deteriorate, shrinking, preventing delivery of blood throughout the body. We should be grateful it was the other leg that was injured."

Wonderful. It was a hard-hitting speech, but one which was needed. He was determined to appear professionally detached at the expense of normal human demonstrations of emotion. No doubt, Moore has been filling her head with hopeful scenarios, where none exist. Sometimes, a good kick up the backside is all that is needed.

Sensing he had Cathleen's undivided attention, Ferguson continued, loving the fact that he had now taken full control of the old dragon. Slain, a more appropriate word.

"Mrs Kennedy, what you see now is the result of ignoring all the warnings given to you throughout the years. Parts of you – the farthest parts – the toes, have succumbed first. If you continue to ignore our advice, soon your fingers are going to die because the blood no longer brings oxygen or flushes out waste matter – or brings white blood cells to fight infection."

Satisfied with his prognosis of a poor quality of life, Ferguson snapped the writing pad shut. The pen went to the top of his tweed jacket, peeping out from the lip of the pocket. The patient would appreciate all he had said – perhaps not now, but certainly later. Moore had a lot to learn from modern doctors. Upfront. On the chin. All the time.

"Have you finished blabbering, *mister?*" said Cathleen, reaching for a cigarette.

Ferguson was taken aback by the venom in her voice. He was about to chastise her for smoking, but quickly decided against it.

"First, I don't drink *liquor.* Never tasted it. So what gives you the audacity to assume anything about me – especially consuming *liquor?* Eh? Eh, *mister?*"

"Well, I certainly didn't meant to –" Ferguson was flustered.

"Didn't mean to my withered arse. You meant ever word uttered from your arrogant little mouth. But let me tell you something, *mister.* A couple of dead husbands called mistakes and a hundred boyfriends called rattlesnakes have given me the universal knowledge of dealing with little pipsqueaks such as you. Coming into my home with your snobbery and hatred of your own so-called profession does not give you the right to think you are superior to me in any shape, shit or form. My amputated toes know more about medicine and doctors than you will ever hope to learn, *mister.*"

To Ferguson's relief, Cathleen stopped talking. He felt exhausted, as if he had just fought some terrible battle with the dragon. He could smell smoke and didn't know if it came from the cigarette dangling from Cathleen's sneering lips or from his arse being set on fire from the dragon's flame.

"I am only here to help you, Mrs Kennedy. That fall you had could have been fatal. Fortunately, your husband was home at the time. He has informed me that he intends to replace the old carpet on the stairs. That's good, but as I told him, there are more fatalities in households than all the plane crashes combined . . ."

Blah blah blah, thought Catherine, ignoring the endless statistics escaping from the young doctor's mouth. If he intended to give her advice, it wasn't working. The only thing he was giving her was another headache.

Cathleen lit another cigarette and groped about the bedside table for an ashtray, fully aware of how much Philip disliked her smoking in bed. Something beneath the surface, a quality that was addictive, enjoyably perplexing but never reassuring, made her feel at times a sensation bordering on destructiveness, but a destructiveness that was positive – at least for her. And that was all that mattered: what was positive and beneficial for Cathleen Kennedy.

"You're Lizzy Ferguson's son, aren't you?" she said, spitting a loose splinter of tobacco from her mouth. It landed on Ferguson's beautiful tweed jacket, just below the magical pen peeping from above.

Puzzled, Ferguson hesitantly replied yes. He was aware of silence now, but entirely the wrong kind of silence. It was the silence of calm waves waiting their turn to swallow ships whole before demolishing them on the hidden rocks.

"Yes, indeed," said Cathleen. "It took a while for my memory to come to my service, but I knew that eventually it would arrive. You all think that old Cathleen's days are numbered, but there's still a lot of fight in the rusty old wreck."

This had become a nightmare for Ferguson. Moore had deliberately sent him here to be ambushed and humiliated by this . . . this creature.

"Lizzy McCambridge was her name back then. One of my regular customers, was Lizzy. God, the stuff she brought me . . ." Cathleen's eyes seemed to glaze at the fond memory. "Funny how you mentioned liquor, earlier on, *Mister* Ferguson, but Lizzy was quite fond of it. Yes, indeed. There was even rumours of her drinking late into the night, shouting at shadows and ghosts. She rarely left the house, in those days. When she did leave, it was only at night via the back streets to the rear of the pub, to purchase some cheap whiskey – brandy being a luxury she couldn't afford in those days. That was before she met moneybags Harry Ferguson, your da. She swilled whiskey straight like a sailor then. You could smell it in her piss." Cathleen chuckled. She should have been a comedian.

The heat in the room was becoming unbearable for Ferguson, who was slowly loosening the top button of his sharp, starched shirt, trying feebly to release the tie that had become a snake squeezing the life out of him. The collar felt like a blade against his throat.

"I remember one day when she came to my shop, crying. She hated that journey into night, hated the young, arrogant barman who told her not to worry, her wee secret was safe with him."

Ferguson saw the door calling to him, telling him to leave now, while the choice was his.

"Does Lizzy still walk the docks, *Mister* Ferguson? That used to be her old hunting ground. Loved the men, did Lizzy, and wasn't a bit shy with them, if you get my meaning." Cathleen winked, a sneaky knowing wink that said: *Don't you worry, sonny. Your ma's wee secret is safe with me. But perhaps not for long . . .*

"Well, I never in all my life . . ." mumbled a devastated Ferguson.

"Unlike Lizzy, eh?" grinned Cathleen. "Always be careful of where you crap, *mister*. You might just walk in it, one day."

Ferguson slammed his briefcase shut and walked quickly towards the door.

"Run rabbit, run rabbit, run run run!" shouted Cathleen, laughing after Ferguson while he ran down the stairs. "Watch the door doesn't hit you up the arse!"

Eventually, Cathleen stopped laughing and decided that today's meeting of minds was the best tonic she had had in ages. To hell with all doctors.

God, she had enjoyed the look on that arrogant little bastard's face, loved deflating it with the sharpness of her tongue. *Wonder if he realises he actually is a bastard? Hmm. Hopefully, I can enlighten him on that if he ever shows his face again.* In the meantime, she would get Biddy to change the sheets. Laughter truly is the best medicine, she agreed, realising the bed was soaking. She had proven that by literally pissing herself.

CHAPTER FIVE

Family in the Blood

"There is no trusting appearances."
Richard Brinsley Sheridan, *The School for Scandal*

*"No passion so effectually robs the mind of all its powers of acting
and reasoning as fear."*
Edmund Burke, *A Philosophical Enquiry into the Origin of Our Ideas of
the Sublime and Beautiful*

PAUL SAT EATING his lunch in the large, ramshackle holding shed of the abattoir – a reprieve from the steam and blood inside the building – alone except for the company of beasts awaiting execution. Thin light filtered through the holes in the walls, barely illuminating their faces.

The unnatural silence suited him, as if watching TV with the volume turned down. Only the soft chewing could be heard – his own, as well as the beasts'. Garbage bags full of animal eyes rested a few feet away, waiting to be shipped overseas as a delicacy. The bags bulged and stretched so thickly that traces of eyes' colours squeezed and surpassed the black plastic, turning it into a rainbow of spheres and lumps. The heavy fragrance of ripe cow dung interlaced with the heady smell of mouldy hay and grain hung in the air, almost visible, punctuated by the pungent stench of fresh blood.

He remembered how he was initially baffled, all those weeks ago, as to how anyone could eat a meal in this hell of a place. Now here he was, munching happily away at his corn beef and onion sandwich, justifying it by reminding himself this was horsemeat and they didn't shoot horses here in the abattoir. They had their principles. Horses were for riding and betting on – not slaughtering. Yet, he had never truly become comfortable with the stares from the cows, their inflated lips and sorrowful eyes. The eyes had the same effect as the dead spooky babies he once saw in McCabe's funeral parlour when he sneaked in one day after school, eight years ago. The babies had all belonged to the same family, killed by some ruthless disease living in the dark and damp homes. Mangler Delaney, who worked during the summer as an apprentice coffin maker for McCabe, had charged him – and all the rest of the boys in town – four Chocolate Logs or two Lucky Bags to sneak in and have a good look at the tiny bundles of flesh with blue, pockmarked skin and bulging eyes. It was the most vile and frightening scene Paul had ever witnessed, but if he had had the money, he would gladly have paid over and over again.

Eight years ago and he could still remember it vividly.

Little by little, all sound in the shed was repulsed. The chewing became quieter, like a munching noise being softly gummed. Paul felt the hairs on the back of his neck rise, the skin on his arms thickening with goose bumps.

He had heard the soft whisper of feet and stopped eating

his sandwich, holding his breath as he tried to detect just where exactly they were coming from.

He knew it must be her and could picture her trying desperately not to make a sound as she stepped on the screaming dry hay, lifting each stubborn leg, placing it before her. He could envision the stress on her face as she softly cursed the protesting legs, cursing their uselessness, wanting to chop them off at the knees.

Paul cleared his throat with one good cough. "No one likes a sneak. They're the lowest of the low," he said, directly to the cow in front of his face. Not only was there fear in the cow's black eyes, but betrayal and bewilderment. "Sneaks have always something to hide. That's why they hide in shadows and whispers. Rather gutless, actually, Miss Cow."

Perhaps there was no one there, after all? Perhaps he had imagined the noise? He felt foolish, talking to a cow, actually giving it a title, hoping it would respond.

"Too good to eat with us?" she finally said, her voice a mixture of anger and loathing.

He didn't turn in her direction. He didn't want to scare her away. Shit, he knew he couldn't scare her at anything. "No, just too lazy. Walking all the way to the canteen doesn't appeal to me."

He felt her weight touch the ground, inching slowly in his direction. She was directly behind him, now. That he could sense. He took a bite from his sandwich and waited.

"You've come a long way from your first day, *Goodman,*" said Violent Violet, stepping from the shadows, wearing a T-shirt proclaiming: IT'S ONLY FUNNY UNTIL SOMEONE GETS HURT. THEN IT'S HILARIOUS.

Disappointment registered in his face. He had deftly avoided Violet each morning through a series of skilful manoeuvres; a pattern developed by working one place one day and another the next. He though – *hoped* – it had been Geordie. He didn't know what he would have said to her, but he would have said something, even though he had only seen her half a dozen times.

"Didn't know you were permitted to leave the office, Violet," said Paul, half-heartedly. He didn't want a conversation with her.

"I could see the terror in your eyes, that first day, Goodman, the look on your face. I had a bet with Shank that you would be gone within a week," she said, snidely, her voice sounding like an annoying insect.

"Just goes to show that you can never tell a book from its cover," replied Paul, placing his sandwich on the ground, appetite gone.

Uninvited, she sat down beside him. "You find me repulsive, don't you, Goodman? You can't even look at my face, can you?"

Paul looked directly at Violet, and then quickly looked away as her locked eyes stared with a self-awareness that seemed strange, as if she wanted to drill holes in his face.

"Or can you? Most people recoil when they see my face, like they just swallowed a cup of bleach. But you're different, Goodman. You want to look at it. Don't you? It reminds you of something. Doesn't it?"

Random thoughts buzzed through his mind, looking for topics to light on. For one terrible moment he wanted to give Stevie Foster's reply that she reminded him of disco days long gone. With caution at first, unsure of his own ability to hold her in conversation, Paul replied, softly, "Spooky babies . . ."

There was silence. Not another word was uttered for at least ten, long seconds that stretched for ever.

"Spooky babies?" Violet remained impassive, then slowly smiled. "Spooky babies. I like that, Goodman. Spooky babies . . ." It was a real smile, and it tightened the devastated skin on her face, closing all the holes living there, and for one terribly brief and revealing moment, Paul could see the beauty that had at one time dwelt there. Now he understood her bitterness, her hatred for the world, and felt at that moment how he would hate the world and all in it if the roles were reversed.

"I've got to get back to work, Violet."

"Shank isn't back until Thursday, Goodman. Relax. When he's not here, I'm in charge. Besides, I need someone to help me with the stocktaking. Shank reckons someone is stealing meat from him without paying. Personally, I don't think anyone would be stupid enough to steal from Shank. He wouldn't look too kindly on it." She smiled her cold smile, and then surprised him by saying, "You're not on his list of suspects, Goodman, so you can stop looking as if you're about to crap your pants."

"Why would Shank leave you in charge? Why not one of the gold hats, like Geordie? She has more control over the workers and they respect her."

"And you, Goodman? Do you respect her? A cripple? I would imagine a man like you would find it very difficult taking orders from not only a woman, but also a cripple?"

"Doesn't bother me in the least. I think she does a great job up there, in the thick of things, never afraid to get her hands dirty or bloody – unlike some people I could mention, sitting in their wee comfortable office." Paul wondered why he sounded so defensive.

"Goodman! Have I touched a raw nerve? Do you mean to tell me that you have feelings for a cripple? That is sick –"

"You're the one who is sick. How can you even talk like that? Don't you know how everyone thinks of –" He was about to say how everyone thinks of you as a freak, also, but luckily held his tongue in time. Or so he thought.

"How everyone . . .? Yes, Goodman? What?"

He licked his lips. They had become parched. There was little point in pursuing this discussion. "Nothing."

"Don't be a coward, Goodman. Say it. Shank tells me you're an honest man. Prove it. Everyone what, Goodman?"

His heart was beating faster, as if he had just downed a gallon of tea.

"Nothing. I was just being . . ."

"Honest? Hmm. Perhaps Shank is right about you after all. An honest man. Who would believe such a creature existed? Certainly not me. Not the freak with the broken face. Isn't that it, Goodman?"

Her words devastated him. He hadn't meant to hurt her. She had made him angry.

"I . . . I didn't mean . . . I just lost my temper when you made fun of Geordie. I don't like to hear people making fun of . . ."

"Cripples?" Violet laughed out loud, startling a group of cows to her right. "Well, for your information, Goodman, if that crippled bitch even thought you regarded her as a cripple, she would kill you." Violet stared at Paul. "I mean that, Goodman. Make no mistake. It's not just her body that's all fucked-up. Shank has her like that."

"Shank?"

Violet looked at Paul, her face tightening. "You don't know, do you? Perhaps you *are* stupid, just like all the rest."

"Know what?" He was becoming agitated and shifted uncomfortably.

"Geordie and Shank are lovers."

A lick of jealousy touched Paul. He couldn't explain it, but he recognised its taste.

"Lovers . . .?"

"I know. Disgusting. They fuck like rabbits."

The word fuck hit him like an axe. It sounded disgusting, obscene, coming from Violet's mouth. "But . . . he's . . . he's her father – your father. How can you sit there and talk like that? Even thought I know you're trying to wind me up, it still sounds disgusting."

Violet laughed, but this time there was ice attached to it.

"Am I winding you up? Or is there truth in what I said?"

Paul stood to go. "I don't care. It's really none of my business, but you shouldn't talk about your sister and father, like that."

"*Our* father, Goodman, and hallowed be his name. For ever and ever . . ."

Paul could still feel her laughter on the back of his neck as he quickly left the shed.

CHAPTER SIX

Strange Encounters, Soon to Be Familiar

"Neither fraud, nor deceit, nor malice had yet interfered with truth and plain dealing."
Miguel de Cervantes, *Don Quixote*

"The innocent is the person who explains nothing."
Albert Camus, *Innocence*

KENNEDY HEARD THE door's chime indicating a customer – or potential customer – just as he entered the hallway to mount the stairs with Cathleen's lunch. He debated whether to bring the soup and bread on up or see to the customer. He decided the latter should be seen to first, knowing Cathleen would ask had any transaction taken place. *She'll be inconvenienced. Fine. Let her soup be cold . . .*

"Yes?" he asked, straining to see the details of the person standing there, framed in the darkened entry of the doorway.

"I called in last week, about the snooker cues," said Paul,

slowly advancing. The cluttered doorway narrowed with his approach.

Kennedy felt a slight pinprick in his chest. There was the slightest tone of grey inside the shadow of the doorway, as if someone was standing behind the young man in the blackness, like an out-of-focus photo. Seconds later, it was gone, forcing Kennedy to question his aging eyes.

"Snooker . . .? Oh yes. I remember. Yes . . . you got me at a bad time. The doctor was in seeing my wife and everything was topsy-turvy. I was a bit rude, if I remember correctly, and I apologise for it."

"No big deal," replied Paul, relieved. "I've had days like that myself."

"Snooker cues?" asked Kennedy, returning to the back of the counter. "Any particular make?"

"Something above a brush shaft. Not too expensive, though," laughed Paul.

Kennedy nodded, opened a larger glass panel and delicately removed a cue.

"Don't have too many requests for these nowadays. I thought snooker was going out of fashion." He placed the cue on the counter before turning to remove two more from their enclosure.

"I doubt if snooker will ever be out of fashion," insisted Paul, handling the cue expertly. "Television has given it a lot of prominence. People no longer regard it as corner-boy stuff."

Placing the remaining cues on the counter, Kennedy smiled. "No, I've never regarded snooker as a corner-boy activity, myself. Enjoyed quiet a few games in my time. Those were the days of more hair, less belly."

"Whereabouts?" asked Paul, intrigued at the thought of this old man, leaning over a table, potting balls. He found it difficult to envision.

"Any place I could get a game, you found me there. Any weather, made no difference. I had a passion for it."

"What happened? Lose all interest? Lose too many games?"

Kennedy thought for a moment. "Got married . . ."

Paul laughed. "I don't think I could allow any woman to come between me and snooker. It's what I live for."

Now it was Kennedy's turn to laugh, softly. His laughter had rustiness to it. "Oh, you only think that. When you meet the right woman, believe me, snooker will go out the window. So enjoy it while you can. The trick is the right woman."

"Is that what happened to you, then? Met the right woman?" Paul held one of the cues in his hand, balancing it between his fingers, feeling the wood soak into his skin, hoping it would tell him something.

"You don't need me to tell you how much the cue you use is of paramount importance to your game," said Kennedy, ignoring the question. He reached for the last remaining cue. "This one, perhaps?"

"It certainly looks the part," said Paul, admiringly, hypnotised by the beauty before him.

The cue was a stunning piece of craftsmanship with a splendid venation of grain – a vitally important aspect of the artisan's craft and pride. The end result spoke of masterful artistic precision. Antonio Stradivari, had he been a cue maker, would have been proud of it.

"How much?" asked Paul, knowing this gorgeous instrument was well out of his financial reach.

"Very expensive," admitted Kennedy. "But well worth the price. Do you prefer light or heavy cues?"

Paul could no longer hear Kennedy. The Tin Hut was full to capacity; television crews were setting up their apparatus, waiting for the star of the show, Paul Goodman, to make an entrance. A 147 break was a strong possibility with this young star. The crowd wanted it, almost as much as Paul.

"We could come to some sort of arrangement," said Kennedy, repeating himself.

"Oh. Sorry. Did you say something? I think I drifted for a moment," said Paul, embarrassed.

"I was saying we could come to some sort of an agreement. Monthly instalments, if that would suit you?"

Paul couldn't believe his luck. This was the cue he had searched all his life for – the Holy Grail of the snooker world – and all he had to do was agree to monthly instalments? Suspicion kicked in. Was this a trick from the owner? Why the generosity of one stranger to another? What was the catch? Was the cue flawed, a hairline crack? He knew the cue also had to satisfy him psychologically. Not being comfortable with it would affect his overall performance.

A look of apprehension appeared on Kennedy's face. Why was the young man staring at him so intensely?

A tapping sound drilled its way down from above, interrupting his thoughts, but Kennedy ignored it, gaining pleasure from the act of defiance. *Damn it, woman. Your soup will wait – as will* you . . .

"Is the cue flawed?" asked Paul.

A puzzled look appeared on Kennedy's face. "I'm merely inviting you to consider purchasing the cue. Does that look like an imperfect instrument in your hands? Are you saying I look like a dodgy character?" Kennedy attempted a smile. "Occasionally, when an item is examined and something odd catches the eye, it does not mean that there is a flaw, but merely an invitation to look again."

Paul re-examined the cue, scrutinising it, suspicious yet thankful at finding nothing, only beauty and perfection. "I think we have a deal."

The knocking from above became louder, impatient, angry.

"You won't regret it," assured Kennedy, reaching for the book of pawn tickets. "I'll expect the first payment at the start of each month, preferably on a Friday. Is that fair?"

Paul couldn't stop smiling. His life had changed for the better over the last couple of weeks; from the new job to this incredible cue, which was criminally underpriced. "I can pay the first instalment today. I got paid yesterday."

"Next month will be fine." Kennedy scribbled something on the ticket, hesitating as he asked, "Your name?"

"Paul Goo –"

"No . . . I only need your first name. You live over near the Half-Bap."

Puzzled, Paul smiled. "Yes, that's right. How did you –?"

"I'll expect to see you next month. The first Friday. Is that reasonable?"

"Yes. No problems there. And thank you. You didn't have to do this for me. I appreciate it."

Kennedy stared into Paul's eyes, but only for a second before quickly glancing away. "Until the first Friday, then. Good day."

Kennedy watched Paul leave the shop, cut across York Street, before disappearing out of view between the chalk-coloured walls of Nelson Street and the redbrick of Corporation Street.

"Damn it," he said, making his way up the stairs. "God damn it . . ."

He entered the bedroom just in time to catch Catherine struggling to get back into bed.

Kennedy placed the cold soup at the edge of the table while Cathleen watched, her eyes smiling with that smug satisfaction acquired over the years.

"Who was that in the shop?" she asked.

Kennedy ignored her.

"Must have been buying or selling an awful lot, the time you spent blabbering away down there? Good job these cheap floorboards are as thin as walls, otherwise I would never know what goes on."

He knew she was baiting him.

"Well?" continued Catherine. "And why did you refuse his payment? Eh? Answer me, Philip Kennedy. What are you playing at?"

Kennedy stood at the bottom of the bed, his fingers tight as a vice, his angry knuckles becoming white, tiny bleached skulls. He felt his hands search for something to hold on to as his fingers curled into fists, his fingernails cutting deep into his palms, piercing the skin.

"Listening in to conversations, Catherine? Ears glued to the floorboards? Is that how low and pathetic you've become?"

"I don't want this soup. It's cold. All that blabbering down there. I'll have Biddy make me something, later," replied Catherine

"You'll take it the way it is. If you were able to sneak out of bed and stick your ear to the floor, you should be strong enough to go down stairs and make your own soup," he goaded.

"I know you are slowly poisoning me, you bastard, but don't be foolish enough to think you will gain my forgiveness. You can ask God to forgive your other deeds, but not this one. Do you hear me, Philip Kennedy? Not this one. I will never forgive you. Remember, I am equally one to be feared." A tidy, perfected sneer appeared on her face.

"Fear? You don't know the true meaning of the word. You talk as if there is order involved, as if you are able to predict things, Cathleen. But nothing can be predicted. There is no order except the order we force on to things."

"I *know* you are poisoning me," she cut in. "Of that, I am certain."

"I can't deal with your so-called certainties, right now. I find it difficult enough to deal with my own. Drink your soup. You'll feel a lot better for it. Trust me."

"Don't patronise me!" she screamed, throwing the bowl and its cold contents at Kennedy, hitting him square on the face and tearing his skin.

Slowly, he removed a handkerchief from his trouser pocket and wiped the blood and soup from his cheeks and chin.

"You're tired," he whispered, and Cathleen could not say it was her he spoke the words to. "But don't ever do any thing so foolish again. I won't be as tolerant."

"Be thankful it wasn't a hatchet!" responded Catherine, lightning fast. "Now, get the hell out of my room."

"Hell? Now *that* is an appropriate word, Cathleen. Just try and get some rest. Doctor Moore will be here to see you, later. We need you out of bed as soon as possible. Don't we?"

She screamed something, something vulgar and tasteless. But it was too late. He had already closed the door behind him.

CHAPTER SEVEN

Boxed in Boxing Clever

"There is no great genius without some touch of madness."
Seneca, "On the Tranquility of the Mind", *Moral Essays*

*"A belief in a supernatural source of evil is not necessary; men alone
are quite capable of every wickedness."*
Joseph Conrad, *Under Western Eyes*

SHORTLY AFTER 11 A.M., Paul was called to Shank's office.

Baffled, a million reasons raced through Paul's head: his timekeeping and attitude couldn't be questioned – he had always arrived enthusiastically each morning; he had worked as hard as the rest of the workers, never complaining, even when given the shitty task of cleaning out the manure pens.

Violet looked up from an outdated magazine just as Paul knocked before opening the door of the office. "Go straight in, Goodman. No stopping at go, no getting out of jail free, do not collect one hundred . . ." she grinned a snide, unfriendly grin, immediately placing Paul on his guard.

Walking through to the next room, Paul was more than a little surprised to see the pugnacious Shank stripped to the waist, lacquered with sweat, bombarding a punch bag with a blizzard of killer punches. Shank's rhino-formed body glistened, forcing the veins on his skull to bulge like shoelaces. The veins upon his forearms were cemented with power and looked ready to explode.

A rhino, thought Paul admiringly, whose own youthful body was formidable and nothing to be ashamed of. Yet he couldn't help but be in awe of the chiselled physique of Shank, the seemingly millions of tiny ball-bearing-shaped muscles riveted to the skin rising angrily with each movement, fanning out over the landscape of skin beneath the lines of tendons matching the swell of muscle.

It was said Shank consumed five pints of animal blood each morning and it was this that had helped create the massive bulk of intimidation. Initially, Paul had dismissed the speculation as mere rumour, gossip and myth. Now? Well . . .

Shank's bodyguard, Taps, seemed to be reading an assortment of sport magazines.

"Leave," said Shank to Taps. "Go get something to eat."

A few seconds later, Shank returned to punching the bag. "Close that door, tightly please, Mister Goodman," requested Shank, never missing a step from his surprisingly nimble movement. "Eyes and ears are everywhere."

With the door closed, Paul felt trapped. The walls seemed to have moved, slightly inwards.

"I am thinking of modernising the abattoir, Mister Good-man; modernising ideas and how we do things in the future," continued Shank. "Behind you in those boxes is the start of the modernising. Open one up. Tell me what you think."

Obligingly, Paul tore open one of the many boxes piled in the corner and removed one of the items. It was a stun gun.

"Notice any difference?" asked Shank.

Paul studied the lethal piece of metal in his hands, clueless as to what he was suppose to be looking for.

"It seems lighter than the ones we have."

"Correct, Mister Goodman. Much lighter. Anything else?"

For fuck sake. "I think . . . there is more of a grip on this compared to the ones we use in the building," Paul replied, awkwardly.

"The main difference, Mister Goodman," said Shank, putting Paul out of his misery, "is that they are cordless." Shank's voice was full of pride. "They are not even on the market yet. So secret they don't even exist. They have been loaned to us by the manufactures so that we may be able to test their effectiveness. Nice, eh?"

Paul nodded. "Unbelievable, Mister Shank. No wires mean that the workers will have more manoeuvrability, won't be getting tangled up."

"Correct, again, Mister Goodman. You catch on quickly. Very quickly, indeed."

"After a couple of clues!"

"I like a man who can laugh at himself. A bit like myself." Shank smiled. "I hear you're a bit of a boxer, Mister Goodman. Any truth?" Shank continued smashing ruthlessly against the battered, threadbare punch bag, his gravity-defying punches buckling its stomach with ease. Without warning, Shank hit the punch bag with a devastating punch, sending it flying backwards in an outrush of air. Yet despite all the exertion, an absence of emotion was in his movement.

Classical music played in the background. Paul didn't know the title, but it was familiar. Familiar, like the echo of a song heard hundreds of times in his life.

"I haven't sparred seriously in years, Mister Shank. I don't have much time for it any more. What little time I have is taken up with –"

Shank snorted. The sound reminded Paul of the pigs they had slaughtered, earlier that morning. "Don't have time to keep your body in shape? Nonsense, Mister Goodman! The body is the vessel upon which we depend to take us to war," smiled Shank, not a friendly grin, but one that seemed to challenge.

The punch bag went spinning as Shank used an uppercut with his left hand. "The body must be maintained to the highest precision and oiled with blood, sweat, but never tears. No, never tears, Mister Goodman. Tears are sacrilege and the currency of cowards." He punched the hapless bag again, quickly steadying it before looking into Paul's eyes. "Some people regard fists as the preferred communication of bullies and thugs. That is their prerogative. I regard myself as neither. I denied myself youth while preparing for adulthood, Mister Goodman, and it was a mistake – probably the biggest mistake I ever made. Now, I am on a mission to recoup some of that loss. Remove your shirt. Show me your skill."

"Here? But I've –"

"Don't be shy, Mister Goodman. Remove the shirt. Show some flesh."

Reluctantly, Paul removed his shirt.

"Not bad," said Shank, admiring Paul's physique. "You've a good build, Mister Goodman. With the right guidance, you can bring it to its potential."

Shank swung the punch bag violently in the direction of Paul's frame.

Instinctively, Paul moved to the side, allowing the bag to brush him before landing a perfectly aimed right to its middle, spinning it back in the direction of Shank, who was now grinning with eagerness at the oncoming leather intruder.

Bam! Shank thundered the bag, watching its staggered return move back towards Paul.

"C'mon, Mister Goodman! Hit the damn thing!" shouted Shank, grinning further. "There's more power in my –"

The bag hit Shank full in the face, knocking him off balance. Before he could regain his composure, Paul sent the bag hurling again in Shank's direction, catching his upper torso with a beautiful wallop that sang joyfully throughout the room.

Shank staggered, but not before the bag hit him again, full in the face, knocking him against the far wall. A lesser man would have crumbled to the ground, but Shank's strength and pride kept him afloat. He was dazed, and Paul wondered if he had hurt him.

"Go in for the kill, Goodman!" shouted a voice from the doorway. "Don't just stand there staring at your fists. Finish him. Give him a good beating."

Violet's voice brought an unexpected stillness to the room. Paul did not know what to say – or do.

"You should have listened to her, Mister Goodman," said

Shank, a grin reappearing on his face. "Never show mercy. That's the crown for fools. Isn't that right, Violet? You wouldn't have shown mercy. Would you?"

"Of course not," she replied and sat down on Shank's leather chair. "I would have killed you, given the chance."

Paul's face registered shock at the words.

"Before you even contemplate doing that, please remove your arse from my chair," said Shank, no longer smiling. "The day your arse becomes big enough, Violet, is the day you get to keep the chair. Now, leave. Mister Goodman and I have some matters to discuss. And don't let me catch you eavesdropping at the door, either."

"You won't," replied Violet, deliberately brushing against Paul as she left, touching his sweat-stained skin with her index finger before placing it in her mouth. "Very salty . . ."

Paul felt his skin creep.

Shank waited until the door closed before talking.

"Quite a girl, Violet."

Expected to say nothing, Paul simply nodded, allowing Shank to continue. "I believe you've become friendly with her."

Taken aback, Paul replied, "I really haven't thought a great deal about friendships, Mister Shank. I haven't had much time on my hands." His throat felt sandpapery. He was straining to suppress his annoyance and could feel the start of acid fermenting in his stomach. Where on earth had Shank got such an outrageous idea about an imaginary friendship?

Removing the boxing gloves, Shank rubbed a towel vigorously against his saturated skin, transforming the paleness into raw-wound crimson. "I do not mistake your hesitancy for reluctance or cowardice, Mister Goodman. I respect it. If I say so myself, I have a good track record of character; of finding that character and honing it. No wastage, Mister Goodman. Remember?"

"Thank you, but . . ." mumbled Paul, wondering if he should be thanking Shank, smelling something wrong with the direction of the conversation. "I really don't know what to say concerning –"

"I suspect you are not far in your thoughts of wanting to achieve great things, Mister Goodman," Shank interrupted. "Can you imagine going through life as insignificant, causing no ripple, no disturbance in the pool of existence?"

Paul could think of nothing to say, except, "No."

"You see, Mister Goodman, I have lived my life driven by principles instilled in me by my mother – God bless her soul. She did not believe in order or institutions. She didn't believe in Church, law or state. She was the *only* woman I ever trusted completely. It was she who taught me that a person had to be self-sufficient, to question everything, to believe nobody if they want to realise their potential." Shank wiped his hands before reinstating the boxing gloves back on his eager hands. "When I was growing up as a youngster, I wore oversized jackets, ill-fitting pants and other bits of random clothing which I scavenged from rag stores or hand-me-downs from my brothers. Each hour of my life I vowed that one day I would be rich, Mister Goodman, and I have neither disappointed nor betrayed that vow. It wasn't easy."

"I'm sure it wasn't," agreed Paul.

"Help me tie these gloves," said Shank, extending his arms outward.

Once the gloves were tied, Shank began to tackle the bag, changing his punching tactics to one of slow, delicate movements, and once again confounding Paul by his nimbleness, the rhythm of which was like the gentle stroke of an artist carefully preparing the canvas before committing to the picture.

Thankfully for Paul, Shank continued talking, unabated. "I am not a stupid man. I know there are men out there – not just in the abattoir, of course – who would gladly give their right arm to marry Violet, knowing they would be well-off for the remainder of their stay on this earth. They mouth great swelling words, flattering to gain advantage. But you, Mister Goodman, are the man I'm looking for: quiet, serious, strong – physically as well as mentally – and you have a certain curiosity mixed with a raw, almost evangelical faith. I remember how you scrutinised the paintings and sculpture in this same office when you first started. I remember how you looked at me as I completed the jigsaw puzzle, probably wondering what on earth a man such as myself would find entertaining about simple jigsaw puzzles." Shank smiled at Paul, knowingly, a smile too close for Paul's comfort. "Violet may not be perfect. She is prone to sudden, sometimes violent, mood swings, a secret preference for the violent outcome. But I think you could tame a lot of the wildness in her, bring out the potential, which I failed to do." Shank reached for a bottle of water, pawing it with both gloves, gulping the liquid down greedily.

Momentarily confused, Paul continued listening absorbedly, speechless, yet still susceptible to the infinite discharge of sounds parading from the mouth of Shank. A parcel of intenseness sat in his lungs and tried to choke off rational thought, as if punishing him for not speaking when he had the chance.

Shank continued before Paul had time to recover. "Let me say that she is by no stretch of the imagination the prettiest flower in the garden. That I know. But even weeds have their place in the clay. Is that correct, Mister Goodman?"

A burning sensation had taken root in the base of Paul's brain, slowly turning out the lights in his skull. He realised that if he didn't speak now, the darkness would render him speechless.

"I'm sorry to disappoint you, Mister Shank, but I do not have any strong feelings for Violet. I don't know where you obtained your information, but it is wrong."

Paul had amazed himself. Where the hell had he grown the balls to talk to the almighty Shank in such a manner?

Sweat trickled down Paul's spine, pooling between his buttocks. He badly wanted to scratch his arse, but thought better of it. Shank could mistake it as an insult.

Shank nodded, slowly, as if reflecting upon this terrible piece of news, and for some inexplicable reason a tinge of remorse touched Paul, as if he had terribly wronged this man who had given him a job and entertained the thought that he, Paul Goodman, was suitable for his daughter, bringing with it the comforts of money and respectability, regardless of how dodgy that respectability may become in the long run.

"There is no fool like an old fool, Mister Goodman. I should never have assumed anything on face value. No doubt, I read the signs wrong and have been punished for not doing my homework on such an important matter. I thank you for your honesty. Other men would simply have lied to keep in with me. More my loss now." Shank slowly removed the gloves, placing them on a nail above his head.

"Mister Shank. I do have . . . feelings, but they . . ." Paul could feel his face burn. He hated it when his face betrayed him. "Well . . . they are for . . . Geordie . . ."

Shank appeared dumbfounded while he ran a hand over the smooth surface of his baldy head. "Geordie? Geordie, Mister Goodman? But she is . . . she is broken, not whole, and I doubt she would be shaped correctly to carry a baby, or make a man happy in bed."

Paul's skin seemed on fire. He didn't think such words were appropriate. Shank gave the impression of discussing one of the cows out in the sheds, not a human being, certainly not his daughter.

"I didn't say I wanted to marry Geordie, Mister Shank, just that I have . . . feelings for her. I doubt if she even likes me, barely tolerates me, if I'm to be honest."

"Likes you? She would love you to death, Mister Shank! Love you to death . . . God, how she would love you! I never . . . I mean . . . Geordie? Well, isn't that a development? Geordie, Geordie, Geordie . . ." Shank continued saying her name, a mantra for all to hear. "I never thought the day would come when someone would have feelings for Geordie. Tell me it's not pity, Mister Goodman. No! Don't! It's none of my damn business!" Shank's dark eyes sparkled mischievously, gleaming like the blue-black sheen of a blackbird's wing.

"That doesn't mean that –"

"We shall meet again, soon, Mister Goodman. Very soon. There is a lot to be considered . . ." Shank's face was beaming. It had the look of someone who had just unearthed an undiscovered Gospel.

Paul closed the door behind him, relieved, as if he had

physically fought Shank and survived. He was damp with sweat.

"A cripple? You sick bastard, Goodman," whispered Violet, who had deliberately turned off the light in her tiny office, camouflaging herself with the darkness, listening to the private conversation between Shank and Paul.

Paul remained silent, his startled eyes diverted to her head, whose details appeared physically impossible, to the neck struggling, attempting to depart from its anchor stationed in the harbour of her shoulders.

"A fucking cripple?" whispered Violet, raising herself slowly from the chair, inching towards him. "You would choose a cripple over me? You're only a pathetic bastard. You find her fascinating. Don't you, you fucking pervert?" she accused "You couldn't handle me. Eh, Goodman? Scared of a real woman, aren't you?" She flicked on a switch, exposing the hatred in her eyes. They appeared damp. "You'll have no peace now, Goodman. Not from me. Camp with the enemy, die with the fuckers . . ."

Paul left the office quickly, squeezing alongside the motionless figure of Violet blocking the doorway, fearful of accidentally touching her as he moved.

The eerily quietness collapsed as he entered the Great Hall of Slaughtering, and he welcomed its noise, its screams and curses. Anything was better than the quietness. Anything was better than the hatred sizzling on Violet's face.

CHAPTER EIGHT

A Darkness of Minds Searching for Light

"The sexual embrace can only be compared with music
and with prayer."
Havelock Ellis

"The meeting of two personalities is like the contact of two chemical
substances: if there is any reaction, both are transformed."
Carl Gustav Jung, *Modern Man in Search of a Soul*

"YOU HAVEN'T EVEN lost a finger, in all this time? Miracles will never cease, Goodman," said the biting voice of Geordie.

Paul glanced up from the carving table. "I don't intend to. So if I were you, I wouldn't hold my breath."

"You'll never be me, so don't hold *your* breath, Goodman," she replied, moving clumsily towards the stairs, in the direction of Shank's office.

"Must have a soft spot for you, Paul," sniggered Raymond,

who was working feverishly on a piece of reluctant meat. "Normally, not a soul gets a word from that little devil in metal – except when she's screaming commands."

Over the weeks, Paul had gathered enough information on Violet to keep well away from her. Thankfully, contacts were rare, except for the occasional interrupted lunch-breaks when she happened to *accidentally* bump into him in the sheds. Paul quickly rectified that by eating in the canteen along with the rest of the workers, much to Violet's chagrin. Geordie, on the other hand, was still something of an enigma. He hated to admit it, but lately she had become more prominent in his thoughts, especially at night, wondering how she must look, naked and twisted, mangled between flesh and metal. He wondered if her flesh was as cold as the metal laying siege to her, wishing it had been her who had come, interrupting his lunch-breaks in the sheds. He wondered if Shank had said anything to her? Had Violet?

"Keep away from the lot of them, mate," advised Raymond, reiterating what Stevie Foster had initially said. "That entire family is bad news. Very bad news . . ."

Yet Geordie remained an itch, gnawing softly, making its presence felt, subtly. Sooner or later, he knew, he would want to scratch it.

"Has Geordie ever been out with anyone? I never see her socialising," inquired Paul, wiping the sweat from his skin, unknowingly smudging his entire face with blood from his wet hands.

"Geordie? Socialising?" A look of puzzlement appeared on Raymond's face. "You're not serious? Who in their right mind would go out with her? Haven't you seen the shape of her?"

"Has she?" persisted Paul, glancing in the direction of Shank's office.

"I couldn't honestly tell you. Why? Feeling kinky?" laughed Raymond, shuddering, mocking a shiver. "You'd have to be, mate. Don't fancy the thought of that, not one wee bit. Her buck-naked, with big pieces of metal sticking out of her legs – or worse – her lopsided arse!"

Paul grinned half-heartedly, hating himself for his cowardice.

Spotting Geordie making her way back down the stairs in their direction, Paul and Raymond quickly recommenced hacking at the miniature pyramids of meat.

"You've become quite a chatterbox since I paired you up with Goodman, Raymond. Do you want me to move you to the tail brigade?"

The tail brigade was the nastiest job in the abattoir, where workers were forced to strip the hair and shit from cows' tails, by hand, leaving the tails gleaming for exporting to foreign lands.

"No, Geordie. I was just –"

"You were just bullshitting, as usual. Watch yourself. I won't give you a second warning," said Geordie, staring into Raymond's eyes until his eyes looked away. "Goodman? Shank says I've to take you with me. We've to pick up some equipment from his house. Let's go."

Once again, contradictory feelings of reluctance and cold excitement ran through Paul as he placed his carving knife on the table, avoiding Raymond's grinning, rather-you-than-me face.

Three minutes later, Paul and Geordie emerged at the back

of the slaughterhouse, navigating their way through the mountains of bloodstained wooden pallets infested with flies feasting on the dried-out liquid.

"Hope you can drive Old Johnson," said Geordie, throwing the keys in Paul's direction.

Old Johnson was an enormous army truck that had succeeded in remaining unscathed during the height of the Second World War, only to be mercilessly battered by the drivers employed by Shank. A bullet to its gearbox would have put the old metal beast out of its misery. Instead, it was forced to perform the impossible on a regular basis: hauling tons of meat to the docks and picking up cheap labour on the return journey.

"I . . . I can't drive . . . never tried," said Paul, embarrassed. Then, as if to redeem himself, quickly added, "No need for it really. Never needed to travel outside of town."

Geordie shook her head. "Why does that not surprise me? A bunch of wasters, the lot of you. Throw me the keys."

A few minutes later, Geordie brought the old truck on to the motorway, cursing the snaky sequence of cars and trucks ahead.

"This is no use," she muttered, turning the steering wheel roughly to the right. "I know a shortcut," she said, smiling. The factory-made smirk on her face resembled that of both Shank and Violet.

They drove where the back roads diverged, stretching over miles of ruptured ground until it was too narrow to hold the lorry's width, eventually halting at an old disused bridge, its wooden structure dilapidated beyond repair.

Paul shook his head. "You're not serious, are you? There's no way you can take the truck across that piece of —"

The truck lurched forward, stopping inches from the bridge's gaping acceptance.

"Serious? You don't know the half of it." Geordie touched the accelerator, slightly, teasingly, and the wooded enforcement moaned under the tremendous weight of the truck's nose.

Paul felt his stomach shift.

The truck moved slowly but steadily, despite the protestation of noises coming from the bridge's creaking underbelly.

With his eyelids tightly shut, Paul breathed slowly through his nose, feeling his fingernails dig deep into his palms. He felt dizzy listening to the gurgle of enforced water, directly beneath.

Without warning, Geordie stopped the truck halfway across the bridge and eased herself awkwardly from the driving seat.

"What are you doing?" asked Paul, alarmed. "We shouldn't even be on the bridge. It wasn't built to take the weight of trucks – cars, perhaps; not trucks."

"Did I ask for your expert opinion?" She popped open the door, slid down on to the bridge and sat on the edge of the wooden structure, her legs dangling puppet-like over the rushing water.

"Why've you done this? Trying to kill us?" whispered Paul, fearful that his words could cause the truck to overspill into the river below.

"Can you smell the river?" she shouted, her voice competing with the force of rushing water. "It smells like shit, doesn't it? Smells just like the abattoir. Smells just like you, Goodman."

Paul couldn't read her expression through the glass. Cautiously, he eased himself over to the driver's side and poked his head out the window. "What are you trying to prove, Geordie? That you don't fear death? Okay. You've proven yourself. Now, can we get off this matchstick structure before we both plummet to our deaths?"

"The truck isn't moving until you get out of it and stand or sit on the bridge. That's my offer. Take it or leave it." Geordie stared up at him.

Paul hesitated, and she glanced away, staring at the water's direction.

"Fuck sake . . ." he mumbled, gingerly edging out of the truck, cautiously placing his feet on the bridge. "Satisfied? Now, can we get off this monstrosity before we end up taking an evening bath?"

Geordie stood and walked towards him.

Despite the noise from the river, Paul could clearly hear the metal surrounding her legs rub against her jeans.

"I hear you've been doing a lot of snooping, asking questions about me?"

Paul felt himself grimacing. He tried to undo his face but she'd seen it. "No . . . not really . . ."

"What do you want to hear?" Her mouth was a knife-edge, ready for ambush.

"Nothing."

"Nothing? Are you sure?" Her eyes became as thin and sharp as needles.

"Yes . . . I'm sure." Was the bridge moving slightly under his feet? Vibrating? He wanted to get off. Badly.

The water surged, turning white on the boulders beneath

them, spraying their faces and clothes. Paul tried to ignore its sound, its terrible power unnerving him. He still enjoyed swimming, but the nightmare of almost drowning in the pool of blood remained.

Geordie walked to the end of Old Johnson. Paul thought he saw her move, craftily, to the side, disappearing. What if she intended to throw him off, pretend it was an accident? Knock him over with the truck? They would all believe her. Wouldn't they? They wouldn't have any other choice, really.

The loud blast from the truck's horn made him jump.

"What's keeping you, Goodman? We haven't all bloody night!" shouted Geordie, perched behind the steering wheel, her face expressionless.

The forty-minute journey took for ever. No words were uttered, although a couple of times Paul felt his tongue moving, ready for the million questions he wanted to ask. Self-discipline saved him from muttering anything, and he was grateful when the house came into view, stationed beside a large field and flanked by a cathedral of skeletal trees.

It was exactly how he had envisioned it: enormous and intimidating – just like the abattoir. It looked as if the same architect had performed the identical layout of structure and brick, giving it a monstrously inadequate-to-live-in look, simply a place for shelter and holding, much like the animal pens. Beyond the house, heading west, was a dirt lane going all the way through the property, like a great, black, hungry snake.

The truck idled as darkness swallowed up the house, and finally the field itself.

"We haven't come here to gawk, Goodman," said Geordie,

awkwardly walking on. "Bring that old trolley from the back of the truck. Shank has a load of new knives he wants brought back."

Paul followed her to the back of the house. An enormous shed sheltered families of cardboard boxes, each numbered, each labelled with its contents and destination.

"You'll find two larger boxes at the back. One will be marked knives; the other should have a seven scrawled on it. Fish them out and put them on the trolley. Think you can manage that on your own?" she asked, walking in the direction of the house, not waiting for his answer.

Over the garden, a filthy village of clouds hung low beneath the former grey ceiling of sky, transforming it to the colour of darkened rust. It was dull, soulless weather painted entirely in grey, mixing with the limitless expanse of light oozing from the land.

Thirty minutes later, Paul glanced in the direction of the house, following the dirt line on the side of the road the entire time, fearful it was his only direction out of this strange and eerie place.

What was keeping her? Did she think he had nothing better to do than wait for her, like a slave waiting for the master's word?

"Here, Goodman. Don't say I never gave you anything." Geordie appeared out of nowhere, startling him. To his surprise, she handed him a beer.

"What's this for?" he asked, puzzled and suspicious. Was this some sort of peace offering, for all that nonsense on the bridge?

"If you don't want it, throw it on the ground," she replied, angrily, looking at him with such ire it pierced his eyes like an unrestrained knitting needle ready to pop them out. "Why can't you simply control that mouth of yours? Question after question. That's your problem, Goodman. Too many questions. Far too many for your own good."

Reluctantly, Paul placed the beer to his lips, tasting only wetness.

"It's not poisoned, or spiked – if that's what you're thinking. I'm not that hard up." She laughed, but it was unconvincing, a trained sound released by the brain's command, not by nature. The sound disintegrated into a bark.

Paul took a more courageous gulp. A few seconds later, the bottle was empty.

"Was that meant to impress me, Goodman? Watch this." Without hands, Geordie picked a full bottle of beer up with her teeth, throwing her head back quickly. Four seconds later, the beer was gone.

Placing the empty bottle on the ground, she wiped the remnants of the beer from her lips, missing a sliver attached to her chin.

Paul felt the urge to reach over and touch the wetness, wipe it from her face. Instead, he simply said, "Okay. I'm the one impressed. Shouldn't we be getting back?"

She ignored his question and handed him another beer. "Plenty of time. Relax. I'm not Violet. I won't bite. Promise."

He accepted the beer, swallowing half the contents before removing the bottle from his lips. "I shouldn't really be drinking. Could easily be minus a finger back at the abattoir." He meant it to be funny, but she ignored his words.

"Violet says you've been sniffing near her. Do you fancy

her?" She had her mouth covered by the bottle, making it difficult for him to discern if she had a smile with the words.

"Violet? You've got to be . . ." He held the word kidding in his mouth. *So, that's Violet's plan, eh? Putting the mix in?* "I don't fancy any person in that place." He sounded defensive. "Don't have much time for a relationship. I practise my snooker every chance I get. I don't know why Violet would think I'm sniffing anyfuckingwhere near her."

"*Wow.* Is that a temper, Goodman? Didn't think you had one in you."

"I just don't like Violet saying things about me that aren't true."

"She's never being backwards in going forward, our Violet."

"That's an understatement," said Paul.

Wind was gathering pace. It had a strange sounding to it.

"So, how much did she tell you about me?" asked Geordie.

"What makes you think she told me anything about you?"

"I know you discussed me with Shank – though it wasn't Shank who told me."

Paul was unprepared for the sudden direction of the conversation. It had all been a carefully planned trap, pretending to pick up supplies at the house. Someone in the abattoir had told her all about the questions – his questions. Nosey Balls. Nosey. Nosey. Nosey. This was why she had him here at this location, her home; this was why she was feeding him beer, loosening his tongue. Evidence. Enough rope and he'd be out of a job, out on his arse.

"Anything I said to Shank was my business." He felt angry having to defend himself, but a cold reality alerted him to be very careful. Extremely careful.

"And you weren't enquiring from any of the workers – such as Raymond?"

Caught by the balls! "Look, you're right, I should have just gone about my duties. I was simply curious." It sounded feeble.

"Curious about me, or the violent sister?" She stared at him, her eyes motionless. "You know what curiosity did to the cat, Goodman?" Geordie brought the bottle to her lips and sipped its contents slowly before dropping the empty bottle at her feet. Before he could reply, she spoke, almost a whisper. "Violet has a ruthlessness in her which is beyond measure. We used to have cats all over this place, in the early days, when we first moved here. Cats, inevitably, bring kittens into this world, Goodman, and Shank soon realised that Violet's ruthlessness could be put to good use. She became quite proficient at drowning all kittens captured, but her problem was – and *is* – controlling that ruthlessness. After the kittens, came the cats . . ."

A finger of ice touched Paul's spine. The beer now tasted like rust in his mouth – rust and blood – yet he desperately wanted another one. Truth be told, coupled with a cigarette, the beer would taste delightful.

"Now you know why Shank never allows her to work in the slaughtering. She sees the killing as pleasure – not necessity."

The beer sat in Paul's stomach. He thought about Violet's words of warning to him; thought it best not to mention them to Geordie.

"Shouldn't we be heading back to the abattoir, before it gets too dark?" asked Paul, hoping to change the conversation. He thought about going across the matchstick bridge again. Surely she wouldn't drive across in the dark?

"She used to turn the gas on in the house, while she sat

there smoking Shank's cigars, calm as the Red Sea, knowing someone would lose their nerve before she did and turn the fucking thing off," said Geordie, ignoring Paul's question. "She could even throw up on command – usually over me."

Paul had visions of Violet vomiting all over him, throwing her head back, laughing like a banshee. For a terrible second, he thought he could smell the poignant stench of vomit. He sniffed the bottle of beer.

"I had a dog like that, once," said Paul, omitting to say it had to be put down for such rude manners.

"I hate to admit it," continued Geordie, "but I'm afraid of her on some level because of her moods and her nature to fight dirty; her reluctance to concede defeat. I realised that it was better to let her win, because she would just keep throwing herself at you, over and over again."

Had she moved closer to him? He hadn't even noticed. He could smell the abattoir oozing off her body, mixing with that smell processed only by women; slightly intoxicating when used correctly. Strangely, it was a smell of comfort and protection, a smell he once associated with his mother, before the dark times came visiting.

"Bring those beers with you, Goodman. We'll sit over there, near the uprooted tree."

They used the old tree to rest against, but placed a healthy distance between each other, fearful of contamination.

"I hope you're not trying to get me drunk, boss?" said Paul, laughingly, regretting it the moment her face tightened into a scowl.

"Think I'm that hard up, Goodman? Think you're something special?"

He thought about remaining silent, but had had enough of walking on thin ice and tiptoeing. "'Why can't you simply control that mouth of yours? Question after question,'" he mimicked.

Geordie froze. Her normally implacable eyes looked at him, sullenly, momentarily confused.

Had he overstepped? Probably. Perhaps he should apologise? Instead, he reached and opened another beer, handing it to her before producing one for himself. He smiled. "These are lukewarm. The next time you invite me to your house, make sure there is plenty of ice." A tingling sensation deep in his chest accompanied the quickness in the small of his stomach, the delicious anticipation of what she would say – or *do* – next. He hated to admit it, but the feeling was akin to something sexual, something forbidden, close to the way an artist experiences the creative process, or the way a snooker player feels, about to assassinate the remaining black ball.

"Who says there'll be a next time, Goodman?" She sipped the beer, but he knew she was covering a smile, a real smile. He wanted to pull the bottle from her lips, stop her from covering what she was not used to.

For the next few minutes, not a word was said. The city moved along outside beyond their knowledge, unheeding, unknowing, uncaring of what they were saying and feeling. Soon it would be pitch dark. Neither seemed in a hurry to prevent it, almost as if they were waiting for it, as if this great cloak of night would help them both to say what they couldn't say, to speak what they never dared, not to anyone bar themselves, alone.

"A magician gets on the stage and starts building all his

apparatus, talking to the audience who are anticipating tonight's performance," said Paul, breaking the silence before sipping on the beer. "Says he can pull a rabbit from out of his hat. No sooner has the old guy produced his black hat than someone from the audience shouts up, 'Big fucking deal. I can pull a hair from out of my arse!'" He took a bigger sip this time, and waited.

Geordie made a sound, like the sound of air being restrained, but he knew he had her.

"In the absence of illusions, reality often works just fine. Ask any magician. Go on. Let it out. You just know you want to piss yourself laughing. Don't you? Go on . . ."

From the top of her shirt, she removed a small brass container, flipping the lid with an audible pop. Seconds later, she was rolling a cigarette, just like a cowboy, joining its paper skin with the dampness of her tongue.

Intrigued, Paul watched, fascinated by her expertise in rounding the homemade cigarette perfectly.

"Here," she said, handing the cigarette to him, her free hand already working on another.

He lit the cigarette, drawing deep its claustrophobic smoke, forcing it down, down deep to his – "Fuck! What the fuck *is* this stuff?"

Now she laughed, loud and natural.

"What?" he pleaded. "What's so funny? What the fuck *is* this stuff?"

Controlling her laughter, she calmly replied, "Marijuana, Goodman. Don't tell me you haven't tried it before, you being a man of the world?" She laughed again, seeing the shock on his face, loving the terror she hadn't even planned.

"Marifuckingjuana! We could go to jail for this. Wait until Lucky hears this. He'll never believe me." Paul stared in disbelief at the cigarette between his fingers, a bomb ready to explode.

"It's no big deal, Goodman. Did you know that Christ smoked marijuana?"

"What?"

"True. It says in John that when Christ went up to the mountain, that there was grass all about . . ."

She was giggling uncontrollably, marijuana relaxing her inhibitions, her anxiety and fears dissipating, if only for the now.

Paul began to giggle also, unaccustomed to the slow drag and pull of marijuana through his body, the mounting sensation of euphoria and promise. He placed his hand on the ground as if to steady himself.

It felt strange, as if he were floating inches above his body. It was lovely. He noticed something odd in the way his words were forming, like they were dull around the edges. It was bizarre.

Geordie inhaled deeply, expertly, watching him smile a half-drunk, semi-stoned smile. She smiled back at him, but he didn't notice; he was floating and finding it difficult to remain on the ground. He wondered what would happen if a night wind came along. Would it take him? Drop him off at sea like a big balloon? He giggled at the thought.

"This is great stuff," he whispered.

"I know. As soon as it reaches the receptors in the brain and organs, usually in less than a minute, its effects can be felt. Especially when sprinkled with a little acid," said Geordie.

"Acid? Will that not burn through, leave a big hole gaping from my stomach?" His eyes were seeing two Geordies. One looked familiar. Sad and angry. The other was happy, grinning, looking cute and pretty, even beautiful. He liked her the best. "I like you best," he giggled, touching the smiling Geordie's face.

"No, *this* acid doesn't burn – at least not in the way you're thinking." She laughed, softly this time, as if not wanting to scare him, wanting him to keep his hand on her face.

"Why this stuff? What's wrong with a good beer?"

"People choose marijuana because it is completely natural and provides much needed relief from a multitude of ailments. The dosage is easy to regulate when smoked, providing just the amount required to be effective. And the side effects are quite pleasant – as you bear witness to. It can also provide effective pain relief from backaches to migraines, thought it is not a miracle cure. It certainly can't make the lame walk, or the crippled whole . . ."

Surrendering his thoughts to Geordie's voice, Paul entwined his fingers with hers. They fitted perfectly together. Better than gloves. More like thin magnets. The scent of marijuana and the unwashed odour of work rested in his nostrils.

The reluctant dying light appeared for a few moments, defiantly, throwing bleeding patches of orange and red on to the withered parchment of patchy grass all about them, before splintering into dazzling streams of almost wet light swelling with bleached-out colour. Moments later, it was gone for good, replaced by crawling darkness. The pale yellows of occasional car lights flashed by, washing out pieces of the house, making it deserted and haunted. It was perfect for ghosts. Naked ghosts . . .

Paul turned on his side, staring at her profile. He lifted his face and her eyes caught his immediately. "You planned this whole thing. Admit it. You wanted me from the first day you spotted me."

"Ha! You wish," she replied, blowing smoke effortlessly into the air.

"I'm going to kiss you," he said, his voice no longer sure, the words slightly slurred. "Will you stop me?"

She said nothing, simply sucked on the cigarette, watching its angry nipple brighten the outline of his face.

He kissed her lightly on the cheek before moving awk- wardly to her lips. He smelt a light mist of perfume rising from her and wondered if that was what she had been doing in the house all that time, putting on perfume? Had she anticipated this, known his feelings? He kissed her harder now, trying des- perately to open her mouth with his tongue, but she resisted.

"Enough, Goodman," she said, gently but with command. It was sufficient to deflate his semi-hardness.

Defeated and angry, he made a movement to go.

"Stay where you are, Goodman. We'll go when I decide."

"Yes, sir, boss. I be waiting. Don't flog me, boss. I a good slave, boss. I don't want to –"

She rolled on top of him and kissed his mouth, hard, part- ing his lips with her tongue, stabbing in and out frantically, like a tiny bird fearful of capture. Her saliva tasted of beer, lip- stick and the sweet sickly taste of marijuana, and he couldn't get enough of their divine, potent mixture. There was a soft purr in her throat, a low frequency gurgle, elevating the mun- dane experience of kissing to the level of something sexual. He felt the weight of her breasts pushing powerfully against him, like two invisible forces holding him in place, teasing and pleasing.

For Paul, the urge to pursue the quickest route for sex took over. His head was swimming. He fumbled for her jeans, but the metal surrounding her stood guard, unwavering, like a medieval chastity belt, frustrating his efforts.

"C'mon," was all he managed to say, before rolling on top, reversing the positions, fumbling at her shirt, popping two of her buttons in the struggle. "I can't get this bastard shirt off!" he screamed. "Help me, for fuck sake," he pleaded.

"No," she whispered through her nostrils, shaking her head. "Find a way." Her tiny eyes scanned his face, watching, seemingly fascinated.

More buttons popped into the air, making good their freedom, until only her bra remained between him and the sight of her breasts.

"By the time I get this off, I'll be too tired to do anything . . ."

She took one last draw of her cigarette, then flicked it into the air, watching it somersault into the darkness. "I suppose I've no other choice, now? I'll do it. Obviously, you've never done this before, Goodman." Within seconds, the bra was gone, her breast exposed, her nipples slightly raised and waxed in sweat.

"Oh . . ." he managed to say.

"Oh, indeed, Goodman," she replied, matter-of-factly.

He kissed the deepness of her neck, snaking his tongue down between her breasts. He was aware of her nipples watching him, as if wondering what awaited them. It was weirdly disconcerting. He thought he saw the left one wink before hiding beneath the heaviness of her breast. *Come and get me,* it said.

"This marijuana does strange things . . ." he mumbled, his voice muffled on her breast, the right nipple giggling with delight as his tongue massaged it with tiny circles. *Stop it! I love it! You're killing me, boy! I love it!* screamed the nipple. "Strange fucking things . . ." He wanted her nude, now – no, he wanted her the way he had imagined her late at night, his hand tight against his penis: he wanted her naked, wrapped in metal, powerless to do anything to prevent him. He wanted to see her mangled legs, bare, covered in scaffolding. He wanted to see the darkness of her hair, between her mangled legs, crying to be touched with his probing fingers.

Finally, Paul managed to unbutton the top of her jeans with his exhausted fingers. Her whispery moan encouraged him to investigate further, and he slipped his thumb beneath the jeans, feeling the elastic top of her panties. For a second he hesitated, as if this were an electric fence daring him to touch it, threatening him with bolts of lightning.

Courage rekindled, he proceeded gingerly, his fingers inching eagerly but warily onwards. He guessed another inch would see him touch the coarseness of her pubic hair. After that, well, he would think it through . . .

Geordie's hand held his, slowly bringing it back to safety. She said nothing, but kissed him, harder this time.

Undeterred, Paul's fingers slowly made their way back down the trail, hoping if they moved quietly enough, she wouldn't notice, until it was too late.

He held his breath. Within seconds, the fingers touched the coarseness of her pubic hair and he felt his heart ready to explode. She didn't stop him and this confused him. This was not part of his great plan. *Is she calling my bluff? Does she know I am practically shitting myself because I don't know what I will find down there, if it will be mangled, will it have its own scaffolding, will it be mushy like a squashed cake?*

Abruptly, he withdrew his fingers and she angrily pushed him away. "Get the fuck off me, you bastard. You gutless tease. Think my cunt is crippled, also? Think it's deformed, impaired, lame, handicapped, physically challenged – all those nice words people such as you use?" Quickly, she covered her breast. "Look away from me. Now!"

Hammered by her words, Paul stammered. "I'm the tease? It was you who pulled my hand away the first time. What do you call that? Eh? I was . . . erect . . ."

"Well then, keep your dick to yourself. But just shut the fuck up. I can't listen to your whining voice, just like all the rest of the whining bastards. I'm sticking you on the tail brigade, starting from tomorrow." She fumbled her bra back on, looking embarrassed by the whole sorry episode.

"No you're not," he retorted defiantly. "You can stick the tail brigade up your own tail – and the job. There are plenty of other places besides the shitty abattoir! I'm going to be the champion of the world one day. What are you going to be? A manipulating tease full of self-fucking-pity? That's your limit and always –"

He remembered waking up, but he could not remember going to sleep. The taste of mud and blood was in his mouth, adding to the total tastes already there. His head seemed to be split in two. The pain was unbearable.

"Are you okay, Goodman?" asked a face which resembled

Geordie's except there were now six faces, all moving in slow motion, splitting into east and west directions.

"What . . . what happened? Oh . . . God . . . my head . . ." He touched it cautiously, praying it was still whole. Dampness stuck to his hair. Blood.

"You tripped. Over that big root sticking from the tree." Geordie knelt beside him.

He looked at her suspiciously and pointed at the alleged offender. "That big root, you mean?"

She nodded.

"That big root sticking out there, the one that couldn't trip up a rabbit?"

"Yes," she mumbled, unconvincingly.

"I thought Violet was the violent one? The one who fights dirty? What did you use? An iron bar?"

"I couldn't help it. You made me lose my temper, saying those things. I thought you liked me."

He touched his head, again. "I do . . . but if that means having my skull crushed . . ."

"Here. This will take the pain away." She held out her fingers, showing him the cigarette.

He moved quickly away from her reach. "No. No thanks . . . That's what started it all. Besides, it really is time to be getting back. My mom needs to be told when to take her nighttime medicine." He felt his face redden. "Sounds daft. Right? A big mommy's boy."

She said nothing for a moment, then: "No. You should be grateful you have a mother. Mine died giving birth to me. I never even knew her."

"I . . . I didn't mean to –"

"I blame Shank," she cut in, catching him off-guard. "He knew it was dangerous for her to have any more children after Violet, but he insisted she try. He wanted a boy, someone to continue his name."

"Is that why you and Violet never call Shank father, because of your mother?

It took a few seconds for her response. "No, he never tolerated us calling him by that tag. He blamed us for our mother's death, blamed us for not being boys. That's why he gave me the name Geordie. Thought that eventually I would morph into a male. Anyway, Shank was in a state of denial at my gender. Worse, both Violet and I suffered from some form of disablement. I was born with a form of muscular dystrophy characterised by gradual deterioration of the muscles. A few more years, I'll be confined to a wheelchair. As for Violet, apart from her over-stuffed head and her hatred and violence, she is pretty much the lucky one between us. She is all woman."

Geordie took a long draw on the cigarette before releasing the smoke slowly down her nose. An audible sigh of relief accompanied the sound. "For a while, I thought that perhaps Shank was right, that I *was* a boy. It is only lately I have begun to develop into anything resembling a woman; little hills of breasts, hair growing in interesting places . . ." She formed her lips into the shape of a disinterested smile. "I don't remember the exact moment when I realised I was different, but as I developed more confidence, I saw the only way to deal with being different was to prove to myself that I could do any task offered me. I took it all as a challenge. But this afternoon was different. I was afraid of what my nakedness would mean to you. I was terrified it would have frightened you, repulsed you."

Paul remained silent, not knowing what to say. He took the cigarette from her hand and inhaled, thinking how wrong she had been about marijuana: there *is* pain it cannot erase.

"If Shank had had his way with me, he would have drowned me as easily as Violet drowned the kittens. It was only years later that I discovered he had forced my mother to take so-called revolutionary tablets that were all the talk at the time; tablets that would strengthen her, helping her to grant him the son he so desperately and selfishly wanted. The tablets, of course, were a disaster. Countless thousands of babies were born with terrible defects, some of which make Violet's and mine pale in comparison . . ."

Dew soaked itself within the earth, and an intense, claustrophobic grey was shifting almost unnoticeably into blackness. Red lights flickered in the new dark and the speckled distance, while Paul and Geordie sat in the old dark for a long time, cigarettes lighting their pale faces.

"They say every girl wants a guy similar to dear old dad." She made a crescent shape with her lips, a fake smile of ice. "I hope you are nothing like dear old *dad*. I don't know why I have told you all this, Goodman. You are the first person all these years I have spoken to, willingly." She inhaled the cigarette. "Don't even think of breathing a word to anyone. I'm not Violet, but I am close . . ."

The malice was no longer in her words, as if she had been drained, mentally and physically. The warning sounded quite feeble.

Paul wished he had another beer. His throat was drying out. The mixture of alcohol and marijuana had laid waste to his inhibitions; now it was turning its attention to his tongue, loosening it. "We all carry nightmares, Geordie, but we smile and pretend that the world is really fine, even though we know how fucked-up it is. I always remember the Saturday mornings, as a kid, when I'd wake up early, sneak into my parents' room and burrow a narrow tunnel between their sleeping bodies. Their bed was an enormous life raft. I would imagine the three of us being the Swiss Family Robinson. But then, everything seemed to change for the worse. That was the day he didn't come home . . ."

"It happens all the time, Goodman, men – fathers – leaving their family. I'm sure he must have –"

"No. You don't understand. My father didn't desert us – he would never do that. Something happened to him, something terrible, when I was a kid, a long long time ago."

Geordie shifted her body slightly, bringing her face closer.

"What? What terrible thing?"

Paul sucked in a piece of air before slowing releasing it again.

"I vaguely remember him getting into a car with a group of men. It was raining that day. I remember the rain bouncing off the windows, distorting his face. I couldn't see his face clearly enough, but I think he looked directly at me, at my mother. I was only a kid, but I can still remember that part like it was yesterday."

"Whose car? Did you know any of the men?"

"No, but I'm almost certain my mother knows. I remember once when I asked her, she placed her hands on my face as if I were a baby. 'Your father was a decent man – not a great man, but a very decent man, and that is a rarity. He was also a courageous man. If you have heard anything about him from any of these people, that he walked out on us, it is lies. Your father did not walk out on us. Do not concern yourself. You must never question me again about this – ever.'"

Again there was silence. Paul shivered slightly in the cold.

"Perhaps that was her way of reassuring you? Maybe she was too embarrassed to admit he left her? It happens all the time, Goodman. I know a couple of cousins –"

"I knew you would say that. Everyone thinks that. But I know that my father didn't walk out on us. All his clothes and belongings were still in the house. My mother keeps them locked in our spare room. Why didn't he take his clothes with him? And if my mother truly believed he walked out on her, why would she keep them, like a shrine dedicated to him. It doesn't make sense, does it? Something did happen, something terrible. As his son, I know; I *feel* it."

"Don't say another word, Goodman. I think we've both said enough."

"It's my mother I'm more concerned about. She gets depressed and does weird things, embarrassing things." Paul felt his face redden. "Some nights I catch her, swinging on my old battered swing in our yard, talking to herself."

Geordie laughed. "If that's the worst thing she does, trust me, it's nothing. I talk to myself, all the time."

"She is always naked."

"Oh . . . well . . . it's nothing, really . . . hairs and holes . . . we all have them. Don't we?"

"Can you imagine the embarrassment? The neighbours seeing her like that? It's fucking horrible. I hate her when she gets depressed. How's that for selfishness? I know she is lonely. I understand loneliness, sort of. It's a sad state, full of dark thoughts. I know I should be trying to help her, but all I'm concerned about is the fucking neighbours and their spying eyes." For a moment, pebbles of anger rested beneath his skin, festering with rage at all the bad memories, then just as quickly were gone, replaced with a tinge of guilt at his prior thoughts of hating his mother.

Geordie made a movement, as if to touch him.

"You can't blame yourself for her depression. And as for the neighbours? Well, if I were you, I'd walk out into the yard, bollock-naked, as well. Jump on your swing, as well. Wave your dick at them. Now *that* would give the nosey bastards something to think about!"

Despite himself, Paul burst out laughing. "I wouldn't have too much to wave."

"Don't be modest, Goodman. Remember, I saw you naked your first day on the job. Not too bad at all," laughed Geordie.

"What a bastard you were. I'll never forget that day."

"It toughened you up, didn't it?"

They sat there, not speaking another word, using the preferred communication that didn't involve talking, like the ritual test of endurance experienced by those comfortable in the knowledge that they have conquered the unconquerable, allowing the silence to harden around them before melting away into abandon.

The tired moon released the faintest blue light, like a light bulb shifting over foil, bringing with it dampness. Yet, still they lingered, as if both knew that this was a magic time, a time to be remembered for ever, a time never to be matched and a time to be savoured for the days of "remember the time?"

It was twenty minutes later before they made a movement, walking in the direction of Old Johnson.

"One day you'll drive this old beast, Goodman. Mark my words," said Geordie, smiling, reaching for the truck's door.

Instinctively, Paul moved to help her ease in, but received a withering look for his troubles.

"Don't. I'm a cripple; not crippled, Goodman. That day hasn't come. Not yet, anyway . . ."

The words made the hairs spike into his neck. Was she warning him of the inevitable, giving him a chance to change his mind, run while he had the chance? What would he do when, eventually, her body succumbed, confining her to a wheelchair for life?

CHAPTER NINE

Going to Meet the Man

*"Whatever happens at all happens as it should. You will find this
true, if you watch closely."*
Marcus Aurelius, *Meditations*

"Lovers' rows make love whole."
Terence, *Andria*

THREE WEEKS HAD now gone, and Paul's relationship with Geordie was slowly becoming stronger. He found himself looking forward to work, knowing she would be there. But deep down inside, something was niggling at him, a voice accusing him of cowardice and hypocrisy. He had yet to introduce Geordie to anyone he knew and wondered if, secretly, he was embarrassed by her psychical appearance. He debated with himself that he was falling in love and that he could never be ashamed of her. Yet, the niggling remained, the tiny voice of reprimand accompanied him to bed each night, accusing.

"Would you come with me, tonight, after work?" he asked, trying desperately to sound casual.

Geordie looked at him suspiciously. "Where and why? You've never asked me to go any place with you before."

"Oh, it's just to the pawnshop, to meet Mister Kennedy. I think you'd like him. He's been very kind to me over the last few months."

"Why not your mother?"

"What?"

"Why not your mother?" repeated Geordie. "Why do you not want me to meet your mother – or Lucky, come to think of it?"

He felt his face burn. "I . . . well . . . you see . . ."

"No, to be honest, Goodman, I don't see. I don't see at all. What you're really saying is that you are ashamed to be seen with me, ashamed of my shape, my walk. You don't mind the incredibly dark holding sheds, or the privacy of my house. Do you?"

"No," he mumbled, wishing he hadn't opened his mouth. The worms were crawling out of the can, all over him. They refused to go back inside.

"Well, tell you what, Goodman, if you are ashamed of me, *you're* not the type of person I want to be with, either. I don't owe you anything for your company."

"It's not that, Geordie. It's . . ."

"I'm looking at the face of a stranger. I don't recognise you. Hate is building up in me. If I were you, I'd get out of my sight, right now before someone sees you speaking to me – and we couldn't have that. Could we? Any chances you may have had with me have just been blown off the hinges."

Everything was collapsing. A coward's payment for a coward's action.

"This is all new to me, Geordie. I've hardly been with a girl my entire life. I'm still not too sure how to handle them – handle you. Just give me another chance. I promise, you will not regret it."

She studied him, her face implacable with righteous anger, her arms folded defiantly. It was ten long seconds before she spoke. "You're on probation, as far as I'm concerned, Goodman. One more mistake –"

"There won't be any more. I promise."

"Okay. But don't mess up." Her eyes scowled, then softened slightly. "Now, where is this pawnshop you are so eager for me to visit?"

"Just outside Sailor Town. Not too far from where I live."

"But what will *Mommy* and Lucky say? Surely they'll be broken-hearted, me not visiting them first?" she whispered, mockingly, her tongue acid.

"We'll do that first, then. Lucky should be in –"

"I'm kidding, Goodman. *Mommy* and Lucky will have to wait to be graced by my presence." She smiled. "Who knows? Perhaps *Mommy* and Shank will fall in love? Wouldn't that be fun? Have a wee Geordie-Paulie-type baby." A smile covered her entire face.

"That's not funny."

"No? I think it's hilarious." She closed in on him and quickly licked the dampness of his face. "You're burning, Goodman. Good. Let that be a lesson to you. But just remember: probation means no more messing up. Got it?"

He nodded, releasing the pocket of air from his lungs.

They stopped at the pawnshop on the way home. The next payment wasn't due for two more days, but if he paid it tonight, Paul wouldn't have to make his way back over on Friday, distracting him from practising for an important tournament on Saturday, over at Whitewell Snooker Hall.

Two years it had taken him to reach this stage of his carefully planned career. He wanted to be on his best form. Joe Watson, manager of some of the biggest names in snooker, would be popping in to eye-up potential players of the future, and as far as Paul was concerned, snooker was his future, his only hope of escaping the soul-murdering drudgery of his existence.

"I was almost about to close shop," said Kennedy, friendly yet with that tinge of nervousness hovering beside him. "Five more minutes and I'd have been gone. And who is this beautiful young lady? You never told me you were dating someone as lovely as this, Paul," smiled Kennedy, staring directly at Geordie.

"This is Geordie. She's . . . we are . . ."

"Boyfriend and girlfriend, I think Paul is struggling to say, Mister Kennedy. You know how shy he is about these sort of things," said Geordie. "Paul never shuts up about you. A pleasure to meet you." She put out her hand.

"No, Geordie, the pleasure is all mine," replied Kennedy, shaking Geordie's hand. "Shame on you, Paul, not letting me know about this beautiful young lady."

"Yes," agreed Geordie. "Shame on you, Paul, you naughty boy."

"Can I get either of you a cup of tea, or something warm? How about a sandwich? I've some nice salmon in the fridge, back there. Would you like some?" inquired Kennedy, looking from Paul to Geordie.

"No, really, Mister Kennedy. It was just that I wanted to get my payment to you. I've a big match coming up on Saturday and I really need tons of practice." Paul removed an envelope from his pocket and handed it to Kennedy.

Without opening or checking the amount, Kennedy pocketed the envelope.

"Geordie? Can I entice you?"

Cheekily, she replied, "Well, time will tell."

They all laughed. Except Paul.

"A big match, Paul? Where's it being held?" Kennedy walked towards the door and pulled down the screen.

"At Whitewell."

Paul could see Kennedy was impressed. Even the old man had heard of Whitewell.

"Whitewell? That *is* big. They say Joe Watson shows his face in there, every now and again, poaching for potential talent."

Paul was impressed with Kennedy's knowledge. "You know a lot more about snooker than you pretend, Mister Kennedy. I'm sure you've met a few of the old masters in your time."

"Ha! Listen to him, Geordie. He makes me sound ancient. I'm not that bloody old – just a rough life," laughed Kennedy, who now seemed oddly comfortable discussing snooker and salmon sandwiches with Paul and Geordie. "I've some old photos if you want to see them, though I doubt you would recognise anyone in them. Long before your time, I'm afraid."

Before Paul could reply, Kennedy disappeared into the shadows of a back room, emerging a few minutes later, covered in dust and speckled in webs.

"Filthy, back there. Never have the chance to . . ." mumbled

Kennedy, apologetically. Seconds later, he sat an old picture album on the counter top. Carefully, he wiped the layers of dust from the plastic, revealing pictures pockmarked with time and neglect. Seconds later, he dove-tailed the pictures out, expertly, like a card dealer or magician.

"Actually, I have had these sitting about to show you. I thought you might be interested in their history, appreciate their time and place . . ."

Gingerly, Paul reached for the top layer of pictures. One more layer remained beneath. "What snooker hall was this? That's not you, is it?" The picture revealed a young man, late twenties, bending his frame, attaching it to a snooker table. He was grinning for the camera.

"That photo was shot in your club, the Tin Hut," replied Kennedy, who seemed to be smiling at the memories; memories long time dead, but now miraculously resurrected by the voice of the young man before his eyes.

"You're kidding me? Shit, the place looked like crap even then."

"Yes," agreed Kennedy. "It really was a dog of a place, but we thought it the greatest spot on earth. When we came together, we were like warriors preparing for battle. We may have been friends before the game, but once that game commenced . . . no prisoners taken."

Engrossed, Paul knew exactly what Kennedy meant. It was how he himself felt before the beginning of each game, a feeling of ruthlessness, each man for himself, all the spoils for the victor, nothing for the vanquished. It were as if a spirit – good or bad – had entered you, and could only be exorcised by the ending of the game, preferably as the winner.

"These pictures should be hanging on the Tin Hut's walls, Mister Kennedy. I'm sure the committee would pay you for them. They're fantastic. A great piece of history."

A tapping from above banged impatiently, annoyingly. Paul thought he had heard the sound the last time he had been in the shop.

"Ignore that sound," advised Kennedy seeing Paul and Geordie's eyes glance in the direction of the ceiling. "That's just an old bird, trapped in the attic. I'll have to wring its neck one of these days."

Paul smiled obligingly, yet feeling awkward and uncomfortable at the harshness in Kennedy's voice. "Well, I guess we'll be running on. We've a couple of errands to do before getting home."

"I've something for you. I need you to hold on for a few minutes more. I'll try not to be long."

Kennedy was gone, heading for the stairs at the back, leaving Paul and Geordie in their own company.

"Well? What do you think of him?" asked Paul.

"I've only met the man for all of ten minutes, and you want me to make a judgement? I've got to be careful of my judgements in future. Know what I mean?"

"I thought that was all sorted?"

"Did you, Goodman? You've got a long way to go before I can ever trust you again."

Within seconds, silence crept into the room, disturbed only by the wooden ticking of a clock above his head. Paul felt a creepy feeling resting uneasily in the room, as if someone or something was watching him. He thought he could hear the muffled sound of an argument coming from some place upstairs and decided it was best to be going. It was late as it was, and he felt sure Kennedy would understand.

"C'mon," said Paul to Geordie, walking towards the door. "I've got to be in the Tin Hut before –"

"Sorry. These thing weigh a ton," said Kennedy, making Paul jump just as his hand touched the door handle.

Kennedy proceeded to open a large mahogany box, placing it atop the wooden counter, unhooking the tiny brass question marks at the side.

"One day, you'll use these on your very own snooker table. I have no doubt about that, lad." Kennedy was smiling.

In the case nestled a complete family of snooker balls, gleaming, pristine, all encased separately and wrapped in silk.

"God . . . they are beautiful . . ." Paul was speechless. Their beauty was overpowering. "They must be worth a fortune."

"Worth more than a fortune, lad. These are the genuine articles. Pure ivory. Not like the manufactured garbage they use nowadays."

Hypnotised, Paul simply wanted to touch them, feel the beauty of their hardened skin.

"Twelve elephants had to be slaughtered to make this set," continued Kennedy. "Twelve great beasts. Can you imagine that? Of course, you wouldn't get away with that sort of stuff these days, and I'm not saying I agree with killing elephants. But . . ."

"Beautiful . . ." whispered Paul, staring at the perfectly sphere-shaped objects of desire. "So powerful, just looking at them makes you feel invincible."

A look of bewilderment crept across Geordie's face. She didn't know what all the fuss was about.

"They're yours, for the asking," said Kennedy.

Paul was taken aback. "I could never afford these, Mister Kennedy. Perhaps one day, when I become a great player. But I wouldn't hold my breath. You'll probably have sold them ten times over by then."

"I'm not *selling* them to you. I'm *giving* them to you."

"Giving? I . . . I don't understand . . ."

Kennedy's face was beaming. He hadn't expected this reaction. It had been worth it, regardless of the cost.

"There is no need to understand. Now, if you don't mind, I'm sorry, I must ask you to go. It's late, and I think I can hear that old, annoying bird flapping about up there." Kennedy smiled. "I hope you don't mind carrying them, but the incentive should alleviate their weight. Don't you think?"

Paul could only nod.

"I'm sure you're very proud of Paul, Geordie?"

"Proud? Oh, ever so," she replied, mockingly flashing her eyebrows lovingly at Paul. "So proud of my Paul . . ."

"Well, it was a pleasure meeting you, Geordie. Don't ever be a stranger. Understand?"

"You'll regret saying that, Mister Kennedy," replied Geordie, grinning. "I love getting a good bargain. I'm sure there's plenty of stuff in your shop to interest me. And now that you know I know Paul, and how proud I am of him, I'm sure a wee discount will be waiting for me the next time I drop by."

Kennedy laughed. "Of that you can be certain. Come by any time, Geordie. Now, goodnight to both of you."

Paul waited until they were a couple of streets away from the shop before asking, "You liked him, then?"

"Hmm," replied Geordie, vaguely. "I don't know. A bit too nice, perhaps. Tried a bit too hard to be nice. Nice people make me suspicious."

"No. He's always like that," replied Paul, defensively. "He really is a kind person."

"Kind to you means strange to me. He rarely looked in my direction, but couldn't take his eyes from you."

"What do you mean by that?"

Geordie simple shook her head. "The jury is still out on Mister Kennedy. I'll see you in the morning."

"What? You're going home already?"

"Don't let the bedbugs bite," she said, cutting across the street.

"No goodnight kiss?"

"Probation, Goodman."

He watched her disappear among the twisted walls of streets, feeling isolated. "I won't screw up again, Geordie," he whispered to himself. "That's a promise . . ."

Kennedy hadn't even given Geordie a second glance because her disability was invisible to his eyes. She would have complained had he been staring at her. He was in a no-win situation. He's a class act. Not a fool like me, thought Paul, torturing himself for his own stupidity. He was lucky to have people like Kennedy and Geordie. He had learned a lesson tonight. One he wouldn't forget in a hurry.

Rain was falling softly. It looked like a downpour was in the making. He'd have to be fast if he didn't want a good soaking. The snooker balls *were* heavy, but his anticipation and adrenaline made them float, like balloons, all the colours of the rainbow. *Unbelievable,* he though, gripping the mahogany box tightly against his side like a thief in the night. *What the hell has come over that old man?*

Chapter Ten

The Hunter in the Forest

"God bears with the wicked, but not for ever."
Miguel de Cervantes, *Don Quixote*

"If you go down in the woods today, you're sure of a big surprise . . ."
Jimmy Kennedy, "The Teddy Bears' Picnic"

FROM THE OPPOSITE side of the road, Lucky watched as tiny bugs bounced off the security lights, their amber glow attracting them like drunks to whiskey.

What the fuck is keeping him? He told me he always finished at five. Lucky was dying for a shit. He wondered how long he could keep it imprisoned.

One more cigarette. If he's not out in five minutes, then fuck it. I'll call over to his house, later tonight.

A few minutes later and the finished cig butt tumbled to the ground, joining a family of others that littered his feet like spent ammo from an old war movie.

At last! Workers began to drift out from the large metal gates of the abattoir. Lucky craned his neck to get a better view, cursing the large angry trucks whizzing by, obscuring his view.

Then, just as Lucky had surrendered all hope, Paul emerged, coat flung over his shoulders.

"Paul! Hey, Goodman, you bastard!" shouted Lucky, waving frantically, his voice competing with the din of traffic.

Paul stood at the gate, glancing at his watch, his ears not capturing Lucky's voice.

"Deaf bastard," mumbled Lucky, taking the initiative to cut across the manic motorway.

Just at he found a safe gap, Lucky's eyes captured Paul being joined by someone else emerging from the abattoir. They seemed to be talking, laughing. A few seconds later, they both turned, walking in the direction of the old gasworks.

"What the fuck . . .?" Disbelief stung in Lucky's voice. His eyes strained to make out the person. He couldn't tell if it was a man or a woman, only that the person seemed to be walking weirdly, clumsily, like a robot learning to take its first steps.

He thought about shouting Paul's name again, but pride kept his mouth firmly shut. Instead, he crept behind the unsuspecting pair, staying securely in the shadowed boundaries of the gasworks' walls.

"I can't believe this. Who the fuck is that?" he whispered, just as Paul and the stranger stopped and peered into the darkness – in his direction!

Had they seen him? Fuck. He felt a real fool now. What would Paul say, catching him spying like a pervert in the night's darkness?

But Paul hadn't seen him. Instead, he pushed the stranger against the wall and – to Lucky's shock – began to kiss.

Momentarily taken aback, Lucky could only stare helplessly as his best mate made movements like a snake coiling in the heat.

"*Bastard . . .*" Why hadn't Paul told him about seeing a girl? Why had he kept this a secret?

Lucky pulled himself back, retracing his steps, cursing himself for not having the balls to confront Paul, there and then.

He cut across the road, no longer caring about the traffic narrowly missing his arse. Blood was in his eyes and all rational thoughts were banished.

"Best of mates, my fuck, you sneaky bastard . . ." On and on he went, mumbling and cursing, not realising he had strayed from the designated route leading homewards.

Its thumb-shaped body unmoving, the owl blended perfectly with the diseased tree. Tiny specks of blood and meat stained the bird's beak from an earlier kill, and a suicidal night bug hovered dangerously close, flirting with death as it licked greedily at the feast's remains.

The owl's eyes pierced the dark, watching and observing.

Not too far from the tree's shadow, a rat's head made epileptic twitches, sensing the *eyes* somewhere close. The rat had already lost its mate tonight to the *eyes*, but the terror in its stomach told it that it had little choice: stay and die; run and perhaps . . .

The skinny rodent moved fast, its tiny feet burning despite the cold. Food was in sight, close. It could smell it, taste it in the air. It knew the *eyes* watched its every move but it no longer cared. It would die soon if it didn't feed.

It came across the decaying fruit just as the owl swooped, its bloody beak now dry and caked. The bird would clean its beak later, after this kill, then rest for the night. It wasn't really hungry, but the prey had shown no respect. Now it would pay.

The talons opened in mid-flight at lightning speed, like a flick-knife zooming in on its target, swooping down with mathematical precision.

The rat knew it was coming but still it fed, feeling its stomach swell with fear and food, as if it knew this would be the last supper, the last pleasure it would ever feel, and it would relish every death-defying second of it.

Without warning, the bird froze in mid-flight, inches away from its target, its feathers in disarray. Something had startled then terrified it, sending it fleeing away from the rat, into the safety of the dark.

"Feathered bastard . . ." Lucky pushed through the bushes, ignoring their biting thorns. The owl had startled him as much as he had startled it, making him jump, his heart pounding wildly in his throat. But the real damage had been inflicted upon his stomach, melting it, making him lose what little control he precariously had. He was ready to explode as panic set in, making his intestines as slippery as mercury.

Quickly, he released his jeans from the belt's enclosure and hunched down, hating his actions for being caught out like this.

The owl hooted, causing tiny sparks to nip the back of his neck. He though of ghosts and weird thing hiding in the woods. "Fuck off, you hooting bastard."

This part of the forest was known as Warriors Field, a place rumoured to be the burial ground of fighters slaughtered in their hundreds by the invading Vikings. It had the perception of strange happenings accurately conveyed in its certainty of location, like a picture framed in the stillness of time.

It was said the bodies rotted to the very core of the ground, fertilising the soil, the blood seeping endlessly into the insatiable wound of the earth, like a dark ribbon brimming with ink. The poppies, which grew here each year, were so beautiful and red some people thought them to be stained in blood. It was said that if you listened at night, dreadful sounds could be heard, sounds of the vanquished screaming for mercy mingling with the unrelenting roars of denial from the victors, filtering through the earth like scattered spiders and cascading waves of melting skulls.

It shamed him, a bit, taking a shit in public, but he had little option, even if it did make him feel like an animal, making his spine burn with the dread of someone seeing him, hunched there, exposed. A few years ago – before his teen years – he literately wouldn't have given a shit about being caught taking a shit.

The dirt beneath his feet charted the passage of others, their footprints wet and perfect. They looked fresh, even in the light's dying breath, making him wonder how long ago they had walked this way? The thin air about his face felt like it could drown an unwary traveller, as if it were placing a plastic bag over him. As a kid, he had always loved the solitary feel of the forest with its fearful loneliness avoided by others – but not under these circumstances. Above, a full moon emerged from ink clouds, glowing like a giant spotlight from an old war movie, reflecting an invisible pool of lamplight, and immediately the entire forest was exposed, shattering his sense of shelter. The glow emitted an eerie colour of chalk and attached itself to the skin of a battered car standing silently, silhouetted, its heavy orange-rust shadow streaking the heads of wild wheat like a great beached whale.

The moon's shape made him think of one of the nude statues he once saw in a book, all fat and naked – just like his arse, at this minute. Under his breath, Lucky cursed the moon, hating its knowing grin and winking, pervert-face staring at him as the air became thick with the promise of rain and something else, something he could not relate to. Not yet, anyway . . .

He was almost finished and quickly looked about for something to wipe himself. He could use a few leaves, but that didn't appeal to him. Not one bit. Once, as a kid, he had mistakenly used jaggy nettles. He couldn't sit down for a week. No, fuck the leaves. That's all he'd need; walking like John fucking Wayne for the next few days.

There had to be *something* he could use.

Normally, old newspapers and wrappers would be littered throughout the forest in tons. *But not tonight, of course,* he thought bitterly. They must have cleaned it up special, knowing he would be taking a shit in the forest, the litter-free forest.

If only he hadn't come looking for Paul. He would still have been at the Tin Hut, finishing another pint, scrounged from a cousin he hadn't seen in years.

What he would give to be back there, in the club's toilet with its nice soft paper and no wind whistling up his arse. He would appreciate wee things like that in future.

"I can't believe there's nothing . . ." he mumbled, knowing a decision must be made quickly. The backs of his legs were tightening and he felt cramps slowly take hold.

What was that? A feathery whisper of night sounds touched his ear, making the hair on his neck rise. *Probably an animal. A hare.* He knew it was his imagination constructing things that hid in the dark, but the noise became heavier, more acute as damp leaves were trampled on. *A badger?* Lucky's imagination ignited. *Rats? Oh, God!* He always hated rats. He thought about the rats grabbing him, biting viciously with their plank-shaped buckteeth. What if they went for his face? He remembered the body of an old homeless man he once saw, down near the docks. Rats had lived on his face for two days, making a nest in it, making him recognisable only by the rags he wore. *Oh, fuck!*

The thought of being found, dead and half naked, covered in his own shit galvanised him as he quickly pulled his jeans up, no time for cleaning, ready to run like hell. Let the dirty bastards try and catch him. He'd show them.

The three figures appeared, like magic, a few feet in front of him, freezing all his movements. Dread swept over him at the thought that it could be someone he knew, someone from town. They'd laugh and tell everyone. He'd never live it down.

He cursed Paul again, the treacherous bastard.

The three figures were talking – arguing? – loudly but inaudible. They looked like men, but it was impossible to be certain. One seemed completely naked. Lucky imagined seeing the bony line of spine snaking its way down to the tip of deflated buttocks, of an arse bristling with its coarse hairs.

Instinctively, Lucky stopped breathing when one of the figures violently pushed one of the figures. Then again. But he wasn't being pushed. The crafty moon emerged again from filthy clouds and caught the lethal sliver shining in the man's hand, just as he plunged it again and again. The screams formed a line straight to Lucky's ears. A ghastly, wounded animal scream. He wanted to cover his ears, block the screams with his fingers, but he couldn't move.

Lucky wanted to stop watching the metal plunging in and out with its sickening dull thud, felt obliged to glance away, but the scene was so strangely compelling he could not close his petrified eyes as the body slumped, disappearing in the night's shadow and blackness, distinguishable only by texture and its ugly jagged shape, stark in the bleak light.

There is a class of occurrences so far from the norm they become surreal, residing in their own realty, occupying where the improbable is commonplace, and this was what Lucky was experiencing as he held his breath for what seemed an eternity, waiting for the silence of the forest to return, quietly, observing the tiny details of this ghastly event.

Blood surged in painful waves while he closed his eyes, imagining bright spatters of crimson gushing from the body, and despite the coldness, tiny freckles of sweat mapped his own body while blue and white sparks danced in his head. He feared he was ready for fainting.

As one figure left the scene, Lucky heard the words "shovels" and "be quick about it – we haven't all bloody night".

Bloody night . . . bloody night . . .

Lucky wanted to vomit, but the strength of desperation forced the food and alcohol back down to were they belonged.

The one who had the knife lit a cig, and that tiny light – in Lucky's mind – lit up the entire forest, screaming for him to be seen.

In the play of light and shadow, the light was pale, yet

bright enough to hurt. Any moment now and the maniac would spin on his heels, seeing him hunkered there like an animal; an animal that now knew too much. Lucky could see the man's silhouette in the fragmented light, and it radiated something so terrifying, something so real it seemed arrogantly autonomous.

A disturbing realisation settled over him as fear heightened his senses: an out-of-body experience was taking place. He noted the man's style of dress. Immaculate. The shoes he wore gleamed in the moonlight, and the he remembered a saying his father always said: *The shine on your shoe says a lot about you.*

He could smell the man, now; smell stale after-shave and sweat and some other smell like a scent he could not describe, only that it hardened the copper-buzz of fear already streaming through his body, warning him that this was pure evil and perhaps he had already died and gone to hell.

Pins and needles were crucifying his legs. He couldn't hold this position for long, even though he knew stillness was imperative. In a moment, it would all be over.

Lucky braced himself, waiting to be grabbed, waiting for the knife that would tear through his flesh. His body would be left, devoured by wild animals, and no one would ever know the truth. They would say he simply ran away from home. He had done that twice before, when he was younger, and now it was coming back to haunt him.

Fuck you, Paul, you bastard . . .

He tried desperately to channel his thoughts positively, that things like this could only happened to someone else, but the darkness in his brain taunted him, laughing at his naivety, telling him that he *was* that someone else, and hurry, make peace with God because the inevitable was about to tumble down upon his head and shitty arse.

The man made a movement forward, and Lucky held his breath as the darkness – that lovely creature – returned, covering him with its blanket, like a protective mother at bedtime.

Momentarily, he seemed to be robbed of all breath, as if under water, and felt pain beginning to swell his head. His face became redder. Any moment now and it would explode, just like his stomach had threatened, all over the place, all over Mister Killer's shiny, something-about-you shoes.

Without warning, the rain began to drench Lucky's face, finding tracks to his eyes, chin and mouth. It was gorgeous. He had always loved the rain. Now he worshipped it. It had come to rescue him. It would chase the killer, bring its righteous thunder and strike him with its lightning streaks of justice.

Only when it stopped did he realise it wasn't rain but urine from Mister Killer's horrible hairy cock pointing straight at him. The yellow shower seemed to last for ever before the sound of a zip ended it all.

Lucky's clothing was completely soaked; his shirt, cold against his skin. In the anxious darkness, he remained motionless, watching as Mister Killer returned to his original spot, tight in the dark, just beyond the hill's ugly facade of knotted root structures and angular, jutting rocks.

He couldn't help it, that sound, that terribly embarrassing sound that echoed like a shot being fired in an empty room. It was his nerves, the fart, nothing else, but he hated the sound more than he had ever hated any sound in his life.

"Who's there?" whispered Mister Killer, instinctively dropping the unlit cigarette.

Silence in the forest but not Lucky's head as night crows tumbled across the field, their feathers gleaming like a wave of black oil coated on the moon. *A murder of crows. Isn't that what a family of crows are called?* He shuddered, wondering if they were an omen as blood pumped at the side of his skull, making it throb. He knew the killer could hear it, pump, pump pumping, screaming to be heard as a soft mist of whispery fog began to rise from the ground like an old horror movie, groping for places to land.

"C'mon. It's okay. Really. We're just having a lark," said Mister Killer, louder this time. "We're old friends. Just had an argument. That's all. I've sent for an ambulance. He's gonna be fine. Things just got out of hand . . ." He was inching his way forward, his weight barely making a sound on the carpet of wet leaves as the thumping in Lucky's head became louder.

"Honestly, I'm not gonna hurt you. Just a little talk. Okay?"

Lucky's chest seemed to have closed. He was finding it difficult to breathe and wondered if he was about to have a heart attack. His father had a history of heart attacks.

"Fuck! I don't fucking believe this!" said Mister Killer. "Miles of fucking forest and I have to walk on some dirty bastard's shit!"

Lucky's face heated with shame at the words. He was about to be murdered and all he could think about was the embarrassment that someone had just stepped in a pile of his warm shit.

"My fucking shoes!" screamed Mister Killer, as if someone had just plunged a knife into his throat. "That was you, wasn't it? That was why you came here. To take a shit. Wasn't it? Your shit is still hot and soft, you fuck." He walked forward a couple of inches. "Now that I've got a good sniff of you, you dirty bastard, I'm gonna be like a bloodhound on your shitty arse. You're still there, aren't you? I can tell. I can *smell* you. I can hear you trying to control your breathing. But that's impossible, isn't it? In fact, the more you think about trying to control it the more it wants to struggle. My voice is making you panic. Isn't that right? I'm getting closer and closer . . ."

Nerves began to kick in as Lucky tried to forge a solid relationship with that which stood outside his own body. He felt a giggle in his stomach and knew he would start laughing like a maniac at the madness of it all. Quickly, he thought of the choices, the careful selection one needs to make, particularly when so many things happen at once, terrible and unbelievable things. He had to make a decision, and make it *now.*

"Fee fay foe fum, I smell shit from someone's bum," hammed Mister Killer, his voice all pantomime, inching his way forward in Lucky's direction.

Stealthily, Lucky eased himself up from the ground. *You can do it. You can beat this bastard, this animal. Take a deep, long breath. Easy. Let it out. Easy. Control your breathing. Good. Very good. Now, get ready, slowly, don't make a sound. Wait! Don't panic. Easy . . . wait until he opens that big fucking mouth of his. Wait . . .*

"Enough fucking about. You're making me very –"

Run! Run like hell! Run like you've never run in your sad wretched life!

The sound startled Mister Killer, knocking him off balance, but only for a moment as he quickly ran towards the sound of bushes and leaves crackling, alerting him to every step Lucky made.

"You've made me angry, now!" he screamed, running directly behind Lucky. "When I get you, I'm gonna kill you. *Slooooooowwwwly!*"

The last word followed Lucky, touching his hair, the skin on the back of his neck. He was disorientated. The darkness, the bony trees all played their part to capture him as he went spilling forward, old haggled tree roots like the thick, ropy trunks of elephants tripping him, the darkness swallowing.

Lucky wanted to get up and run, but his energy was sapped. Defeated, he no longer cared. He just wanted it over with, quickly. The killer would probably slice his body up before dumping it with the one in the ground. His disappearance would remain a mystery, a topic for discussion in weeks to come.

"I know you've stopped running," said Mister Killer, his voice making Lucky cringe as he rolled herself up into a ball, tight against the tree's hollow in such a way that his body seemed to be contained almost wholly within the trunk. "That's good. You made me angry when you ran. But that's okay. We've stopped running. Right?" Mister Killer allowed his voice to cascade, listening to its echo return to him like a homing pigeon. "Look, I'm sorry I scared you – fuck, you scared me, too, hiding in the shadows." He attempted a laugh, but it sounded rusty, disused and foreign. "I'll make you a deal. You tell me you're sorry for scaring the shit out of me and I'll apologise for scaring the shit out of you."

Lucky could smell that smell again, and refused to open his eyes. He knew Mister Killer was staring into his face, knife trapped between half-rotted teeth and fetid breath.

Withered leaves cascaded to the ground, where they spread like tiny brown birds, settling all about him, as if trying to camouflage. In the silence of the dark he heard the sound of a thousand tiny fibres breaking, as footsteps came closer.

Mister Killer manoeuvred slowly, as if listening intently to every sound oozing from the forest floor. But the only sound was of the leaves settling back into their places.

"The bastard could still be here, watching me," muttered Mister Killer, but there was defeatism in his voice. "Wishful thinking . . ."

As he turned to leave, something caught his eye, something gleaming. He bent and picked it up.

He held the find closer to his face, allowing the moon to become a lamp. A smile crept across his face. "Okay, you win – for now. But you better keep running until you recognise the horrible futility that one day soon I will find you . . ."

For a second, Lucky wanted to let himself slip into defeated unconsciousness as he battled with a part of him that wanted to linger, differentiating between reality and almost serenely, in the past of safe childhood days; days where bogeymen and monsters did not exist. But he knew that if he were to survive this nightmare, then he would have to muster strength – strength he was not certain he possessed.

The old wood became quiet and dark, waiting for him to move. Only sporadic animal sounds – and all of the other unfamiliar noises or the even less familiar natural sounds of the forest – broke the stillness. Living things were everywhere, but he was dead. He knew that now. It was only a matter of time.

CHAPTER ELEVEN

Whispers Never Fade

"All for one, one for all."
Alexander Dumas, *The Three Musketeers*

"What counts is not necessarily the size of the dog in the fight –
it's the size of the fight in the dog."
Dwight D. Eisenhower, *Dogs*

"I NEED YOU to come over to my house, immediately," said Lucky's whispering voice on the phone.

Paul had been dreading this. Lucky would force a guilt trip on him, asking – demanding – to know why he hadn't been about, lately.

"I've only just got in from work. You'll have to wait until I –"

"No, it can't wait, for fuck's sake. Can't you give me a few minutes of your precious time? I need to tell you something . . ." Lucky's voice didn't sound right.

"What's the big mystery?"

"I don't want to discuss it on the phone."

"Don't be daft. You're sounding like –"

The phone went dead.

For a few seconds, Paul stared at the lifeless phone in his hand before slowly replacing it in the cradle. Had he detected uncertainty in Lucky's voice? What had the idiot gone and done now? The Tin Hut, no doubt. Bet he's run up a tab under my name, the fucking wanker. Nah, Terry wouldn't entertain that, at all. What then? Paul racked his brain, trying to think of the worst case scenario. Had Lucky burrowed money? Was that it? Did he expect Paul to pay it off?

The filthy streets, with handbills fluttering loosely from crumbling walls, conveyed a strong sense of abandonment and loss. Not even a ghostly reflection of an onlooker in any of the tenement windows. Rain was falling rapidly, but with a hushed silence normally associated with snow. The evening wasn't cold, but Paul was feeling the chill of despondency soaking through to his skin.

A few minutes of walking found him standing outside Lucky's house. He knocked at the door but received no answer. He thought he saw a curtain move slightly at the window. He knocked again, louder this time. He checked his watch. He hoped whatever this meeting was about wouldn't take long.

The door opened. Lucky peeped from behind it, his eyes scanning the dimly lit street.

Unnerved by Lucky's strange behaviour, Paul enquired, "What's going on?" He tried desperately to sound casual.

"Slam the door behind you. Make sure it's shut."

"Will this mysterious meeting take long? I've got a lot of

practising to do."

"Snooker, snooker, snooker. Can't you forget about it for one fucking minute?" Lucky walked into the kitchen. Paul reluctantly followed. Something wasn't right in Lucky's tone of voice, his attitude.

Paul attempted a fake smile, but it quickly melted once he had a good look at Lucky's face. The damp interior of the kitchen did little to ease the apprehension visiting his stomach. "You look like shit. What's wrong?"

"Here. Take a beer. You'll need it," advised Lucky, handing Paul a beer from the fridge. "I need something a wee bit stronger." From the top cupboard, he removed a bottle of Jameson.

"Haven't seen you drinking that stuff in a long time," said Paul, wearily. The last time Lucky had consumed whiskey, he started murder in the Tin Hut, culmination in the barring of both him and Paul for three long months. He promised Paul that he would never touch the stuff again.

"'Haven't seen you drinking that stuff in a long time,'" mimicked Lucky, mockingly. "You're beginning to sound like some old lady friend."

Reluctantly, Paul took a sip of beer. He wanted his head to remain clear, so he rested the beer between his hands, waiting for Lucky to say or do something.

Nervously, Lucky began to massage the label on the whiskey bottle, while words began to tumble from his mouth.

"I went looking for you, Tuesday night, over at the abattoir."

"The abattoir? Why?" Paul looked puzzled.

"Why? Because I hadn't seen you in almost a week. That's

fucking why. I wanted the two of us to go out for a drink. I even borrowed a few quid for the occasion." Lucky smiled miserably, and immediately Paul felt like Judas.

"I know I haven't been about much lately, mate, but I've been doing a lot of overtime at the abattoir, and stuff. Don't worry, though, I'll make it up to you."

Lucky sipped the whiskey. "That's the first time you've ever lied to me, mate," accused Lucky. "I guess that's what happens when you allow a woman to wedge herself between us. How long have we been best mates? Ten, twelve years? You're seeing a girl, and I'm cast to the side like a dead dog. That's not right, mate. Not right at all."

"Look, you shouldn't be drinking that stuff. Remember the last time you –"

"Will you just shut the fuck up! For once, stop your moral slobbering and think about me for a change." Lucky made the remaining contents of the glass disappear before refilling it.

Paul knew it wasn't good, whatever was coming next. Had he hoped to start a fight with his best friend, just to be able to walk out of the room, not hear a thing, not get involved? A few weeks ago, that thought would have been unimaginable. But that was before he met Geordie . . .

"Okay. Have it your way," replied Paul, trying desperately to sound calm. He sat back on the sofa, lit a cigarette and watched the long stream of pale liquorice smoke drift aimlessly to the ceiling.

"I went over to your work and spotted you. I saw you coming from the entrance." confessed Lucky.

"You saw me? Why didn't you shout?"

"I did. You didn't hear me – or pretended not to hear me.

You were with a girl – at least I think it was a girl!"

Paul's heart skipped. "How long were you spying on us, in the dark?"

"Spying? Who the fuck was spying? That beer's gone to your head. You've become paranoid."

Paul envisioned Lucky hiding in the shadows, shocked at Geordie's body, sniggering. Quickly, he tried to calm the burning blood rising dangerously towards his skull. It had been a long time since he had experienced this sensation. Usually it accompanied him into the ring, seconds before a fight, transforming him from human to animal. He had always detested the sensation but – oddly – now welcomed its return. Lucky wouldn't know what hit him if he said the wrong thing now.

"Okay, you weren't spying. Seems strange, coming all that way to see me, only to ignore me once you did." Paul's face had become tighter. His fists balled automatically. He wanted Lucky – his best friend since childhood – to say the wrong thing. He wanted to beat him to a pulp, teach him a lesson for spying on them.

Lucky tipped the neck of the whiskey bottle on to the edge of the glass, watching the amber liquid spill and fill. He stared at the glass for a long time before saying, "I was . . . I was fucking jealous. Okay? Happy now? I was fucking jealous of her being with you. I'm your mate. Not her."

A calmness eased into Paul's blood and bones, and the anger was suddenly replaced with remorse. "Ah, Lucky . . . you'll always be my best mate. Don't you see? Nothing will ever change that. Just because I'm seeing a girl, doesn't mean –"

"I saw someone murdered," replied Lucky, so softly Paul

had difficulty hearing the last word.

"What? Did you say murdered? You saw someone get their shit kicked in?"

"No, I mean murdered. *Murdered.* Dead. His throat cut . . . his body stabbed . . ."

There was silence in the room. Paul's heart had moved up a notch.

"Were you drinking? Maybe you –"

"They fucking murdered him! Don't you understand? I witnessed it, stone cold sober. Okay, maybe not stone cold sober, but I know what I saw."

Paul's lips felt dry. He licked them.

"Why wasn't it in the papers, or on the TV? Surely it would have been on the –"

"They buried him, out at Warriors Field. That's fucking why."

"*Buried?* You saw them bury him? Are you sure?"

"No, I ran as fast as my fucking legs could carry me. I was alone . . . terrified. I only wanted to save myself. I just wanted to run and run and run. But they were talking about getting shovels . . ."

"They?"

"There were a couple of them. Maybe more. I can't be certain."

Paul tried to think.

"Look, okay, let's say you were right. But there's nothing you – we – can do. We can't get involved. If you go to the cops, you're dead. You know that, don't you?"

"The killer knows someone saw him kill . . ." whispered Lucky.

"What? What do you mean? You said you ran away."

"I did fucking run, you wanker, but I slipped, right on my shitty fucking arse. I couldn't do anything else but hide. He kept getting closer, calling out to me –"

"Tell me you're winding me –"

"– telling me that every little thing was gonna be okay. Just come out. We were only having a bit of a lark . . ."

A bone popped in Paul's neck. It was loud in the room's quietness. "He didn't see you, did he? Otherwise, you would-n't be sitting here now. All you've got to do is keep your mouth shut. Understand?"

"I know who did it."

"What?"

"I know who did the murder."

Paul licked his dry lips, again. They felt like sandpaper.

"Don't tell me his name. I don't want to know. Anyway, you can't be certain of –"

"Kojak."

"What?"

"You know, that bald-headed cop from the old TV shows? Sucks on a lollipop? Massive baldy head? Isn't that how you described him? We couldn't remember his fucking name. Remember? Well, old Kojak made my shit come out quicker than a greyhound with six legs."

"You're saying it was Shank? Even as a joke, that's dangerous."

"It's no joke. I know who I saw."

Paul shook his head. "It was dark. You can't be one hun-dred per cent sure."

"Dark? Yea, but I was so close to the bastard I could almost reach and touch him. Do you want me to describe his cock? I got a good eyeful of that horrible beast – excuse the pun – while he pissed on top of me. The next time you see him, ask him if he is circumcised. That's how sure I am."

Something cold and slimy had found its way into Paul's body, housing itself inside his stomach's lining. He was fearful of moving, as if any sudden movement would alert it. The blood seemed to have siphoned from his head into his feet.

"What the fuck have you done, Lucky? Do you realise the shit you're in?"

Lucky remained silent. No smart remarks. No excuses. His face remained expressionless as a marble statue. Only the flush of whisky made his skin seem real.

"How many people have you told this to? The truth," continued Paul, nervously, steeling himself for the answer.

"I'm not that stupid. You're the first. I haven't breathed a word to a soul. Why would I? I haven't been able to sleep. I keep hearing the poor bastard's screams. Horrible. Even more horrible, I keep hearing that bastard Shank's whispering voice . . ."

"You're dead. Know that? If word reaches Shank that you know – think – he is somehow implicated in a murder, you're dead."

"Go on. Keep saying dead. It's almost as if you want me to be fucking dead. If I hadn't went searching for you that fucking night –"

"Don't. Understand? Don't try and lumber me with the guilt trip. It's your moronic actions that got you into all this shit. Do you even realise the danger you've placed yourself in? I've seen Shank, up close and fucking personal, and believe me, he is not a pretty picture at the best of times."

"So have fucking I," said Lucky, flippantly. "In the fucking woods. Any other wise words of encouragement?"

Paul realised that panicking Lucky would only add fuel to the uncertain fire. "Look, we don't even know if this is true. There's a possibility that you were mistaken, that you thought it was Shank because of his reputation. It happened at night. Right? Surely the darkness would have been an obstacle? Your eyes could've been playing tricks, couldn't they? And why has no one even spoken of it? Not even a whisper?"

Lucky allowed Paul to exhaust all possible theories before talking. "I know you're doing this to reassure me, mate, and I honestly do appreciate it. I'm sorry for what I said earlier, about you not showing up and all that shit. That was a load of nonsense. But you're only clutching at straws. Do you want to hear something else, something so funny you'll piss yourself laughing?"

No, he didn't. He wanted to be in the Tin Hut, having a laugh, playing snooker. He wanted to be a million miles away; away from Lucky.

"I lost my gold chain; my *good luck* charm."

The muscles in Paul's face loosened. "The one with Lucky engraved on it?"

Lucky nodded reluctantly. "Who says God doesn't have a sense of humour?"

"Oh fuck . . . where? Don't tell me you lost it in the forest?"

"Okay, I won't tell you I lost it in the forest."

"Stop fucking about."

"It must have come off in the panic, while I ran. It was only when I got home I realised it was missing."

Paul reached for the beer. He drank it quickly, feeling the

rush hit his neck, scorch his throat. He coughed then spluttered, forcing some of the beer's remnants through his nose. "Shit . . ."

"Are you okay, mate?" asked Lucky. "Take another sip, easier this time. It'll help stop –"

"You're not telling me the whole story about the gold chain. Are you? There's little point in holding back, now. You've practically told me you saw Shank murder some poor fucker in the woods. I don't think anything else will come close to that bit of information. Will it?"

Lucky coughed, clearing his throat. He glanced at the remaining segment of whiskey in the bottle.

"I . . . I think Shank picked it up . . . I'm not a hundred per cent certain, but . . ."

Bubbles of anxiety burned in Paul's stomach, like an overstrengthen laxative. He wanted to run to the toilet.

"Picked it up . . .?"

"It's like a flashback. I can't be certain, just flashbacks of Shank holding it to his grinning, rubbery face."

"That's *enough*," hissed Paul. "I don't want to hear any more of your story. I don't want to hear his name being mentioned, ever again." For a moment, Paul thought that Lucky was ready to cry. Shit, he felt like crying himself. But what good would it do?

"What are you going to do?" a sliver of suspicion toned Lucky's voice. "You wouldn't . . ."

"Wouldn't what? Go on and say it. Hand you over to Shank? You bastard. Is that what you think of me? Perhaps you're right. Perhaps I should hand you over. He'd love me for that. Already treats me like the son he never had."

"I'm sorry, mate . . . I . . . I'm just scared. That's all."

"Scared? You should be. One massive pile of shite. That's how scared you should be." Anger was quickly replaced with remorse. "I'm sorry, Lucky. I know you're crapping them. So am I. So am fucking I, but that's not going to help either of us. Is it?"

"No . . ."

"We're going to have to think of something; something fast."

Lucky nodded.

"We'll have to play this tight to our chests. Okay?"

Lucky nodded, again. He was becoming good at nodding.

"On the plus side, Shank may not even have an inkling of the chain's significance. Maybe he didn't pick it up. If he had, you probably wouldn't be sitting there now."

"Thanks," mumbled Lucky, his face tired and haggard. "Those straws you're clutching at really makes me feel so safe. But you know as well as I do that eventually Shank will figure it out. If you believe all these nightmare tales about him, that it's impossible to take a shit without him knowing its weight, then you know I'm fucked. Any other reassuring words of wisdom? Like, get the fuck out of town, Lucky, while you still can? I'm your best mate, Lucky, but I've got to save my own arse first?"

Paul shook his head. "Calm down. Together, we can work something out. The thing is not to panic and to stop that whining. We're in this together. For better or for worse. We've got to find a safe place for you, until the dust settles a wee bit."

"Sounds like you want to marry me," said Lucky. "The Two Musketeers. That's us. All for one, and one for all. Isn't that right, mate?"

Paul smiled, reluctantly. "Yes. All for one . . ."

"Just like the old days, eh?"

Paul nodded. "Just like the old days."

"You know I wouldn't let anyone touch you, don't you Paul?" said Lucky, a crooked grin stitched to his face. "I'd kill the first fucker who even thought about it."

Cramps were beginning to take hold in Paul's stomach. He needed to take a shit, real bad. He was now an accomplice. He'd be dead if Shank found out.

If?

When.

CHAPTER TWELVE

A Secret Should Remain Just That

"I know that's a secret, for it's whispered everywhere."
William Congreve, *Love for Love*

"The leader of the enterprise a woman."
Virgil, *Aeneid*

THE HOUSE HAD a constant coldness to it. Even in warm nights, wood perpetually burned in the enormous fireplace, sizzling and crackling loudly, spitting out angry sparks upon the wooden floor.

Geordie and Paul were immersed in shadow, as if they had been welded together in a dark silhouette.

"Weeping demons," said Paul. "That's what my mother always calls sparks. Weeping demons. Said they're the tears of the condemned . . ."

"I saw sparks coming out of your arse one night, Goodman. What the hell are they called? Farting demons?" she giggled.

"Have you been drinking?" he asked, puzzled. "Marijuana? That's it, isn't it?"

She giggled again.

"No. It's called contentment, Goodman. You should try it sometime."

Paul did not reply.

"You've been so moody lately," said Geordie, "that I've decided you've been punished enough. I'm granting you clemency. Your probation from this day onward has now been scrapped." She kissed him playfully on the cheek.

Paul would have loved hearing that news a few days ago, but Lucky's predicament had dampened all emotions in him. An erection was out of the question. He hadn't slept in days. Food was no longer enjoyable. Everything had become irrelevant, and he cursed Lucky, again.

"That's great news, Geordie," he replied, smiling forcefully.

"When it's awfully quiet like this, you can almost hear the house breathing, as if it is a living thing," whispered Geordie. "Listen."

Paul listened and the sounds became muffled, more soothing than he had imagined.

Geordie was right; you could hear breathing, rolling across the floor, gently licking the windows, penetrated the walls and rooms.

"I couldn't live in a house this big," said Paul, spooked by the sounds.

"You big baby! Scared the bogeyman will get you?" she laughed, and moved quickly to force herself on top of him. "Besides, you did say you wanted to marry me, one day, didn't you? Or at least you hinted that to Shank. So, this will be your home for quite some time, Goodman."

More sparks echoed in the dark.

"Speaking of Shank: are you sure he won't be home tonight?"

"He'll be back on Tuesday, at the earliest. So just relax. He's on some sort of business trip. There's no one here but us mice. Violet is still at the abattoir, doing the books. You're talking midnight before she gets home. Feeling better? Feeling horny?"

When he didn't say anything, her voice became serious. "What's wrong?" She squinted to read his face. "I thought you'd be rushing me up the stairs, ripping my panties off. Instead, I see a troubled face."

Geordie seemed to have developed an instinct for his emotions that allowed her to grab hold of them before they filtered through his skin. Lately, he had been able to gauge her frame of mind, also. It was uncanny, the similarities.

"What's wrong, Goodman? Why are you like this?" she asked.

No particular reason except the profound sense of loss that my life could come to a dramatic finish, any day now . . . "Nothing. I'm just tired and stressed out a bit. I've got a tournament coming up . . ."

"I've got a great remedy for stress. It's in my medicine cabinet, next to my bed. No, actually, if I remember correctly, it *is* my bed." She laughed, giggling shamelessly, and he couldn't resist it, couldn't control the emotions bubbling up inside.

"Geordie . . . have you heard of anything strange happening lately, over the last few days?"

She stopped laughing and her forehead lined. "Strange? What do you mean by strange?"

He stumbled over the next few words, trying to sound casual, hoping to blunt the edginess in his voice.

"Have you heard of anyone hurt – seriously hurt – in the abattoir?"

"No . . . nothing serious. Just the usual cuts from the clumsy bastard not paying attention. Why? Why do you ask?"

"Nothing serious, at all? Any fights, if not in the abattoir, perhaps outside. Drunks fighting with knives? You know, too much booze in their veins?" He tried to laugh at the last sentence, but the laugh caught in his throat.

"Fights?" She looked at him oddly. "I don't know what goes on outside the abattoir – nor do I care. If some idiot wants to prove his manhood, then let him. A few cuts never hurt anyone, Goodman."

"Not a few shaving nicks, Geordie. I'm talking about someone being killed, accidentally, in a knife fight."

She shook her head, and smiled slightly. "Have you been watching reruns of *West Side Story*?" Her smile became broader, and suddenly, irritatingly, she began to hum the theme music of the movie, bringing her face closer to his, her voice louder and louder.

"Stop it. Okay?" He eased her away, annoyed. "Look, if something happened, something like someone killed, it wouldn't look good for the abattoir or Shank, would it? There have to be an investigation by the police. Wouldn't there?"

It was her turn to become annoyed. "What is all this about, Goodman? You've started to ruin what was going to be a great evening for us. Know that?"

Fuck you, Lucky. How I'm beginning to hate the thought of you and all your fucking about.

"Has Shank been behaving . . . strangely . . . I mean . . ." Paul's voice trailed off. He couldn't find the words; he didn't want to find them.

"Shank? Why Shank . . .?" Geordie stiffened. "What's this all about, Goodman? If you don't tell me the truth and stop treating me like a moron, then you're heading out that door, and we are finished for good. No if ands or hairy fucking buts. Got that?"

Once again he could detect that hint of menace in her voice; knew that if he didn't tell her everything, he would surely lose her for ever.

Paul nodded, and the reluctant words stumbled from his mouth.

"I'm in serious trouble . . ." He sounded just like Lucky, pathetic and whiney. How he hated him at that moment

Geordie's face transformed from anger to concern. "What kind of serious trouble? What's wrong? There are no secrets between us, Goodman. If you love me, then you must trust me. Otherwise . . ." It sounded like an ultimatum.

For the next ten minutes, Paul's voice was detached while he relayed Lucky's terrible night in the forest. At one point, he heard her breathing strangely, trying desperately to control herself. When he finished, she spoke quietly but harshly.

"You're a bastard, Goodman. No one knows better than me what Shank is capable of doing, but murder isn't one of them," she said, furiously.

"I can only tell you what Lucky said he saw. You've got to believe me, Geordie."

"I don't got to do anything, Goodman. You said yourself that you're stressed out. Stress does strange things to people. Believe me, I've been full of the stuff at one time or another. It messes with your head until you don't know what day it is."

"But Shank murdered some guy, years ago. He could do it again."

"Oh, that old rumour," she replied sarcastically. "Shank never killed anyone in his life. I've heard those rumours myself at some time or another. The last I heard he had killed six men over a pair of socks."

"This is serious."

"I'm serious. Yes, he might have beaten a couple of men until they were an inch away from death, but he has never murdered or killed anyone, Goodman. This you must trust me with. Okay? Surely if anyone has an axe to grind against Shank, it's me. Right?"

Paul nodded.

"And how come Shank is going about his normal duties in the abattoir? Wouldn't I have notice something? Wouldn't his behaviour have changed in some way?"

Paul sighed. "I suppose so. It's just . . . I don't know. Perhaps you're right."

"No perhaps about it. I want you to forget all about this field trip your so-called friend had. If you ask me, he was probably sampling the magic mushrooms littered about the place. Maybe this so-called friend Lucky can't handle competition? Maybe he perceives me as a threat and wants to cause problems between us? Did you think of that?"

Reluctantly, Paul nodded. No matter what Geordie said privately about Shank, the man was still her father, and blood was always thicker than water. But what if she was right? What if this was Lucky's perverse way of trying to cause problems, pretending to have seen something in the forest? Surely, Geordie would have detected something about Shank's moods if the man had just murdered someone? Worse, if he thought someone knew he did it?

Doubt was now creeping into the equation. Had Lucky manufactured the entire thing? Was he spaced out of his head, munching on mushrooms, fuelling the hoax with his bitterness?

"I don't want you to mention this nonsense ever again. You're not *that* gullible, Goodman," said Geordie. "In fact, you're quite shrewd when you wish to be. From here on in, it is you and me. No one – and I mean *no one* – must be allowed to come between us. Agreed?"

Her words administered balm, lifting a great weight from his shoulders. Secretly, he had wanted to hear those exact words, clear his conscience. "Agreed."

Geordie eased herself off the sofa and walked in the direction of the door, stopping directly beside it. For a heart stopping moment, he thought she was about to throw him out of the house, but the way she looked at him was an invitation. She opened the door, pausing in such a way Paul knew he was supposed to follow.

"Trust me, Goodman. In about an hour, you'll be laughing at all this." She held out her hand. "And I better be laughing, as well. Or, at least, smiling . . ."

They walked down the hall instead of taking the steps up to her room – much to Paul's disappointment.

"Close your eyes," commanded Geordie, opening the door of a room foreign to him.

Obeying, Paul felt a bit silly. "Can I open them now?" he asked impatiently while been ushered inside.

"Almost," said Geordie, and he knew from the sound of her voice that she had to be smiling. "Now!"

Opening his eyes, Paul's immediately focused on the single item dominating the enormous room.

"Geordie . . ." He was speechless, making her laugh.

"Well? What do you think? Do you like it?"

A full-length snooker table spread majestically along the centre of the room. It obviously had seen better days, but to Paul's incredulous eyes it was the most beautiful table he had ever seen.

"Where did you . . . where did you get this? Am I dreaming, Geordie? If I am, please don't pinch me."

She pinched him playfully on the arse. "No, you're not dreaming, Goodman. Do you like it? It's ours. One of Shank's old customers had it turning to dust. He gave it to Shank as payment or something like that. And even thought it gutted me to ask Shank for anything, I asked him for it – for you. Happy?"

He could hardly hear her. Tomorrow he would set about cleaning it, brushing it lovingly like a thoroughbred. The cloth looked in pretty good shape, but he'd have to get a professional in to make sure the entire table was level, no runoffs. He would bring the snooker balls given to him by Kennedy. Perhaps Geordie would let the old man visit, just so Paul could show off, show Kennedy his talent? Who said dreams don't come true? If Geordie hadn't been standing beside him, he doubted if he could have controlled his emotions.

"There is a catch, Goodman," said Geordie, her face deadly serious.

"There always is," replied Paul wearily. He knew this had all been too good to be true. "What is it?"

Geordie smiled. "You teach me how to play snooker."

He kissed her, holding her tightly. "Reluctantly, I accept."

"Reluctantly? By the time I'm finished with your balls, Goodman, you'll not know if they've been snookered or potted!"

They both laughed, falling to the floor, fumbling with buttons and zips.

Within minutes, all thoughts of Lucky's dilemma were gone. The forest? What forest? All Paul could think about was beautiful Geordie laying beneath him, naked, cupping his balls, feeling their texture, their weight. Truth be told, he was finding it hard to remember his own name at this particular moment . . .

Somewhere in the great hall of the house, a phone was gently lifted from its cradle. Fingers silently tapped in a number. A few seconds later, a muffled voice of a woman could be heard.

"He's not here. I'm afraid you've got the wrong –"

"Listen, you old bag," hissed the secretive voice. "Get Shank on the phone. Otherwise, you *will* be afraid. Tell him his daughter is on the line. It's an emergency. *Now.*"

CHAPTER THIRTEEN

Twisted Sister? Pussy Cat?

"Never explain – your friends do not need it and your enemies will not believe you anyway."
Elbert Hubbard, *The Motto Book*

"The master of the monstrous . . . the discoverer of the unconscious."
Carl Gustav Jung, on Hieronymus Bosch

PAUL'S EYES RESTED on the severed pig's head. It looked surrealistic, more so now than that first day he had entered Shank's office. The pig's smile seemed terribly real, as if it were having the last laugh at his expense. Real and terrible . . .

The unexpected call to Shank's office, just as Paul readied himself to go home after his shift, threw him into a state of uncertainty. A part of him had the feeling that this call wasn't in regards to anything negative, but it was so unexpected that he felt that something unpleasant was quietly waiting to happen. He had no other option than to ride the storm. That was three hours ago . . .

He now sat in one of the chairs in the room, his hands and ankles fettered with rope.

Directly behind Paul stood Taps, unmoving, speaking not a word. Geordie sat opposite, watched by Violet, her glaring eyes drilling into the back of her sister's skull.

Shank had just finished his tea, and a tiny mist of grey filtered from the remaining tepid liquid in the cup. A scene entered Paul's head. It was the Mad Hatter's tea party. He thought he heard the Cheshire Cat whisper: *We're all fucking mad here, you know* . . .

"Mister Goodman, in life there are always two paths. One easy; one hard. A stupid person will always take the hard path, making it difficult to find the way home. The smart person always locates the correct destination. You belong to this family, and I would certainly feel proud to have you as a son-in-law. I can see you running this place – or, at least, a significant part of it. You are someone to lead the workers to their potential. All I ask from you is a small piece of information. I'm sure you wish no pain on any of us, because I know this has all been a mistake," said Shank, leaning back in his chair, his fingers laced behind his massive bald head. "One who makes no mistakes makes nothing, Mister Goodman. There is nothing to be ashamed about making mistakes. We all do it. Where is your friend, Mister Short?"

Paul swallowed the spittle resting in his throat. "I don't know. I haven't seen him in ages, since I started working in –"

Shank closed his eyes. It was a sign for Paul to control his tongue, not to insult with such clumsy lies. Shank appeared to be whispering under his breath, counting, as if trying desperately to control his temper.

"I have become utterly mystified at the emergence of the situation and dilemma facing us. Things we do not know make us speculate. Information, no matter how delightful, is always dangerous in the aftermath. Surely you understand the futility of withholding information? Disloyalty to the family is not permitted. This rule is not flexible; it is nonnegotiable. Yet honestly, I can say to you, hand on my heart, that I still believe an accommodation can be found. Wouldn't you want that, Mister Goodman? An accommodation to suit us all?"

"Don't trust him, Paul," said Geordie, held by her sister. "He'll kill you once he has obtained all the information from you."

In a flash, Violet had a meat hook pressing against Geordie's neck. A tiny dot of blood appeared on the white skin. "You're such a selfish bitch. Always the me me me," accused Violet, glaring into Geordie's face. "The rest of this family have never entered into your considerations. Have they? Always the me. Me me *meow.*" Violet hissed into her sister's face. "*Mefuckingow.* Remember, Geordie? The kittens at play? Do you remember how cute and cuddly they were before going for their nice swim in the bucket of dirty rainwater? Remember how I used to chase you, holding their stiff tiny bodies in my hands? Remember that annoying fucking meow and how you always complained it gave you the shits? But it was always left to Violet to bring silence to your ears. Strange, it was always easier for you to kill a bull than it was to kill a kitten. Ha! I have never been able to figure that out. Perhaps you're trying to prove something to yourself? Just remember that I have no qualms, either. Don't ever forget that. And don't think for one moment I'll allow you to destroy this family. Do you understand?" She pressed the hook tighter.

"Why are you taking his side? He has never loved you *or* me. He has hated us both from day one."

Violet smiled and a sliver of panic began to move in Geordie's stomach. Geordie called that particular smile the preparation smile, a coffin handle smile. Something ominous was always certain to follow.

"Because I was the one who killed the fucker in the forest."

Paleness attached itself to Geordie's face while Violet allowed the silence to fester, loving the reaction, waiting for the right moment to continue.

Geordie opened her mouth slightly as if to say something, but the words never came.

"While you slept in your comfortable bed, dear *Kitten,* we were out *burying* the bastard who wanted to *bury* us. He was going to tell about the rotten meat. We would have been finished. And as usual, it was left to Violet to squeeze the kittens. Poor crippled Geordie wouldn't have the stomach for it, only liked to profit from it. Isn't that right, *Kitten? Isn't it?*" she hissed.

"Enough, Violet. We do not need discussions from you," said Shank, calmly, yet menacingly. "Place the hook away from your sister's throat. She is not the enemy here. No one is – yet. Isn't that right, Mister Goodman?"

The unknown can be a knowingly frightening place, but Paul was still focused enough in his conscious mind to understand the direness of the situation. He couldn't acknowledge what Lucky had told him. They would kill him – kill them both. Probably kill Geordie, also.

"If she isn't the enemy, why didn't she tell you about that bastard spying on us?" countered Violet. "Had I not come home early that night and heard every little word of betrayal, we would be in deep shit, right now. We don't need him or *her*, Shank. Turn Goodman into fertiliser. I would get great pleasure from that."

"Have I asked for your opinion?" Shanks glared at Violet. "But you could be correct. Perhaps I have been mistaken. Your stubbornness can be quite lethal, Mister Goodman. I hope you're prepared for the consequences." Shank glared at Paul before shouting to Taps. "Connect the ceiling hook. See that it's secure. We don't want any accidents, do we?"

Taps smiled and began to harness the pulley to a wooden beam directly over his head. A heavy-duty hook dangled from it like an inverted question mark.

"Leave him alone, Shank!" screamed Geordie, lunging at her father, before being grabbed violently by Violet. "No one is going to say anything. You've got him the way you always have people: terrified out of their wits."

"Everything is in the hands of Mister Goodman. If he makes the right choice, he will prove he is part of this family. If he doesn't, then I'm afraid he leaves us with little room to manoeuvre . . ."

"You will have to kill me as well, Shank," said Geordie, calmly. "If you kill them, you better make sure that I am dead. If the cops don't get you, I promise you that I will."

"You will go home now," said Shank, looking directly at Geordie. "Taps will accompany you until you calm down. You know that everything being done here is for the good of us all. Don't you?"

"I hate you, Shank. I've always hated you, for what you've done to us, what you did to our mother –"

Taps lifted her, immune to the kicking and punching, and pushed through the door. "I'm sorry about this, Geordie. But orders are orders."

Shank waited until quietness had returned before talking directly to Paul again. "Remember when you first started in the abattoir, Mister Goodman, you saw that saying from William Blake in my office?" Shank pointed to the maxim attached to the wall, directly above Paul's head.

Paul did not answer.

"No? Let me refresh your memory. '*It is easier to forgive an enemy than to forgive a friend.*' Well, I was fool enough to regard you as a friend at that time, someone to be trusted. Now? You placed yourself against my face, and that has only one conclusion. It's time for all of us to get serious."

Shank eased his bulk from the fat chair and walked over to the dangling hook, and tested it with the strength of his pull.

"Do you know how Saint Peter met his martyrdom, Mister Goodman? No? Well, according to legend, he was crucified upside down. He said he was unworthy to be crucified like Christ."

Paul held his breath while his nerves pulled tighter on a knot resting in his stomach. Sour food was moving about inside. He desperately wanted to vomit.

Shank's immediate movement caught Paul by surprise as the chair was pulled from beneath him, sending his body crashing to the floor. Effortlessly, Shank lifted him by the ankles and pinioned him upon the hook, his feet held in the angry nose of its curve.

Terrifyingly effective, Shank's movement was over in less than five seconds.

"Now, Mister Goodman, we can go about our work without any interruptions." Shank removed his shirt. He was perspiring, slightly. An odour was nesting in his skin; not body odour, but something more repulsive; something toxic. "Quite soon, most of the blood in your body will drain to your head. It is not often that both mind and body are taken to their limits, but you could be unfortunate enough to experience that tonight. You will feel dizzy and light-headed, as if the very essence of yourself is being shredded to nothing. That's to be expected. In a few minutes, the brain will be doing little calculations, deciding on where to distribute the remaining blood in your system. Because you are now inverted, there is only one channel where the brain can possibly flood: the area surrounding your throat . . ."

Paul felt the blood beginning to pump, downwards. He had seen this process performed in the abattoir, when apprentices were initiated into blooding piglets, preparing themselves for bigger, stronger livestock later on in their careers. He remembered how the blood always shot outwards, almost in a tangible, straight red line. All it took was a tiny nick from a finely honed blade . . .

"Violet?" Shank nodded to his daughter.

As if reading his mind, Violet smiled, reached and unlocked a small cupboard ensconced in the wall, revealing a tribe of lethal-looking knives, paradoxically beautiful in their ugliness.

"You're privileged, Goodman," said Violet, her words sniggering in Paul's ears. "We only use these on special occasions."

Paul could hear her grinding the blade, sharpening it. The sound screamed in his ears.

"Please, Violet . . . I'm begging you. I've never done anything to you . . . I wouldn't do a thing to harm the abattoir. You've got to believe me."

Shank went back to resting in his leather chair. He opened a drawer and removed a cigar from its box. "You can't beat Cuban," he said, more to himself than anyone in the room as he snaked the cigar along his nostrils, inhaling gently before his thumb rolled over a lighter, scratching out a flicker of a flame.

Violet shook her head as she gazed at the inverted Paul. "I warned you, Goodman. Sleep with the enemy . . ." She grabbed one of his ankles and instinctively Paul began to wiggle and shake, rocking the hook to and fro as he felt the coldness of the blade touch his skin.

"Please, Violet! You don't want to do this!"

"Oh, but I do. You just don't know how much . . ."

Paul could hear the tearing as she guided the blade down the leg of his jeans, stopping only when the highway of blue material ended at his waist. "Stop wiggling, you fucking cowardly worm!" She moved quickly to the other leg, slicing her way through. "Hey presto!" With one good jerk, Violet pulled on the ragged jeans, tearing them off completely.

Violet feigned a gasp. "You naughty boy, Goodman! No underwear? You never struck me as the commando type." She touched his languid penis, allowing it to rest on the flatness of the blade. "Not bad, Goodman. Almost the length of the blade. Balls could be a bit bigger, mind you, but all in all, not too bad. I guess that's why crippled Geordie has been smiling, lately." She laughed and quickly turned her attention to his shirt, disposing of it in less than ten seconds, the blade zigzagging through the cheap material.

Completely nude, Paul could no longer talk. Something inside him had died, studding his tongue against the roof of his mouth. He felt like the edges of his sanity were on the move, spiralling out of control. A growing pressure swelled in his stomach, like a balloon being filled with water. The sensation moved along his gut, stabbing down into his bowels, seething, pushing through his arse.

"You've shit yourself, Goodman! You've shit yourself upside down! Not too many people can boast of that!" Violet laughed until tears were in her eyes.

Paul closed his own, feeling pain and shame. He didn't care if they killed him, now.

Violet pushed him, gently but firmly, watching him swing back and forth, like a pendulum. "Tick tock, hairy cock, shitty arse Goodman. Time is running out. Fast . . ."

CHAPTER FOURTEEN

Dance with Me, One Last Time

"Our freedom as free lances . . . We shall have no time for dances."
Louis MacNeice, "Thalassa"

*"Always do sober what you said you'd do drunk. That will teach you
to keep your mouth shut."*
Ernest Hemingway

L UCKY PACED THE floor in the upper room of his cousin's
house. He hadn't slept in days and was becoming more
edgy with each passing hour.

What the fuck was keeping Paul? He said he would call
over, the first chance he got, let him know what was happening – if anything. *Just keep your head low for a while, mate. As
soon as I hear anything, I'll let you know. Probably tomorrow, at
the latest . . .*

But tomorrow didn't come. The two days – caged up in
this stinking room – most of it spent in darkness – was doing

his head in. He had to get out, get the air about him. He had to find Paul . . .

Chalky headlights suddenly lit up the room and then were gone, startling him for a second, forcing him to stop pacing. He crept to the window and eased the curtain to the side.

Outside, a car rested in the street, exposed by the light from a street lamp. The car's metal skin was waxed in rain droplets the colour of blue ink, making it look like a hastily drawn oil painting. He tried to see if someone sat in the car, but the doorbell interrupted his concentration.

Fuck!

Tiptoeing, he crossed the room and eased opened the door, just a sliver, just enough to be able to listen if not see the late night caller.

In wasn't unusual for Lucky's cousin, Jim-Jim, to get visitors at this time of night. Jim-Jim sometimes ran poker games, late into the night, and sold illegal cigarettes and any other black-market items that could help bring in some income, no matter how small.

What was that? He heard something; steps dangerously close. Someone was coming up the fucking stairs! He sucked all the air in, holding his breath.

He closed the door, gently, but kept his ear firmly to it. He speculated that it was probably Jim-Jim and a lady friend – no doubt the same noisy one from last night, all grunts and moans.

His face reddened slightly thinking about last night's performance. He shouldn't have been listening, of course, but it was difficult not to. All that noise. They were hardly fucking miming!

Someone knocked on the door. Fuck! Lucky's heart went mad in his head. He tried to control it, but it was impossible. Gingerly, he edged away from the door, tiptoeing backwards, doing a moon dance.

The door was rapped again, this time with a bit more urgency. The door handle turned, craftily, as if not wanting to be heard.

Lucky's lips moved, but no sound came out, as if he were starring in a silent movie.

The door opened, slightly. Light bleached in from the landing.

"Mister Short?" Lucky could see a hand reaching for the switch. A second later, the room came to life in light.

"Who are . . . who are you? What do you want here? Where's Jim-Jim?" Lucky squinted his eyes, sheltering them from the stinging light angling in from the opened door. He could barely see or make out the man standing before him, but something in his gut warned him to be wary.

"Jim-Jim? Oh! Yes, he's downstairs, in the parlour. He was kind enough to allow me to come up and talk to you."

"Jim-Jim wouldn't allow anyone up here . . . what did you say your name was? I didn't catch it, the first time."

"At the minute, we need only be interested in *your* name, Mister Short. You *are* William Short?"

"William? Oh, him! You've the wrong cousin, I'm afraid. He's in the Tin Hut playing snooker as we speak, that wanker. A lot of people mistake me for him." A weird, plastic grin appeared on Lucky's face.

"Oh? Perhaps you're right," said the man. "You see, I only wanted to return this to him." The man opened the meat of his massive palm, revealing a gold bracelet. "*There's only one Lucky,* it says on it. Your nickname name isn't Lucky, either?"

Lucky swallowed hard, and his Adam's apple stuck out like a robin's egg. He tried to swallow again, but couldn't. He shook his head.

"Pity. A wasted journey, I suppose." The man shook his head, also, and then smiled. "Tell you what. Could you do a favour for me? It would save me a lot of time and bother."

"If . . . if I can . . ."

"You know what he looks like. You can give him this for me. Tell him an old friend found it for him, keeping it warm, like." The man dangled the bracelet a few inches from Lucky's face, slowly swinging it like a hypnotist.

Lucky's hand slowly extended. He hoped his hand wasn't shaking too much.

The man's quick movement startled and mesmerised Lucky.

"This shouldn't take more that two minutes," said the man, calmly cocking an enormous looking revolver at Lucky. The gun made the sound of a knuckle being cracked. "Don't do any funny stuff and we'll all be away out of here before you can say Humpty Dumpty crapped on a wall."

"What . . . what's this all about? What do you want with me? Who . . . who *are* you?"

"Oh, I'm sorry. I thought I had already introduced myself. My manners have become atrocious, lately." The man smiled stiffly, and magically the words YOU ARE LYING appeared on his gums.

Oh fuck . . .

"People call me Taps. Heard of me?"

A sound came from Lucky's arse. "I've . . . I've sort of heard of you. But what . . . what do you want me for?" Lucky tried desperately to control his breathing. He wondered if he was to be shot here, inside Jim-Jim's house? He farted, again, twice.

"Mister Shank is having a wee get-together. A party, you could say. He's invited you."

"Really? That's very nice of him, and I really would love to go, but as you can see I'm not suitably attired for a party." Lucky's teeth began to chatter.

"You don't need to be dressed for this kind of party, Mister Short. The car is parked outside. You'll be there in a jiffy. Wouldn't want to disappoint Mister Shank. Would we?"

But the nerves in Lucky took over. He had flashes into the future of straddling a wheelchair for the rest of his life, pushed by reluctant friends and disapproving relatives. Last week, before all this madness began, was probably his chance to have danced in the Boom Boom Rooms. God, how he loved his dancing. Then the terrible thought entered his head: murdered? What if–

But his thoughts were interrupted when Taps touched him on the shoulder, and the entire scene became surrealistic as Lucky bolted for the door, follow by the ponderous enforcer.

Lucky made it down the first flight of stairs, taking the steps two and three at a time. He was already on the last flight by the time Taps had covered the first four steps at the top of the stairs.

"Mister Short, I'm warning you!" screamed Taps, ploughing down the remainder of the stairs. "Don't force me to shoot . . ."

But this threat hyped Lucky's nerves even further, sending him scurrying down the stairs, faster, out the door and past the nose of the car stationed outside the house.

He would wait until he was a few streets away before finding a phone. He'd have to warn Paul. What if they already had him? What if Paul was already dead, chopped up and buried in some dark and lonely place, over beside the abattoir, in the shitty forest?

Lucky wanted to weep. It was his entire fault. What an idiot he had been. Why had he ever taken a shit in the woods? His thoughts were interrupted when the door of the car swung out, violently smashing against his legs, forcing him to the ground.

"Wanker," said Violet, emerging from the car, looking downwards at him. She smashed the sole of her boot into his face, crunching his nose, peppering bloody dots all over his clothes.

He vomited, narrowly missing the nose-breaking boots, and while Taps roughly bundled him into the car, disregarding the broken and bloody nose, Lucky believed he had never felt pain like it in his life. And just as he found the strength to move, Violet kicked him again, more forceful this time, knocking him out.

CHAPTER FIFTEEN

Every Picture Tells a Story, Don't It?

"There is only one corner of the universe you can be certain of improving, and that is your own self."
Aldous Huxley

"What madness is it to be expecting evil before it comes?"
Seneca, *Epistoloe Ad Lucilium*

LUCKY AWOKE TO pain. The surrounding gloom frightened him for a moment as he tried to clear his foggy mind, trying to remember what had happened or where he was.

He could hear a voice, calling his name. It was a soft voice, a reassuring voice.

"Mister Short? I hope you enjoyed your nap?"

"Where . . . where am I?"

"With friends, Mister Short. Genuine friends." Lucky heard a wink in the voice.

Blood had hardened and darkened on Lucky's face. It felt like he needed a shave. The stench of the place was everywhere, and despite his nose being broken, he could smell it, taste it resting in his throat. Thankfully, there was nothing left in his stomach as his eyes began to clear, exposing the figure sitting in front of him. There was little doubt in his mind that the figure was that of Shank.

"At last we meet, Mister Short. The last time we met, it was rather . . . hastily."

Each time Lucky glanced at the baldy head, he couldn't help having terrible flashbacks of Shank's baldy circumcised cock, glaring at him in the forest, keeping its eye on him. A quiver ran up Lucky's spine.

Shank continued. "I'm sorry about the unfortunate incident with your nose, Mister Short. An accident, I believe?"

"What . . . what is it you want?"

"Want? I want to show you some pictures, Mister Short; tell me what you think of them, describe them to me." From a drawer, Shank produced four Polaroid pictures and placed them face down, on the table.

"Pick one, Mister Short."

Reluctantly, Lucky's fingers strolled along the top of the table, touching one of the pictures, before gently easing it out.

"Good. Now, look at it, please."

Lucky turned the picture over. His lips curled in distaste. A large piece of bloody meat sat staring at him from the picture. A carcass of a cow, perhaps, covered in shit?

"And the next one, please," said Shank, his voice soft and encouraging.

Lucky repeated the process until all four picture rested

there, glaring up at him. They all looked to be the same pieces of horrible bloody meat, each taken from a different angle.

"What do you make of those, Mister Short?"

Make of them? What the hell did that mean?

"I . . . don't know . . . meat, all bloody, ready for a butcher's shop?"

Laughter sounded behind him, and for the first time, from his peripheral, Lucky saw the figure of Taps and that other bastard, the one who smashed his nose.

"Well, after all, this is the abattoir, Mister Short. Bloody meat is what you expect. Wouldn't you agree?" asked Shank.

"I suppose . . ."

Shank stood, then walked towards a large, opaque plastic screen which was centred in the room, dangling from the ceiling. He indicated for Lucky to come over, stand beside him. "Suppose, Mister Short?" Shank pulled back the edges of the screen. "I don't suppose at all."

There on the ground, shaped like a bloody "S" was the horrible piece of meat from the picture. To Lucky's horror, it moved, slightly, squirming in its own blackened blood.

The air in Lucky's stomach began to spin, looking for food, hoping to toss it through his mouth.

"Fuck . . ." Lucky stepped back a couple of inches, realising he was standing in chunky red and black liquid.

Without warning, the meat reached and touched Lucky's shoe.

"Fuck!" He kicked it away. "What the fuck?"

There was more sniggering from Violet and Taps.

"You don't recognise him, Mister Short?" said Shank.

"Him . . .?" Then it came, the shock, hitting him full force in the throat. "Paul . . .? Ah fuck . . . Paul . . ."

A sound whimpered from the meat; its fingers made a slight movement in the blood.

Shank ripped the screen from its encasement. "Yes, Mister Short. That is Mister Goodman. Now, I think it's best if you sit down. You look as if —"

"You baldy-headed cunt! What the fuck did you do to him!" Lucky made a feeble attempt to swipe at Shank, but his fist was quickly grabbed by Taps, who pushed him back, in the direction of the chair.

"Sit your arse down," commanded Taps, forcing Lucky into the chair. "Don't talk. Not yet, anyway. Not until Mister Shank requires you. And when you're asked to talk, make sure you tell him everything he wants to know. Understand? Everything . . ."

When Lucky didn't answer, it was left to Shank to break the silence.

"It's okay, Taps. Something tells me that we can do business with Mister Short. He looks a far smarter man that Mister Goodman."

"Why? Why did you do that to Paul? It wasn't his fault. He knew nothing. He was just trying to protect me. He's my best friend."

"Best friend?" chided Violet. "Is that what he is? Then why did he tell us everything, right down to the room you were staying in?"

Lucky shook his head. "You can't try that shit with me. Paul would never tell, no matter how much you fuckers tortured him. He won a gold medal at the Olympics, for boxing.

Know that? Beat the shit out of Mangler Delaney. Bet you did-n't. He can take your best fucking shot and spit it right back at you!"

Shank nodded, as if agreeing. "All I ask is that you tell me how many others were told, about what you *think* you saw in the woods."

"Others? What others? There are no fucking others."

"Taps? Please secure Mister Short. It seems he is as unwill-ing as Mister Goodman."

As ordered, Taps tied Lucky to the chair.

"I know Lucky is only your nickname, Mister Short," said Shank, approaching the chair. "I'm told people say you were born with a horseshoe up your backside. Is that correct."

Lucky mumbled, a feeble grin on his face, the words sounding through his broken nose, "Some even say it was an entire stable."

Shank smiled. "Good. I like a man with a sense of humour. But let me tell you something for nothing, Mister Short: luck never triumphs over reality, and I guess someone just left your stable door wide open, because you've run right out of luck. But that can all be rectified with the right answers."

"Otherwise, you will be sliced and diced like the little frog you are," replied Violet, bringing her face closer to Lucky. Her hand held a meat hook. "Perhaps you have more sense, Lucky Ducky, than your so-called friend. He didn't care shit about you. He would've let us kill you first. My advice to you is save yourself, tell us how many other people know about what you saw in the forest," she whispered. "Just give us the names of the other people."

Violet's voice had become so soft Lucky strained to hear

what she was saying. She could easily have been a mother whispering a bedtime story to her son.

"C'mere. Closer. I want to tell you where the others are hiding," whispered Lucky, his voice barely audible.

Violet turned to Shank and grinned. He couldn't get the names, but she had secured them. He'd be raging. "Who are they and where are they hiding?" asked Violet, impatiently.

"Right up your scraggy, smelly hole," he giggled, uncontrollably.

Baffled, Violet stood back in amazement at the madness that had just escaped from Lucky's mouth. Shank shook his head.

Angry at being made a fool of, Violet plunged the hook towards Lucky's head, drilling it for his eyes.

Only the sudden movement of Shank's feet tripping Violet prevented the hook from finding its intended target, imbedding itself into Lucky's thigh instead.

"Don't be so stupid," growled Shank, staring down at the figure of Violet on the ground. "He's no use to us dead, you fool."

Rising, Violet stared at Shank. "Don't call me that again. I don't like it. I don't allow anyone to call me a fool."

Ignoring her, Shank turned his attention to Lucky.

"Not much brains, Mister Short, but you do have balls. I respect that. Balls. But I can't allow such insolence." He twisted the hook deeper into Lucky's thigh, until he felt metal against bone.

The shrieks coming from Lucky's mouth were chilling, like a dog severed in half.

"I think it is safe to say the application of justice has been done," said Shank, removing the bloody hook from the devastated leg. Blood flowed freely from the wound, but Shank made no action to prevent it. "Blood and time are both running out for you, Mister Short. Your life is entirely in your own hands. I hope you understand that?"

Shank nodded to Taps, who opened up a box and removed two items, one of which was an electric drill. Taps plugged it into the wall and flicked the switch.

"Did you know that primitive people believed that madness was a sign of demonic possession? They drilled holes in the front of the skull to serve as a gateway out of the mind," said Shank, touching the drill's trigger, its whirl screaming in the room. "Very primitive, but effective . . ."

Lucky's body was beginning to get cold. He felt exhausted, resigned. He wanted it all over with.

Shank held the second item inches from Lucky's face. The items were shaped like the figure 8 with long metal rods attached to it. Tiny teeth hugged the inside.

"Do you know what these are?"

"No . . ."

"Gelding tongs, Mister Short. The latest model. Pristine and ready for action. Are you sure you don't wish to help us? No? Very well. You leave me with no other option, I'm afraid. Violet?" Shanks handed her the gelding tongs.

Violet smiled a bottle-in-your-face smile. "I'm going to take such delight in removing your baggage."

A shiver touched Lucky spine, making his balls shrivel.

Chapter Sixteen

Tidying Up All Loose Ends

"Execute every act of thy life as though it were thy last."
Marcus Aurelius

*"The thought of suicide is a great source of comfort: with it a calm
passage is to be made across many a bad night."*
Friedrich Nietzsche, *Beyond Good and Evil*

KENNEDY SEALED THE letters. One was address to
Cathleen, the other to Paul. He debated whether
they should be left on the table for Biddy to find in
the morning or left somewhere in Cathleen's room. The latter won out. Biddy would open the letters, reading them thoroughly, deliciously spreading their contents for all to see and
listen to. No, Biddy could not be trusted. He had learned that
lesson the hard way. Catherine couldn't be trusted either, but
she was certainly the lesser evil of the two as far as gossiping
was concerned.

The house felt dank, amplifying the mouldy odour of the old carpeting. A nice warm fire would kill most of the smell, but there was little point in any more mundane habits.

In the kitchen he filled a bowl with soup, accompanied it with some bread and a small glass of orange juice. He couldn't help smiling. Cathleen would sniff suspiciously at the contents.

Moments later, Kennedy entered the bedroom.

"It looks like a storm gathering strength," he said, placing the tray on the side table.

Cathleen ignored him, eyeing the tray vigilantly. "What on earth is *that?* I didn't ask for any of that health food garbage, did I? Did you put sleeping tablets in that? Think I'm as bloody daft as you look?"

He saw fatigue on her face and considered abandoning any lengthening of conversation.

"I'm concerned that you are not eating."

"Very concerned, are we? Perhaps it's the soup you've put the pills in? How many? Bet you didn't even bother to count them? Just poured them in. Old Cathleen doesn't know what day it is. They'll say she did it herself. Silly old woman. That poor man, now a widower. And pigs will fly." She swiped angrily at the tray, knocking it across the room. "I'm not hungry. Besides, I've told Biddy to come over and make my meals in future. You're not to be trusted, Philip Kennedy. Not one bit. I don't know what's going on, but I know something is."

"Don't play the martyr. You're no more innocent than me, my dear. You know exactly what's going on. You took something belonging to me, thinking it would empower you to keep me here." He laughed. "I am not going to harm you, Catherine. Not now . . ."

Catherine looked at him, her eyes tight with suspicion.

"You intend to leave me. Don't you? Bastard. For better or for worse. Remember those fine words?"

"I never agreed to them. You did," he retorted.

"I won't let you leave. You'll have to kill me. Otherwise, I will use everything in my power to keep you here."

"A prisoner? Is that it?" He wanted to laugh at the irony of it.

Traffic could be heard in the distance. There was the sound of dogs barking.

"Lately, I've begun to feel like an hourglass, sand running out. Running out a bit too fast, telling me something . . ." said Kennedy, surprised at this admission to his wife.

Cathleen snorted. "An hourglass, you say? I was thinking you're more like a giant balloon, all the hot air escaping through your arse."

She seemed alive again, purged and ready for action.

This is her most dangerous, he thought, when she can convince people to trust her again. He had given her the chance to be civil, but she had slapped it away, just like the tray. There was no point in pursuing this discussion. It would only take an unpleasant turn, and a quarrel right now would be disastrous.

For the next few minutes, not a word was said, as if both were simply content to listen to the other breathe, waiting for the other's blunder, or trap.

"There were times I thought I felt something for you again," said Kennedy, breaking the silence. He needed to exorcise the remaining amount of words assembled in his head, needed the next discussion to be on his terms. "But there were other moments; moments when I was so stressed by fury and hatred of you that I wanted to kill you."

"You've never loved me," accused Catherine.

"I never once told you I never loved you," said Kennedy. Cathleen wasn't to be loved. Respected, yes. Loved? Indeed, he would have found it difficult at the moment to refute that there was at least a trace of truth in what she was saying.

"You never once told me you did," retorted Cathleen, lightning fast, a mischievous gleam in her eyes, ever the pragmatist, yet excited in these rare glows of moments long gone.

He would have encouraged her with a smile – a negotiating smile – but he was far too raw for that.

She continued. "I had a terrible pain last night, unlike any other I've had to face. Yet, when I awoke this morning, the pain had subsided. In fact, it had totally evaporated, and the permanent throbbing in my side was no longer permanent. It was gone."

Kennedy sighed softly, believing he was in for the usual monotonous self-pitying lecture, but was rammed by the force of the continuation in Cathleen's next three words.

"I am dying," she said matter-of-factly, a voice flat and apathetic, almost as if she had not meant him to hear her. "I know this now because Moore told me two weeks ago, but I suspected it much earlier."

She turned her head away, her eyes catching the last fusion of the day's dying strings of coloured lights.

For a moment, Kennedy was confused. She had cried wolf so many times, yet something in her voice alerted him.

"Don't be silly. You'll be burying me, when the time comes. God knows what garments you'll force my corpse to wear," he grinned woodenly, feeling uncomfortable by the conversation's direction, approaching her bed cautiously. "The realities, for you, are still as endless as the possibilities; possibilities you have always strived after." He wanted to touch her head, her face, but couldn't. "You have always been an extraordinary woman, a strong woman."

Shadows began flittering across the room. He eased the lamp's glare on her bedside table while placing the letters beneath her pillow, hoping she wouldn't open both, believing she would.

Night sounds were gathering outside in the street, but even they could not disturb the stillness and fullness of that which now confused and infuriated him by its utter unfamiliarity. He was a stranger in his own home, yet familiar too, in that frightening way when the past that you so desperately want to forget suddenly comes calling.

Kennedy made his way down the stairs, switching off the lights in each room. Only the eerie orange glow from the living room, caused by the remnants of hot coals from the hearth, remained, guiding him expertly towards the box – the box that had long faded from recognition but which was brought to his attention the day he was searching for the snooker balls for Paul. He was convinced it was fate playing its shrewd hand, a harbinger laughing at him, asking if he thought all had been forgotten – or *forgiven?*

Cautiously, he removed the box's content and was immediately pleased by the condition of the sole remaining item. He had always been good at his old job – when he was young and willing, unquestioning – and the proof was in the pudding. Oiled and ready, black and shiny, the old gun rested like a fat, contented eel in the palm of his hand. He was confident of its perfect working condition. In its own paradoxical way, the ugly piece of metal was beautiful, created flawlessly with inlays designed to exact tolerances and unparalleled precision and efficiency. It still hummed of lubricant when he handled it, the weapon feeling heavy yet light when balanced on fingers, admiring it like the young man who had once balanced a snooker cue, countless aeons ago, calculating the possibilities, the pros and cons.

He placed the weapon down, alongside the book of *Don Quixote,* opening a page at the designated place. He reread the paragraph, loving the formations of perfect words. *I shall never be fool enough to turn knight errant. For I see quite well that it's not the fashion now to do as they did in the olden days when they say those famous knights roamed the world . . .*

A few minutes later, he closed the book for the last time and walked towards the large front window, opening it. He closed his eyes and listened to the sounds of the rain and tiny creatures flying home to safety. The wind sneaked in to the room and entered his mouth, tasting like withered crusts of bread.

Reluctantly, he opened his eyes, thinking he should feel something – the touch of a hand, cloth against his skin, but he felt none of it. Instead, he felt numb, as if a part of him had been amputated – like Cathleen's toes – and he could no longer find it, could no longer remember, what part was missing, only that it felt wrong.

Mixed emotion – regret tinged with an equal amount of self-justification – slowly began to build. He brushed all self-debates aside. He no longer had to be in the mood for them, no longer had to tolerate their intolerable whining, their predictable dilemma and sanitised versions of memories fading, growing dim and blurred.

Knocking was sounding somewhere in the house. He smiled. *Cathleen, Cathleen, Cathleen. A nuisance, if ever one existed.* He placed the weapon to his skull, tightly, almost drilling it against his skin, feeling its weight press against him, simultaneously terrible and reassuring.

The tension in his knuckles had transformed into tiny skulls about to pop from their enclosure. Every nerve in his body tingled with adrenaline while the night closed in all around him, getting darker and deeper. There was no light except what glowed from the rusted ashes nestling in the fire's open mouth.

Obligingly, Kennedy fixed his eyes on the wall opposite, his mouth slack. He cocked the hammer, and the sound did not disappoint. He was now lost, overwhelmed by events and memories no longer controlled by him.

Kicking now followed the knocking – fierce, impatient kicking. Windows were being banged, ready to be caved in. Why was he listening? Let someone else worry. He smiled. He had more pressing matters at hand, in his hand, pressing against his skull.

Pull it. Hurry. Pull the trigger. Soon it will all be over. Soon . . .

In the distance, he could hear his name being echoed over and over again. It sounded like a ghost.

CHAPTER SEVENTEEN

Quixote and Sancho

"For fools rush in where angels fear to tread."
Alexander Pope, *An Essay on Criticism*

"Wheresoever you go, go with all your heart."
Confucius

THE DARKNESS SURROUNDING the abattoir sat waiting, patiently. It had no place else to go for at least another couple of hours, before the early morning light came to relieve it from its duty.

Geordie's face was a pale spot framed by the fragment of moonlight creaking in through the broken stones marshalled all along the makeshift tunnel – the one-time pathway leading to the back of the abattoir. It had remained idle for years, after the crumbling stonework had fallen, killing one of the workers making his way home on a Saturday afternoon. Always a favourite shortcut, it now lurked officially unused, condemned as too dangerous. Too dangerous, even for cost-cutting Shank to consider keeping as a legitimate entrance.

Geordie cursed silently to herself. The noise from her leg braces seemed to be a million times louder than usual. Regardless of how she tried to cushion the noise, the scrape scrape scraping sound of metal against cloth became keener.

"Stupid crippled legs," she hissed to the figure walking cautiously behind her. "Great idea? Right? A stupid girl and an old man coming to the rescue, taking on Shank and Violet, rescuing a stupid snooker player because he's loyal to a half-witted mate who got him into all this shit . . ."

Kennedy knew frustration mustn't be permitted to sabotage their efforts – no matter how pathetic it looked. He was unwilling to consider the possibility of his own death, at this particular time. Otherwise, the hopeless situation of trying to rescue Paul would become direr. For a split second, something derailed his focus and he needed an anchor, something that would tether him to the familiar. He could hear Cathleen's voice, mocking and laughing. *Quixote rides Rocinante, and Sancho rides his burro Dapple. You are the perfect pathetic bastard, always chasing windmills. Always the windmills . . .*

An orange bulb, blackened by dirt and bugs, threw urine coloured light into the tunnel. If the tunnel was officially closed, it was obvious to Kennedy that few of the workers obeyed the yellowing warning sticker at the entrance.

Cautiously, Kennedy breathed the entombed air within. It reeked of the spew that was human excrement, piss and a smell not unlike that of decaying rats, hugging the inside curve of the tunnel in a kind of paralysis. Manure, muck and dead blood all banded together, joining forces. Kennedy could taste it in his mouth. It wasn't pleasant and gave off some kind of vibration, like a tuning fork punctuated by too much feel.

As he progressed, his eyes adjusted to the cobwebbed-filled interior. They were greeted to the sight of carcasses of dead birds carpeted on the ground, their fragile bones gleaming like hulls from tiny ships caught in rocks, each blending wickedly into an origami of shadows and repulsiveness. The ever-skilful rats had been proficient in stripping the flesh. It was a massacre, a feasting of the dead, and he was baffled how creatures of flight could have been captured so easily. Used condoms, their loads drooping like Dali's pancake clocks, hung over the edges of loose bricks and rusted beer tins. Old, corroded water pipes hissed and spat in his face, blinding him periodically. Dark and dank narrow spaces had never bothered him, but he was finding it difficult to stay orientated. Geordie's self-criticism – balanced against the uncertainty of whatever lay ahead – wasn't helping the situation. The need to maintain a calm demeanour was paramount.

"You wouldn't have come to me if you thought for one moment I didn't stand a chance against your father," whispered Kennedy, hoping to keep Geordie's confidence high. "We have the advantage of surprise on our side. It's a good weapon to have."

Geordie snorted in exasperation. "If you're trying to instil confidence in me, I'd advise against it. You're the only one in this stinking town I know. I was hoping you could get some other people together, save Paul from Shank and Violet. I couldn't call the cops – not on my own family; but if I'd known you were going to act out your Lone Ranger fantasies, I wouldn't have gone banging on your door, either. And talking of weapons: that antique you have in your hand doesn't actually fire, does it? If you think you can bluff your way out of this, then we're in bigger shit than I thought. You should have grabbed one of those iron bars when I asked you." Geordie made a motion with the mangled piece of rusted iron in her hand. "I can get to Violet with this, no problem. It's your part of the plan I'm worried about. Actually, it's the fact that we have no plan is causing me to worry."

Kennedy forced a grin on his tired face. "There's an old saying that snowflakes are one of nature's most fragile things, but just look what they can do when they stick together."

"Snowflakes?" Geordie laughed scornfully. "Ever see what a flamethrower can do to snowflakes? Well, that's how I regard Shank. A human flamethrower. You better be prepared to get your arse burnt. I just wish we had another way of changing this."

Kennedy continued smiling, granting soft relief to the silence surrounding them.

Geordie's silence prompted him to ask. "Tell me the truth, Geordie. Why did you think that by coming to me, I could help?"

She sighed. "Do we need this? I mean, right now?"

"It might help me more than you could ever imagine."

A crafty wind came rushing down the tunnel. Geordie shivered, slightly.

"That night, those few weeks ago, when I first met you, I saw how you looked at Paul."

A puzzled look crawled into Kennedy's features. "How?"

Geordie cleared her throat. "I don't think you really want to know my gut-feelings on that night."

In the darkness Kennedy composed himself, dreading what Geordie might know – might think she knew.

"I'm always interested in feelings, Geordie. Especially those that come from the gut. Most times, the gut is more perceptive than a million eyes."

Hesitantly, she continued. "I thought . . . that night . . . you wanted to have sex with Paul."

Kennedy laughed, relieved. "Sex with Paul?"

Geordie sounded embarrassed by the disclosure. "That was my first impression. You seemed overly . . . keen. Afterwards, I put it down to simple nerves. Perhaps you were always like that, meeting people . . . meeting *young* people."

"And has your impression changed? Or do you still believe I'm some old pervert chasing after young boys?"

Her tone changed. "No, I no longer feel that way, at all. I think perhaps you love him, but not in the way I thought. I think you've become a sort of, you know, father-figure to him."

Kennedy did not reply. He listened to the last sentence, over and over again, in his head.

A sense of silence, reinforced by the tunnel's density, settled all about him. He could smell rain and mud, and it stank like blood, but his eyes were excited over the dark rings that had formed under them over the past two years.

What seemed like an eternity ended with the door to Shank's office coming fully into view. They walked toward it, moving stealthily, carefully avoiding the jagged sheet of light quilting eerily from the office window. Rain was coming down, hard and filthy, its pellets as black and round as rabbit dung. A great deluge was drowning the building. The strong stench of decayed meat crept inside Kennedy's mouth. He breathed in that smell as if he'd been born to it.

"That's it," whispered Geordie. "That's Shank's office, but there doesn't seem to be any noise coming from it. You don't think something –"

"I want you to pay careful attention to what I am about to say," cut in Kennedy, prohibiting her from saying the unthinkable. "I need you to walk in, as calmly as you can manage, and beg your father to forgive you, that you didn't mean to run away. You didn't mean to doubt or question him. Tell him you were confused and apologise for distrusting him."

"What?" whispered Geordie. "Apologise? You really are flaky – as flaky as your snowflake theory. Shank doesn't understand words, only violence. He wouldn't believe a word from my mouth –"

Geordie was unprepared for what came next, the Jekyll and Hyde transformation of Kennedy's features, his voice, his entire being.

"*Listen*," he hissed, grabbing her tightly by the throat, his voice radiating a low but steady warning. "*This is not a game, little girl. Not a game of hide and seek, peekaboo, or all-ends-well. Understand? Paul Goodman is not the only one in danger. We all are. Now, you will do exactly as I told you. I don't care if you have to cry or kiss and hug that bastard, but you will do as I say. If you don't, I'll break your skinny petite neck, drop you right at this spot. Do you understand, little girl?*"

Kennedy tightened the grip on her throat, hating the terrible necessity of inflicting fear into Geordie's hate-filled eyes. Geordie would never forget the look on Kennedy's face, something terrible and indescribable at that exact moment as he stared at her, his eyes burning like embers. Later, she would remember that look as the glare of a killer weighing up in a split second how he deemed to dispose of a body.

A slight movement from her head told him all he needed to know. All blood had drained from her face, transforming it into a powdered death mask hue.

"Your tears are tools; manipulators that can procure us confusion and vital seconds. Sometimes, that is all one needs – a few precious, but vital seconds. Now, little girl, if you truly love Paul Goodman – and I believe you do – a few tears is a small price to pay. Don't you think?"

Geordie nodded, slightly, her face a grimace of pain

Boldly, he reached out and stroked her hair. In another time and place, it would have seemed a nice, innocent gesture, perhaps reassuring. Not here. Not now. He meant it to terrify, exchanging one fear for another, ruthlessly and efficiently.

"Good. Very good. Now, just ease the pressure on your fingers. I'm going to remove the bar from your hand. You will not say another word to me. The next time I hear you speak will be when you are facing Shank. It's up to you how all this ends. All up to you . . ." whispered Kennedy, his face an arrangement of weird and delicate features, of calmness and callousness, known by the few as a war face, the face of death.

Geordie pushed away from him, and he watched as she disappeared in the direction of the entrance. He admired her, admired the natural courage she possessed, her strength and determination. She would hate him, after this – not that it mattered. He didn't want to think of possible disasters. Not this time. Not ever again. He had moved beyond the boundaries of reflection.

Something was returning to him, to his brain, surging like a confidence of power, of possibilities unambiguous in their definite conclusion. There would be no going back. It was too late for that. Much too late.

He calculated the passing of one minute before stepping expertly out of the tunnel, allowing his eyes to focus on any tiny obstacle limiting his field of vision. Feeble stars cast alternating wisps of light and shadow in the area, bringing to life images of industrial wasteland: stacks of hay were predominant, along with the giant cutting machines used to detach the animals from their vital parts; a gaggle of discarded tools rested against the side of the building. Years of rain had cemented them to the ground, rendering them totally useless. A family of battered trucks lined the outer perimeter of the office, collaborating with their lesser cousins, the forklifts and cement mixers.

He could see the office up ahead. Lights glowed in windows; shadows flittered across tightly pulled shades. The night was closing in all around it, painting it darker and darker.

If Geordie's information was correct, there would only be Shank and her sister, Violet, holding Paul hostage, along with some unlucky bastard called Lucky. And not forgetting some brute known as Taps.

Kennedy's face was cleaved by the long spine of the moon's silvery reflection, giving his appearance an eerie, distorted look of two faces meshing into one. He carefully stepped forward, sneaky as an old fox reaching for a snoozing chicken. He could almost sense the steps of the entrance and could hear voices, muffled and secretive. He forced his brain to pursue every possible conclusion with the same ferocity of anticipation gnawing at his stomach. His pulse quickened. The gun in his hand felt good; reassuringly good, like a friend, lost now found. It was supportive, intoxicating with arrogance and self-absolution. He marvelled at how calm he felt and had to admit: *There's no feeling on earth quite like it; sure as hell feels good.*

CHAPTER EIGHTEEN

A Strange Mix of People

"Above all things, never be afraid. The enemy who forces you to retreat is himself afraid of you at that very moment."
André Maurois

"I wanted you to see what real courage is . . . It's when you know you're licked before you begin but you begin anyway and you see it through no matter what."
Harper Lee, *To Kill a Mockingbird*

TO KENNEDY, THE slightly opened door served duality as an immediate invite and a challenge. He pushed it open, quietly, sneaky as an old fox. Unobserved by all, his eyes consumed the room and all its occupants. Geordie was arguing with – screaming at? – a man, probably Shank. Something about Paul; something about killing him. A burly figure – Taps? – was examining knives, proudly displayed atop the table.

So much for his order of pleading, begging if necessary. If a young girl had little respect for his threats, what chance of Shank fearing him?

Shank stood over a naked figure, pinioned to a chair. A shape lay on the floor to Shank's right, motionless, curled up like a question mark. It was naked also. In the dim light, he wondered which was Paul, which was Lucky?

"You've killed him, you bastard!" screamed Geordie into the face of Shank before being grabbed unceremoniously by the hair, the eager fingers of Violet digging themselves deep down to the scalp, ripping the skin.

"Shut your sad treacherous mouth, before I shut it permanently," hissed Violet, forcing Geordie to the floor. "Move and I'll cripple the rest of your useless body." Violet held the meat hook against Geordie's skin.

"That wouldn't be very ladylike, young woman. Would it?" said Kennedy, pointing the gun directly at Violet.

Violet froze, startled by Kennedy's unexpected appearance; but it was the face of Shank which held surprise and shock, looking at Kennedy with utter disbelief and sheer hatred at being caught off-guard by an intruder who had the audacity to come, uninvited, into his kingdom and point a weapon at his face, as if he, Shank, were nothing. Worse: insignificant.

Taps remained motionless, but Kennedy's peripheral watched his fingers resting on the knives.

"Now, if you don't mind, release Geordie's hair and quickly release that horrible looking hook from your hand. Otherwise . . ." Kennedy waved the gun, slightly.

Reluctantly, Violet allowed the hook to slip from her hand.

"Good," said Kennedy. "Very good. Now, stand over in the

far corner, your face against the wall. Fighting in school will not be tolerated. And we certainly do not allow meat hooks, young lady."

For a moment, Violet appeared to be calculating what to do next. Her face was a ball of anger.

"I'm not going to count to three. I don't believe in Mexican standoffs. I'll simply shoot you in the knee." He cocked the weapon and pointed it directly at Violet's leg.

"Do what the man says, Violet," commanded Shank.

A couple of defiant seconds passed before Violet complied.

"Good. Now we're getting somewhere," said Kennedy.

"And you are?" asked Shank, calmly, not a care in the world. His bare knuckles were raw, covered in blood. He stood, towering over the limp, bound body of Paul, whose face had been used as a punch bag, barely recognisable. Small pools of blood rested, glued to Paul's skin, mixing with bruises and distortions of bones.

Kennedy saw his own distorted reflection on the surface of the limpid blood pooling at Paul's feet. The image of the battered Paul infuriated him with its mixture of brutality and hopelessness. He tried to ignore the cold in his stomach.

"That's irrelevant, at the moment. What I really need from you are not questions, but simple compliances. Ease yourself slowly away from the man you've just beaten the life out of. Raise your hands while doing so – and pray. Pray you haven't killed him." Kennedy's voice was strong. He wondered if it fooled anyone in the room?

"Do you know who I am?" asked Shank, reluctantly easing himself away from the battered body. "Know anything about me? If you do, you're either a fool or a very brave man."

Refusing to be distracted by the calmness of Shank's voice, Kennedy watched Violet closely from his peripheral, trying desperately to identify patterns or movements, anticipating the unexpected. "I am exceedingly afraid and trembling," replied Kennedy, smiling. "So, I guess that rules out the very brave man."

Shank's face measured out a small grin – just enough to acknowledge Kennedy's words. "Perhaps we are all in for what will hopefully be an intriguing evening?"

Taps made a slight movement, undetected by everyone in the room. Everyone except Kennedy.

The shot sounded like an explosion in the room's confine. The bullet hit Taps in the chest, startling everyone but Kennedy.

Taps staggered forward, slightly, in slow motion. Kennedy fired once more, hitting the enforcer in the throat, buckling him to the ground. A few seconds later, the jerking body became still.

"You killed him, in cold blood," accused Shank, staring at the gun in Kennedy's hand.

"That's the best way to kill anyone," replied Kennedy. "When they least expect it."

It was always going to be either Shank or Taps. Kennedy had calculated – rightly – that he could handle two protagonists; three was pushing it. He had already decided to eliminate one of them, long before he stepped inside . . .

Violet edged away from the dead body.

"I wouldn't make any more movements, *Violet*. Not until I have everything under control. I won't hesitate to use the gun again."

"A gun," jibed Shank. "The preferred weapon of cowards and barbarians."

"Correct, Shank," retorted Kennedy. "That's my name. Mister Cowardly Barbarian." Kennedy took stock of his surroundings, of the weird skeleton-like statues; paintings equally as weird, though beautifully rendered; the walls containing a cornucopia of knives, each imbued with the unpredictable power to slit a throat, sever a head, all within an effortless blow. He could feel an old sensation coming back, consuming every nuance that was him, the feeling he had tried to suppress all these years, and it felt good, damn good, god-like good. It had been years since he had felt so alive, so useful.

"Blake?" said Kennedy, admiring the amateurish yet almost perfect reproduction of biblical scenes.

Shank nodded, his face slightly flushed with pride. "You're familiar with the great man?"

"Familiar? No, not exactly. I've come across his work, over the years. I have to admit, his paintings, in this place, seem appropriate."

"You'll never get out of here alive," said Violet, seemingly agitated by the conversation, the calmness oozing from the mouths of Kennedy and Shank. "We have workers arriving soon. The day shift starts in less than an hour. They'll never let you leave."

Kennedy could recognise parts of Shank in the girl. There was also a slight resemblance to Geordie. Big eyes, bleak but sharp. Defiant. *There is something to her, something that draws the eye in, like uncompleted beauty. Only the smattering of those tiny scars ruined what could have been,* thought Kennedy. *She looks like someone who needs an almost daily fix of anger . . . just like Cathleen.*

Those same bleak and defiant eyes left him with little doubt: she hated him, could possibly kill him if given the chance.

"Leave? Who said anything about leaving? I quite like it here, the unusual surroundings. Now, I must ask you to refrain from talking, commencing from here on in." Kennedy spoke to Violet, but his gaze remained on Shank. He could picture Shank's brain calculating the pros, weighting them against the cons, could practically see the gears spinning in his head. *He's a gambler. A gambler willing to take risks. What is he thinking? What will he try? Hurry, Kennedy. Get that old, dilapidated brain of yours in motion. He looks like he's going to call your bluff. He knows you're a fool, only good for chasing windmills. Hurry, he's coming right at you, a speed train, right up your arse.*

"You look like a smart man, Mister Cowardly Barbarian," said Shank. "Nobody in this room has to die. Nothing complicated. In fact, very simple: I get a little information, and all is right as rain. I will even go as far as to forget this personal affront."

Kennedy nodded, as if agreeing. "Geordie? Remove one of those knives from the wall."

In her eagerness to comply, Geordie's awkward movements combined with speed and clumsiness almost stumbled into Kennedy, knocking him slightly to the side.

"Easy, girl. Time taken is time saved. Cut the rope from Lucky's feet, first. I don't want him falling forward, in case he has internal injuries."

Shank's face registered surprise. "Geordie . . .? You know

each other?" The surprise turned to a begrudging acknowledgement. "You used her as a Trojan horse . . . very clever, Mister Cowardly Barbarian. Very clever, indeed. You have my admiration."

Kennedy ignored Shank's words.

Gingerly, Geordie did as asked. "What next?"

"Check his pulse, his heart – anything," commanded Kennedy.

Fatigue had engraved itself firmly into Geordie's face, and for a moment, Kennedy reconsidered seeking her help. The whole situation was becoming discouraging. For a moment an intense wave of nausea rose in his stomach; a sense of something slipping away from him.

"He doesn't appear to be breathing," replied Geordie.

"Just like you, soon, *Judas,*" spat Violet. "You conniving little bitch. You had this planned all along, bringing strangers here to destroy us because you've never been part of this family. Well, you've turned your back on us for the last time. I should have fixed you a long time ago."

Kennedy stared at Violet, his head shaking disapprovingly. "You know what you did; and if you don't, then you'd better think about it because I'm not going to tell you." With his gun, Kennedy cracked Violet on the side of the head, her face contorting in a grimace of inevitability as it witnessed the single blow. She collapsed, groaning.

"I did warn her about talking . . ." The strength of the blow was unintentional, and for a moment Kennedy wrestled with an apology, but quickly decided an apology would imply unintentional force, and that could construe weakness. Shank gave the impression of being the sort of man who could smell weakness a mile away, and an apology in this situation would be disastrous. "Actually, truth be told, I was looking for an excuse to whack her. One less to worry about."

If it bothered Shank, his daughter being knocked unconscious by an intruder, he didn't show it. His face remained impassive, impossible to read. *A cold fish, indeed, our Shank,* thought Kennedy before allowing a wry smile to creep on to his own face. *A cold fish indeed, our Kennedy,* boomeranged a voice from the past.

"Are you after money? Is that it? Blackmail?" asked Shank.

"Blackmail? You've lost me."

"Such a liar." Shank's facial expression changed. Not a smile, just a hint of one. "Blake said, 'A truth that's told with bad intent, beats all the lies you can invent.' So, you either know, or don't want to know, and the only reason why you wouldn't want to know is because you intend to kill me."

"I know you're scum, but that wouldn't necessarily mean I would be able to blackmail you. Would it? And killing you? Well, that all depends on how you conduct yourself in the next few minutes."

Shank shook his head, seemingly amazed by the boldness uttering from Kennedy's mouth.

"He's breathing!" shouted Geordie. "Paul's breathing!"

Relief eased into Kennedy's face.

"Geordie?" said Kennedy. "Do you know where the keys are to any of the vehicles outside?"

Geordie nodded. "They're usually kept in a small box, over beside the table. The forklift keys are kept there. The truck keys are kept upstairs. Will I get them?"

Kennedy thought for a moment. "No. We don't have the

luxury of time. Use the forklift. I need you to drag Paul out, perch him on top of the forks, if need be. Just get him the hell away from this place and to the nearest hospital. It's slow, but it'll get you there eventually. It's his only hope."

"But, he's ripped apart from the inside. We'll kill him if we move him," replied Geordie.

"He'll die if he remains here. At least he has a chance. Talking is eating precious time. Just take him."

"What about his friend, Lucky? What will I do with him," she asked.

"You'll do nothing except what I instructed you to do. His friend is no longer with us, I'm afraid."

Clumsily, Geordie pulled on Paul's arms, slipping and sliding in his blood. He moaned. It was horrible to listen to.

"God . . . Goodman," she whispered. "There's no other way . . ."

"But there is, my dear," said Shank. "It's not too late to rectify this mistake. Do you want him to kill me? Is that what you really want? Am I such a terrible father that you would gladly see me killed, murdered? You're my daughter. Don't ever forget that. I may not have shown a lot of love, but that is my nature. You know you were always my favourite, always the one who would eventually take over the business. Violet would never have had the brains for it, would never have been able to communicate with the workers. She would have destroyed all that I built. Only you could have guaranteed the continuation of the factory, my name. Only you."

Kennedy feared she was at breaking point. She appeared confused by Shank's unexpected words, as if they were what she had wanted to hear all the long years.

"I don't believe you, Shank," said Geordie, her voice a whisper.

"No? Then believe this: you are signing my death warrant, the moment you walk out that door. We both know that. He will –"

"Talking talking talking," said Kennedy, angrily. "Just get the hell out of here, you silly little girl! Hurry!"

To Kennedy's relief, Paul moaned, stammering a few words through clenched teeth and busted lips. "Just do . . . just do as he says, Geordie. You're doing great . . ." His words of encouragement faded.

Geordie quickly linked her arms with Paul's, desperation granting her strength.

It seemed like an eternity, but less than a minute later, they were gone, much to Kennedy's relief.

Kennedy waited until he heard the sound of the forklift fading before talking.

"Things happen, Shank, blending together sometimes, in a complex pattern of events called destiny. And that is what we have in out hands at this very moment. Destiny. Everything in its place; a place for everything."

"You must be suffering from insanity," said Shank.

"I don't *suffer* from insanity. I *enjoy* every minute of it."

Shank smiled begrudgingly, almost admiringly. "You never intended for one second to allow me to live. Did you?"

Kennedy knew that a momentary lapse in his strategy would allow awareness or compassion to interrupt his momentum or activate his conscience. He could no longer afford the human side of his nature to lead, and slowly permitted the animal to take control. "I would prefer not to hear your words. I respect you, Shank. I respect how dangerous you are. But tolerance isn't high on my list of priorities at this particular time in my life."

"And Violet? What do you intend to do with her? Murder her as well?"

Kennedy considered the question. "No. I just need the organ grinder. The monkey can go free."

"I wouldn't call Violet a monkey. She wouldn't be too happy with that description. No, not one bit," smiled Shank.

Arrogance was seeping back into Shank's voice.

Too late, Kennedy realised why.

"A monkey? Is that what I am?" whispered Violet into Kennedy's ear, seconds before hitting the trigger of the stun gun. It sent him reeling, buckling and jerking, a puppet captured on invisible string. The wound at the side of his head was penny-wide and penny-deep, and his hand instinctively moved to touch it. Bewildered, he watched as blood dripped softly from his head, pooling in a small, inconspicuous puddle, spilling on to his chest.

He heard another pop from the stun gun and felt his left knee go on fire. It felt like acid.

"You threatened to shoot me in the knee. Didn't you?" said Violet, watching Kennedy squirm on the floor in agony. "Never threaten. Do."

Shank smiled with approval at Violet before directing his words towards Kennedy.

"You really are a stubborn sort of bastard," said Shank lighting up a cigar, grinning as Kennedy pulled his devastated knee up to his stomach in a foetus position. "Not only can these little guns stun a bull – they can kill it, if the correct spot is hit. Violet purposely hit that spot of yours, just above the left ear. Had she meant to kill you outright, I'd be speaking to a dead body." Shank inhaled the cigar, his nostrils flaring at the pleasant aroma. "I'm sure the pain devouring your body at this moment is so terrible you don't know if it's a shave, shit or shower you need. If you really concentrate, you actually *can* distinguish one pain from the other. The knee probably fells the worse. That's the brain's defence mechanism kicking in, fooling you that all is A-Ofuckingkay. Like the captain of a sinking submarine, it is issuing orders to the lower ranks, telling them all is under control. Your brain is actually pissing itself. This is a continuous process, without end, before death." Shank dislodged a fragment of tobacco from his tooth, examined it, and then wiped it on his pants. "You have my admiration, Mister Cowardly Barbarian. In another time and place, we could have been friends. A terrible waste. A terrible waste, indeed. Do you know something strange? I don't even know your name."

Standing silently, the stun gun dangling by her side, Violet stared at the door where Geordie and Paul had disappeared a few minutes ago.

"Don't worry about them. They'll not get too far – not in a forklift," said Shank, smiling at her reassuringly before turning to the topic of Kennedy. "You shouldn't have shot him in the head. That was stupid. He might have told us who else knows. We could have interrogated him. I doubt if he's anything other than a vegetable, now. Have you ever listened to me? Didn't I warn you about that dangerous pleasure you take in hurting for the sake of hurting? Hurting is something done for profit."

"Did you mean what you said, to Geordie?" asked Violet, confusing Shank momentarily. Bloodshot collected at the corners of her eyes. Her face was scarlet.

"What? Did I mean what? Oh, that shite about being the favourite? Of course not. You know –"

"You said I wouldn't have the brains."

"I don't have time for this nonsense," replied Shank forcefully. "We'll talk about it after we –"

"You said I would have destroyed all that you built. *You* built? Without me carrying out your every whim unquestioningly, your every order, you would have had nothing. Geordie was always your favourite, wasn't she? Never did a thing to help the family, but always your favourite."

"Later, I said," replied Shank, dismissively. "Right now, we've got to –"

The black tiny mark on Shank's naked skull oozed a wisp of smoke, like a spent volcano. Tiny droplets of blood trickled down the side of his face. To his credit, he did not collapse immediately. Psychically, Shank was stronger than Kennedy. He staggered back from the horror of calmness that lit up Violet's face. It was angelic. Perfect control. He could hear something when she moved her lips, but not words. He couldn't comprehend how such a tiny hole could generate such pain, and so much blood. It was sprouting in a tiny arch, like a fountain pen release.

Shank placed shaking hands on the table as if to steady himself.

It took another two shots from the stun gun to put him on the ground. Three in all, to Kennedy's two. The third shot, the killer.

"You defeated yourself, Shank. Pushing me to the limit, leaving me with little choice other than to turn on you. You unintentionally freed me. Now, I don't need you," said Violet, leaning to touch him, noticing the unruly pool of shadows coalescing as light splintered in from the window preying on both downed bodies. "I don't need any of you."

Walking calmly towards the table, she sat down and opened the cigar box, separating a cigar from the enclosure. She lit it, inhaling it perfectly, just the way Shank had inhaled so many times under her watchful, envious eyes. Tiny greyish smoke streams emerged from her opening lips. Within seconds, the cigar's aroma filled the room. "I guess my arse is big enough now."

Kennedy's gun lay bridged between his own body and that of Shank's. It lay there useless and unused. He wished he could laugh at the irony of bringing it with him, but all he could do was breathe deeper, taking in the exquisite aroma of cigars. Ink was seeping into his head, forming behind his consciousness, escalating into blackness behind his eyes. Dark lights vied for his attention, telling him to stay alert, breathe easier while an omnibus of memories began to filter into his brain. He could feel his heart slowing down and, strangely, a calmness flowing throughout his entire body, a reassuring calmness foreign to him most of his life. He could see the face of Shank staring in his direction, eyes unblinking like those of a cobra, adoring the silence of his own death.

Kennedy's eyelids became heavier, and he could hear sounds crashing down on a beach mixing with the cut of late autumn winds. He closed his eyes, listening to the waves breaking themselves upon the rocks while seagulls screamed for food. The lazy fragrance of salt and sand filled his nostrils. The wind rushed towards him, and he opened his mouth to see what the wind tasted like, and it ran into him, like a ghost, pulsing through his veins, making his every thought infinite. It rendered him motionless, like the stillness of an ice sculpture.

It made him smile.

Violet hastily snatched the keys for Old Johnson, in the upstairs' office drawer. She couldn't recall how long she had been out cold – only that Geordie and Goodman were gone. The forklift, Shank had said? If so, hopefully she could still catch them before they could do any more damage. *That treacherous bitch*. What she would give to have her and her gutless boyfriend by the throat . . .

Before leaving the office, she bent and retrieved Kennedy's gun. "Don't mind if I borrow this, do you?" She smiled at the staring corpse before kicking it in the head, then made her way out to the back, where Old Johnson rested in the moonlight. She climbed in, slammed the door shut, and tested the ignition.

Old Johnson coughed and spluttered.

"C'mon, you piece of shit!" Violet pumped the pedal. She wanted to ram her foot right through the floor, hurt the old truck, which seemed to be part of the conspiracy to destroy her. "C'mon!"

A ball of black smoke escaped from the exhaust, followed by two loud bangs. She pumped the floor, gritting her teeth. The truck shuddered, then growled into life.

She hit the gears and, within seconds, was thundering out the gates, missing them by inches.

Turning left, she cut through Warriors Field, smashing

down a "Private Grounds. No Trespassing!" sign. She hoped there were lovers fucking each other in the darkness, hiding in the long, filthy grass. She hoped to squash them, like worthless bugs, beneath the wheels.

Her head was swooning. Possibly the aftershock of that bastard hitting her on the head? *He won't be hitting anybody any more*, she smiled. *Fucker.*

But as the minutes ticked away and the expanse of remoteness became endless, doubt began to creep in. Had she left it too late? What if they had taken a different route?

Then, just as hope began to fade, in the distant darkness two red dots could be seen. They disappeared for a few seconds and then returned, shining brighter than before, like a lighthouse bathed in fog.

Violet's heart began to beat with anticipation. *It's them . . . it has to be.*

It was a vehicle of some sort, small and slow – painfully slow. The forklift? It was moving clumsily, its brake lights screaming in silent outrage each time they were called upon to act, as if the driver were a learner, terrified of the dark. Or simply a driver being careful not to hurt a passenger?

The bridge. They're heading for the bridge. Violet pushed her foot all the way down, ignoring the tearing sounds screeching from the engine. She could smell the clutch burning, mingling with rubber from the tires. The engine was overheating, but she no longer cared. She had only one thing on her mind . . .

Geordie had heard the sound long before she saw the headlights beaming in the distance. There was no mistaking Old Johnson's coughs and splutters. She had tested the old beast too many times to be mistaken. But who was driving it? What had happened back at the abattoir? Was it Shank driving the old truck? Violet? It couldn't be Kennedy, could it? What if it was? What if he was coming to help her get Paul to the hospital?

"Geordie . . . ?" mumbled Paul.

"It's okay. We're almost there. Across the bridge, the hospital is waiting. Almost there." she lied.

The forklift entered the bridge just as Old Johnson came into view.

Violet's mind calculated as the forklift came into perfect sight, exposing both Geordie and Paul. She had two weapons at her disposal: the gun and the truck. She would combine them. Ram the forklift, and then shoot both bastards in the head. She didn't have the luxury of capturing them, bringing them back to the abattoir. Too dangerous and risky. She would have loved that, making Geordie watch as she did things to the dying Goodman; things Geordie could only dream about; things only real women could do.

Geordie's heart beat so brutally that it took her breath away. She was finding it difficult to breathe as panic closed in on her as Old Johnson entered the bridge.

Then it happened.

The bridge began to sway, and then buckled violently. Large chunks of wood splintered, tore, before ripping themselves apart, scattering in every direction.

"Hold on, Goodman! Hold on!" screamed Geordie, coaxing the forklift, squeezing every single effort from it as she tried desperately to control its awkward manoeuvres.

Old Johnson slowly came to a halt, careening in slow motion against the eastern side of the bridge, tearing a gapping hole in the wooden structure.

Geordie felt the entire bridge quake. She waited for it to collapse, hurling them to their doom in the darkened water, below.

Relief. Sheer relief. The forklift touched solid ground, launching them forward just as the rest of the bridge collapsed, spiralling downwards, taking Old Johnson with it.

Dismounting from the forklift, Geordie watched as the old truck bubbled, half submerging itself upon the family of boulders, before slipping further into the water.

Panic rose in her chest. Who had been behind the wheel? Could they get out of the quickly submerging truck?

A face appeared fleetingly at the windscreen of Old Johnson. It was Violet, her face grey and glassy, frightened. She was banging on the window, the sound soft as damp cardboard. Her lips were moving, but all Geordie could hear was the sound of rushing water, angry rushing water.

"Violet!" Helplessly, Geordie stood as the truck tilted, sliding downwards at an incredible speed, disappearing under the water. "Violet. . . ." She wanted to vomit, but nothing came, only sour liquid and belching. She squeezed her head between her hands, sandwiching it, hoping to stop the silent screams trafficking in her head, trying to erase the image of her drowning sister.

CHAPTER NINETEEN

A Little Bit of Reading Goes a Long Way

"Pray you now, forget and forgive."
William Shakespeare, *King Lear*

"An odd thought strikes me – we shall receive no letters in the grave."
Samuel Johnson, in James Boswell, *The Life of Samuel Johnson*

FOR HOURS IT seemed as if Cathleen had screamed his name, commands, orders and curses. The banging from the door was ceaseless. "Where the hell are you?" she shouted, dragging her tired body out of bed, sweating and wheezing. "Philip? Answer the door, you bastard. I know you're trying to torment me, but it will not work. Do you hear me?" One minute later, just as she neared the door, crawling, it came crashing in, almost taken from its hinges by the shoulders of three heavy looking policemen. She knew he was gone, even before they opened their mouths, their faces acting out the part of heralds of sorrow.

"Get out! Get out of my shop!" she screamed, over and over again.

Two days later, she read his note. To call it a letter would be too generous, and Cathleen was not in a generous mood.

Cathleen

There is very little to say to you, only that I am sure you are relieved by the outcome of my action.

This letter makes me feel like I'm having a conversation with you, but just in my head, a conversation of no interruptions, no bickering. It is marvellous, and you should really try it some time.

There was a time though, when life was filled with emotion and anticipation was everything waiting just beyond the next corner and vibrant colours seeped out of everything that was life, when everything was semi-perfect just like one of those summer days, when we first met, lined with moments of surprising, touching beauty that somehow obscured the more.

Despite our differences and the regular misery of our relationship, you are an exceptionally good woman even though I have been trying to dissuade myself from this very opinion for years now, with some slow and limited progress.

On a more pressing and necessary issue, suicide is covered by the insurance policy, so that is an added benefit. I have double-checked that fact, so let them tell you nothing different. Once you get up to par for stocktaking, you will notice that the collections of books have disappeared. I decided to donate them to a worthy cause – and you know how much of a fool I am when it comes to worthy causes . . . I did not want your anger to burn them – that would be so wasteful – and you would only have regretted doing it, once you calmed down.

I have left a letter for Paul Goodman, the young man who has been purchasing snooker items. He will be in the shop next Friday, the first of the month, to make payments which are no longer necessary as I have finished off the payments myself (no, not from your money). Please ensure he adds no further money to the shop's coffers.

The letter for him is extremely important, and I would appreciate it if you could see that he receives it. It will clear so many things up for him, things that perhaps should be left behind in the past, yet need to be told in the present. I had neither the courage nor inclination to tell him face to face while I lived, and like the coward I am (was) have left it all to paper and ink.

Ask Biddy to pardon the unpleasantness I left for her. I'm sure it was a shock for the old dear finding me sprawled out that way. I'm certain she fainted. I did it in the kitchen knowing it would be a lot easier to clean up, afterwards. Don't say I wasn't considerate to her. Or you . . .

Philip

Ps: Destroy the item you stole from my cabinet. I should have destroyed it a long time ago.

Catherine had wanted to kill Kennedy herself, once she heard what he had done, over at the abattoir, acting the hero, dying for strangers, refusing to live *for her.* Then she wanted to kill him again, reading the letter, damning him for wanting to commit suicide *because of her.* Had he hated her that much? Despised her the way she had despised him?

"Mrs Kennedy? Can I bring you up some soup," asked Biddy, timidly entering the bedroom. "Mrs Kennedy?"

"What? Oh . . . no, you go on home, Biddy. Perhaps you'll be good enough to call in tomorrow. I must get better now. So many things to do . . ." whispered Cathleen, calculatingly low, as if she were on her deathbed.

"Don't you worry about nothing, Mrs Kennedy. I'll be at your side for as long as you need me. It would be my pleasure," lied Biddy, smiling a perfect melancholy smile.

"Thank you, Biddy. It's great to know there is still someone I can depend on," said Cathleen, sighing, returning the smile and the lie. "Just make sure you slam the front door downstairs. That new lock makes me nervous. I don't trust it."

Cathleen waited until an almost ideal silence returned to the room, quieted along with the curtains fluttering at the window. The only sounds that penetrated seemed far away and insignificant: the soft hum of traffic could be heard, but other than that, an almost perfect nothing, a negative hum that swallowed the sounds it made.

In the dark she lit a cig, refusing to break the chain.

A small evening breeze teased her hair while she studied the unopened letter resting on the table, almost admiring the two perfectly formed words on the envelope's paleness: Paul Goodman.

She tapped her fingernails against it, debating, wrestling with the curiosity of a cat, desperately trying – half-heartily – to convince herself not to do what she knew was inevitable.

Slowly, expertly, she eased the envelope's lip apart, careful not to tear; extra careful to leave no traces of forced entry.

Teasing the pages out, she rested them on top of the table before making herself comfortable with the goose-feathered pillows firmly against her back.

There was a feeling coursing throughout her entire body, a feeling she hadn't experience in a very long time, the feeling of power held within while some one else's secrets were about to be exposed.

Dryness covered her lips and she licked them before commencing. She hoped this letter was longer than the note she had received. She hoped it would last all night . . .

Paul

Hopefully this letter will find its way to you, unopened and unread, though something tells me it probably will have been consumed by someone else's preying eyes before reaching its destination.

"Bastard," mumbled Cathleen.

Only one thing will be certain: once you have read the letter's contents, your perception of me will have changed, utterly and for ever, for the worse.

It is said that in the dead of night that man is prey to his truths, when guilty secrets begin to emerge from their unpleasant retreat, torturing. I have found that to be totally true.

In a lifetime, people develop certain beliefs that they cling to, even at their peril. Often these beliefs are defective, but they are felt as truths until something happens in life to bring about a realisation that, perhaps, they have been wrong. No one likes to admit a mistake, but what if that mistake lasted a lifetime? Think how difficult that acknowledgment would be.

I was your father's executioner, murdering him for a crime he did not committee. At the time, the "evidence" against him for being a police informer seemed overwhelming. I had no qualms about carrying out my duty. Three good men had died because of the information your father allegedly fed to the enemy. In those days of guerrilla warfare, madness reigned supreme. Normal, decent men committed inhuman and cruel acts. No side was blameless.

It wasn't until two years after the terrible deed of killing your father was it learned that the real informer, a highly respected member of our organisation, had set him up. To add insult to injury, this creature was permitted to die peacefully in his bed (he died two years ago in Italy) because no one was prepared to acknowledge the devastation caused by such a senior figure.

Strangely, I had read an interview by Kim Philby, a few weeks prior to the terrible event. You're too young to know who Philby was, but he worked as a double agent for the Russians during the Cold War, setting up his comrades to be killed for his own dirty deeds. His words in the interview were chilling and quite prophetic: to betray, you must first belong . . .

If only I had thought about those words a bit more cautiously. Your father was a low ranking member of our organisation. He never would have had access to the high level information given to the enemy.

Initially, I justified my act by simply claiming it was done under orders, in a terrible time, when terrible things were done. Little comfort to you, but they say conscience is the ultimate guide, even while men deceive it, trying to transform it into something acceptable. I can honestly say my conscience has tortured me all these long years, my own nightmares consuming me to the bone. The dead, I discovered, can talk volumes . . .

These last few months, I have been overwhelmed by those events and memories I'd thought long since erased from my consciousness. As the years gain momentum, the memory becomes more and more suspect and open to error, but your arrival at the shop was the beginning of the end for me. Many times I wanted to scream in your face what I had done, wanting you to find a weapon to kill me.

For more than fourteen years I have held a stretch of sand in my mind. There is, on the south bank of Greenwood Beach, a tiny *cottage, long gone to rot. A few times I struggled with myself to approach it, search where the old well used to be. Only three weeks ago, I walked along the beach, seeing the ruin in the distance, telling myself to do the right thing by digging and searching until I found your father's body. But no. It wasn't to be.*

I know nothing can be done to rectify this terrible tragedy. All I can offer is remorse. But is remorse enough to gain absolution? Only you can answer that, Paul. Always remember, there is no revenge so complete as forgiveness.

Philip

Engrossed, Cathleen only noticed her surroundings when she managed to drag her eyes from the letter, her gaze falling aimlessly into the distance. She had been sucked into the very fabric of the letter, mesmerised by the words.

She read it twice – as was her fashion with other people's mail – and it struck her deeper than the actual contents of the letter left to her by Kennedy. She closed her eyes and thought of him briefly. She could hear the murmur of his voice oozing from the page; picture him sitting downstairs, beneath his books, writing this terrible, devastating letter.

For a brief, secret moment, Cathleen was overcome with a regret rarely acknowledged, but this feeling quickly filtered from her, replaced by the wasting anger of dead years.

She replaced the letter in its enclosure and, with damp tongue, sealed it for its rightful owner, never truly believing she would ever meet him.

CHAPTER TWENTY

A Meeting of Battered Souls

"What wound did ever heal but by degrees?"
William Shakespeare, *Othello*

"Widow. The word consumes itself."
Sylvia Plath, "Widow"

"THERE IS A young man and woman looking to speak to you, Mrs Kennedy. Should I show them up?" asked Biddy.

"Are they selling something? Tell them we're not –"

"No. They're not selling. They want to speak to you about Mister Kennedy's death." Biddy crossed herself, before continuing. "The young man says his name is Paul –"

"Goodman," intercepted Cathleen. She smiled a nervous smile, a smile of acceptance and anticipation.

"Shall I show them up?" asked Biddy.

Cathleen seemed in a trance. "Yes – no, wait. Tell them to

come back within the hour. It'll give you time to freshen the room up. Speaking of which, the bedpan needs emptying."

"I'll be back in a tick, Mrs Kennedy. I'll let the young people know what you said," replied Biddy, turning to go back down the stairs.

"And some nice scones for our visitors, Biddy. Plenty of raisins in them. I've grown quite partial to raisins. Not as runny as the prunes . . ."

Biddy waited until she had left the room before mouthing secretively, "Not as runny as your stinking arse, Mrs Partial Prune."

Almost one hour later, Paul and Geordie were shown into Cathleen's bedroom. Windows were partially opened, allowing the faintest of breezes in.

"Well?" asked Catherine. "What is it you want to see me about?"

Paul's face retained dying scars, their paleness resembling tiny strips of paper. He forced a smile and the tiny strips whitened. Remnants of stitches still hung ghoulishly from his busted lips.

"My name is Paul Goodman, Mrs Kennedy. This is my fiancée, Geordie –"

"Yes yes. Get on with it. What do you want? I haven't all day," interjected Catherine.

Geordie's eyes narrowed slightly. She stood holding her newly acquired crutches. Paul had the terrible vision of Geordie cracking Catherine over the head with them.

"We've come to offer our condolences, Mrs Kennedy, and to tell you how Mister Kennedy died, saving our lives," said Paul.

Cathleen's eyes locked on to Geordie.

"What is wrong that you need crutches?" asked Cathleen, impertinently, continuing her stare, ignoring Paul. "Have you broken your leg, also?"

"No," replied Geordie. "A childhood ailment. I need crutches when climbing stairs, now." Paul had warned her about this old woman, but for the sake of Kennedy's memory, she had agreed to restrain herself.

"And you navigated the treacherous stairs just to visit me?" If Cathleen was appreciative of Geordie's Herculean effort, she showed no indication. If anything, her look was one of contempt.

"To offer my condolences, actually," corrected Geordie.

"A bit reckless and stupid, don't you think?" replied Cathleen, smiling like a cobra.

"The stairs? I've conquered bigger obstacles in my time. The bigger the better. I enjoy being reckless," replied Geordie, a mongoose preparing to strike.

Paul sensed things were turning nasty and quickly cut in. "You don't need me to tell you how your husband was a hero, Mrs Kennedy. He saved my life, as well as Geordie's."

Catherine snorted. "A hero, eh? Perhaps if he hadn't acted out his fantasies, he'd still be here in the real world, helping to run this shop, help pay the bills – most of which were caused by his generosity." She looked away from Paul and stared directly into Geordie's eyes. "It was your father and sister, wasn't it? The police told me. It was you who came to the shop that night, banging and banging. Wasn't it?"

Geordie nodded. "Mister Kennedy was the only person I knew. I didn't want him to go to the abattoir. I thought he would get help from somewhere."

"Help? Ha! Pathetic Philip could hardly help himself." The statement was full of brutality, void of mercy.

"We must be speaking about a different person," said Geordie, defensively. "The man who was with me that night was more than capable of defending himself. He was more than a match for Shank. I never saw anyone stand up to Shank the way he did, that night."

"You knew him for how long? An hour? A day? And you've become an expert on Philip Kennedy?" sneered Catherine. "Did you know he was ready to blow his brains out – what little brains he had – all over my kitchen? Oh, did I shock you? I thought you already knew that, you being such an expert."

Paul and Geordie stood there, numb, disbelieving.

Geordie's mouth made a movement, as if to contradict, but nothing materialised from it.

"Ironic, isn't it?" continued Catherine, unabated. "You probably prevented him from committing suicide here, only to bring him to his death, over at the abattoir."

Like an angel sent from heaven, Biddy pushed open the door, steam rising lovingly from a teapot. A tiny squad of scones encamped themselves beside it.

Biddy placed the tray down and spoke directly to Geordie. "Now, young lady, sit you over here, beside Mrs Kennedy. What are you doing standing, anyway?" she smiled, friendly. "If you're waiting for Mrs Kennedy to ask you to sit, then I'm afraid you'll be standing the entire visit. Isn't that right, Mrs Kennedy?"

Cathleen glared at Biddy. "Why don't you make me up a nice prune juice for later on, Biddy? Make it an *extra large glass, please.*" The last four words came out like a hiss from a leaky radiator.

Biddy mumbled something before disappearing out the door.

An awkward silence had now settled into the room. Only the sound of Paul slurping his tea could be heard. Geordie's tea and scone remained untouched.

"Geordie's gonna have a baby," said Paul unexpectedly, his face flushed with pride. "If we have a boy, we're going to name him Philip, in Mister Kennedy's honour."

If Paul thought Catherine would be happy at that little titbit, he had miscalculated.

"Isn't that nice? I'm sure he'll be well pleased – wherever he is," replied Catherine. "To be frank with you, I don't approve of babies having babies. I don't approve of babies, at all. Thank God I never had the urge to have any."

Paul glanced at Geordie. A storm was building in her face. Any second now, she would release it. He shouldn't have opened his mouth.

"I think it's time we went," said Geordie. "I'm sure Mrs Kennedy needs her rest."

"You're beginning to sound like my doctor, little missy. And if there is one thing I do not need, it's another doctor," said Cathleen, scornfully. "Doctors? *Doctators,* is what I call them. Little *doctators.* I've had my fill of them and their damn pills, their expensive advice . . ."

"At least we have something in common," replied Geordie, positioning the crutches under her arms, ready to go.

"And that is?"

"Our healthy disrespect of doctors. Mine told me it was unwise to have a baby, spoke to me as if I were some sort of strange creature from another planet, void of all human emotions. Told me – *ordered me* – to have an abortion. Advised it wouldn't be *sensible* to have another disabled being on this earth. I wasn't too long in letting him know what he could do with his advice."

"I'm sure you did," said Catherine. "Yes, I'm sure you did."

Had a slice of respect crept into Catherine's tone? Paul thought he detected it while setting down his cup, placing it on the table beside the window.

Cathleen's eyes instinctively caught the movement. The letter, address to Paul Goodman, rested on top of the table-cloth, face down, just beside the lamp. It had sat there, all this time, as if waiting for its rightful owner to return and claim it.

The red flush entering Catherine's face when Paul's fingers accidentally knocked the letter to the floor did not go unobserved by Geordie.

He bent and picked it up. "I'm sorry about that, Mrs Kennedy. Guess I'm not used to being invited to tea," smiled Paul, sheepishly, extending the letter towards Cathleen.

Catherine said nothing, staring intently at the outstretched hand and the letter in its grasp.

"Mrs Kennedy? Mrs Kennedy?" asked Paul, startled by the dead look on Catherine's face. "Are you okay? Should I call your maid?"

"It's addressed to you," said Catherine, her voice a whisper.

"To me?"

"It's from your hero."

"My . . .? From Mister Kennedy?" asked Paul, puzzled.

"Yes . . ."

"I don't understand."

"Not now, perhaps," said Catherine. "But you will."

Open it. Discover the real Philip Kennedy. Tell me if you still think he's a hero. Go on. Open it now. Read it aloud. Let me see your devastated, hero-worshipping face . . .

"Let's go, Paul," said Geordie, her voice recognising something not quite right with the scene unfolding before her.

"Oh. I almost forgot," said Catherine, hurriedly stretching over to reach for the drawer. But the suddenness of her movement, coupled with weeks of inactivity, strained her withered muscles. With a determined grunt, she overcame the stitches of pain in her rib cage and eased open the drawer. "You might be interested in this, also. Funny thing is, Philip Kennedy thought he had lost it. Searched high and low for it, he did, with no success. All the time it was down the side of my bed. Can you believe that for a coincidence? Perhaps if he had looked there . . ."

"What is it?" asked Paul, taking the item from Catherine's hand.

"Some sort of tape, I believe. Probably some of his favourite songs on it. I'm sure you'll find his taste of music . . . interesting."

Paul glanced at the tape before putting it in his pocket.

"Thank you, Mrs Kennedy. I'll always treasure it."

"Good for you," said Catherine, her voice hollow and faraway, no longer directed at any one in the room. "Good for you . . ."

Epilogue

*"The thoughts of a prisoner – they're not free either. They keep
returning to the same things."*
Aleksandr Solzhenitsyn, *One Day in the Life of Ivan Denisovich*

"The grave hides all things beautiful and good."
P.B. Shelley, *Prometheus Unbound*

S A CHILD, Paul loved to listen to the wind while he
waited for the school bus in the mornings. But this
wind, skimming across tumbling sand and angry sea,
made the hair on the back of his neck feel funny. It made him
feel tired and strangely old.

He watched families gather up their belongings, leaving
empty boxes and bottles to litter the beach's sandy tongue.
Parked cars shimmered in the evening heat, all silvery and
scaly, like stranded salmon captured upstream upon the rocks.

At last, he took a deep breath, placed his finger on the
"play" button, and squeezed the sound from the tape, conscious of its whispery whirl. It crackled, like webs set on fire,

and his heart began to beat furiously anticipating what he had heard a hundred times already, over the last few days.

For a few seconds, only the sound of a chair being disturbed could be heard as the tape whirled its white noise. Then came sporadic coughing in the background. There was another sound in the background, faint and faraway. Upon his initial hearing, he hadn't quite captured what that sound had been. Now, after numerous playbacks, he knew it to be the sounds of gulls and crows fighting over food; fighting over dead things . . .

"Your name?" asked a voice from the tape. Paul tried to picture the voice's owner. What did his features look like? Angry? Calm?

Silence. Some coughing. Then . . .

"Thomas . . . Thomas Goodman. Most people call me Tom . . ." There was a quiver in the voice, a nervous hesitance.

Paul's heart never failed to reach his throat each time his father's voice sounded on the tape.

From his pocket, Paul produced an old black and white photo of his father. His father was smiling in the picture, arms folded, not a care in the world. Paul's mother stood awkwardly beside his father, smiling shyly, her face partially hidden from the camera's eye. She looked so young – they both did.

Paul tried to push his memory back, tracing the very first time he had heard his father's voice. He couldn't recall. In all truth, he was probably too young to have remembered it. Now, hearing it on this – this nightmarish device – it stunned him into silence and a realisation of such a vast expanse of time, only revealing itself in tortured words, his father's voice a flimsy shadow living in hell, and it sounded so heartbreakingly terrible it infuriated him, eclipsing his sorrow.

Initially, upon reading the letter from Kennedy, Paul had been confused. Was it the rambling of an old man contemplating suicide, his faculties dulled by an unbalanced mind? What if the words were from the sick fingers and mind of Catherine Kennedy, her jealous and bitter world tunnelling through her broken, hateful body?

He believed not a word of the letter at first, almost tearing it up in defensive anger of Philip Kennedy, the man he regarded as a hero. But then came the tape, piquing his curiosity as it sat on the kitchen table, glaring at him with its hollow, owl's eyes.

How much money were you given?

There was an immediate lull in the tape's continuity, then came the voice, again.

I keep telling you. I wasn't given any money. I don't even know – argggggggggg . . .

Urgently, Paul hit the stop button. He felt dizzy, again. All his blood had been summoned to one spot. Every night for a week now, he found himself shocked awake with a pounding heart. Why was he tormenting himself, over and over again?

Geordie had asked that same question, but he couldn't answer.

He pulled his mind back to what was going on around him, focusing on gulls hovering in the distance, thinking how he could just sit here for a very long time, especially in late summer, when the wind gets a bit blustery and the gulls come out of the sea mist, swooping up and down in their quest for food.

The sun began to slowly spill into the earth, bringing the beginning of tomorrow's cool wind bleeding northwards. The breeze off the beach felt cold on his face. White patches of foamy water hissed in his ears. He could smell ozone, could smell the keen smell of starched linen, and it made him think of his mother, dressed for church on Sundays, and it made him feel so terribly alone.

No. A million times no. I did not – arghhhhhhhhhhhh . . . bastards!

Bastards, thought Paul. *Bastards.*

Time slipped by, unnoticed, and when the sun finally died, the sky was still light from where it shone somewhere else, leaving fingers of silver and red across the sky. A new moon began to appear, ghostly, sickly thin.

Closer to shore, roiling swells broke the moon's reflections into a thousand tumbling pieces, while Paul's eyes darted from surf to sand, searching for a telltale glint, a clue. Something. Anything . . .

He thought about Lucky, his terrible death, and what if he, Paul, hadn't told Shank everything he wanted to know, albeit under torture? What if he hadn't mentioned it to Geordie while Violet listened to every word? What if . . . what if . . . what . . . if . . .

He became as still as death as he listened to the tape one more time, remembering Shank's quote from Blake, that is was easier to forgive an enemy than a friend.

From his pocket, he removed Kennedy's crunched-up letter and flowered it out. He lit it, allowing the flames to lick greedily at the tape, sizzling it into a blackened blob of plastic.

He remembered Shank's quotes, but thought Kennedy's more appropriate, wiser: forgiving is not forgetting. It's letting go of the hurt, and that once forgiving begins, dreams can be rebuilt.

Over the last few days, Paul had felt like something was being torn down and rebuilt inside him. Kennedy had found his redemption in the abattoir and Paul had forgiven him. Now it was time to forgive himself.